T0102088

THE EXPENDABLE MAN

DOROTHY B. HUGHES (1904–1993) was an American mystery writer and critic. Born Dorothy Belle Flanagan in Kansas City, Missouri, she received a bachelor's degree in journalism from the University of Missouri and worked as a reporter before attending graduate school at the University of New Mexico and Columbia University. In 1931 her collection of poetry, *Dark Certainty*, was selected for inclusion in the Yale Series of Younger Poets. The next year she got married and it was not until 1940 that she published the first of her fourteen mystery novels, *The So Blue Marble*. For four decades Hughes was the crime-fiction reviewer for *The Albuquerque Tribune*, earning an Edgar Award for Outstanding Mystery Criticism from the Mystery Writers of America in 1950. *The Expendable Man*, published in 1963, was her last novel. "I simply hadn't the tranquility required to write" while caring for her family, she later said. In 1978, however, she published *The Case of the Real Perry Mason*, a critical biography of Erle Stanley Gardner, and that same year she was recognized as a Grand Master by the Mystery Writers of America. Among Hughes's best-known books are *The Cross-Eyed Bear*, *Ride the Pink Horse*, and *In a Lonely Place* (which was made into a movie directed by Nicholas Ray and starring Humphrey Bogart).

WALTER MOSLEY is the author of more than thirty-four books, including the best-selling mystery series featuring Easy Rawlins. Among the many honors he has received are an O. Henry Award, a Grammy, and PEN America's Lifetime Achievement Award.

THE EXPENDABLE MAN

DOROTHY B. HUGHES

Afterword by
WALTER MOSLEY

NEW YORK REVIEW BOOKS

New York

THIS IS A NEW YORK REVIEW BOOK
PUBLISHED BY THE NEW YORK REVIEW OF BOOKS
207 East 32nd Street, New York, NY 10016
www.nyrb.com

Library of Congress Cataloging-in-Publication Data
Hughes, Dorothy B. (Dorothy Belle), 1904–1993.
The expendable man / by Dorothy B. Hughes ; afterword by Walter Mosley.
    p. cm. — (New York Review Books Classics)
ISBN 978-1-59017-495-1 (alk. paper)
1. Mystery fiction. gsafd I. Title.
PS3515.U268E96 2012
813'.54—dc23

                        2011043843

ISBN 978-1-59017-495-1
Available as an electronic book; ISBN 978-1-59017-509-5

Printed in the United States of America on acid-free paper.
10 9 8

For my friend, Charlesetta

THE EXPENDABLE MAN

1

ACROSS THE TRACKS there was a different world. The long and lonely country was the color of sand. The horizon hills were haze-black; the clumps of mesquite stood in dark pools of their own shadowing. But the pools and the rim of dark horizon were discerned only by conscious seeing, else the world was all sand, brown and tan and copper and pale beige. Even the sky at this moment was sand, reflection of the fading bronze of the sun.

It was good to be out on the road, away from the banging of the town on the other side of the tracks. Driving into Indio after six of an early May evening, the sun-blazing of the earlier hours of the day had become an invisible cloud of heat which lay heavily, suffocatingly, upon the town. Noise had intensified the discomfort, and there was noise—the kind which only a covey of teen-agers in spring could engender. Their cars roared and popped and spluttered, their car radios blared above the din, while their voices screamed and shouted over the combined cacophony.

Hugh's intent, on driving in, had been a stop at an air-cooled drugstore. But once he had seen the size and temper of the invading young people, he settled for a drive-in restaurant. It had been a mistake, this he knew once he had parked. Almost immediately the jalopy which had cut across his way not once but often on his entrance to town, came rocketing back up the street and swung precariously into the drive-in's court. The car was crowded with high school youngsters; he didn't count them, only observed they seemed to be spilling over the sides of the open chassis. He shut his ears to their din and waited for one of the serving girls to bring him a menu. There were three of these girls, dressed in red band-uniform type trousers and wilted white shirts, topped with bolero-length jackets of the same red. Two were no more than teen-agers, the third a little older.

He waited for some time. He would have quit the place but he hadn't eaten since noon. If he were going through to Phoenix tonight, he'd have to eat something now. Between here and Phoenix, there wouldn't be much opportunity. Therefore he waited, refusing to be driven away by the vulgar young people or the disinclined help.

Eventually, as he knew eventually it would happen, the less pretty of the young waitresses came to his car and thrust a menu at him. He ordered a bacon and tomato sandwich and iced coffee. It was too hot for anything more. There wasn't an undue wait for the order to come and it wasn't bad when it came. The jalopy had roared off with thunderous pipes before then, and he was allowed to eat in peace. Nevertheless he'd been relieved to get out of the town, to cross the tracks into this empty sand world.

He switched radio stations until he found a Los Angeles one with good pop records, lit another cigarette, and settled back into a comfortable driving position. In spite of the heat in Indio, it wasn't too hot on the desert here at sundown, not the way it would have been in summer. Most evenings were still cool, the nights chill, on the desert in May. It should be the same in Phoenix—hot days, cool nights, perfect weather.

He had wound through the small canyon outside of town, and was moving on to the long desert plain, when he noted ahead an extra shadow in the tree shadow marking a culvert. It looked as if there were someone resting under the tree. It couldn't be possible, here, close to fifteen miles out of town. There wasn't a car in sight in either direction, and there was no habitation of any sort in any direction. Yet it looked like a person's shadow.

It was just that. The shadow, raised up from its haunches, waited for his car to approach. He knew better than to pick up a hitchhiker on the road; he'd known it long before the newspapers and script writers had implanted the danger in the public mind. Most assuredly he would not pick up anyone in this strange, deserted land. But he reduced speed when he approached the shadow, the automatic anxiety reaction that a person might step in front of the oncoming car. He passed the hitchhiker before he was actually aware of the shape and form; only after he had passed did he realize that this was a young girl. From the glimpse, a teen-age girl. Even as he slowed his car, he was against doing it. But her possible peril if left here alone forced his hand. He simply could not in conscience go on, leaving her abandoned, with twilight fallen and night quick to come. He had sisters as young as this. It chilled him to think what might happen if one of them were abandoned on the lonesome highway, the type of man with whom, in desperation, she might accept a lift. The car was stopped. He shifted to reverse and began backing up.

As soon as the girl saw that he had stopped, she scooped up her belongings from the ground and started running toward his car. Hugh spoke through the open window. "Do you want a ride?"

She didn't answer at once. She stood there looking through the window at his face. She was a teen-ager, she might have been one of the girls he'd seen at the drive-in. She wasn't pretty; her face was just a young, thin, petulant face, too much lipstick on the mouth, wisps of her self-bleached hair jutting from beneath the gaudy orange and green scarf covering her head. She was wearing tight green slacks. A boy's shirt, too big for her, hung almost to her knees; a dirty white shirt pin-striped in blue. She carried a boy's jacket, a high school club jacket of maroon and gold. She also carried a box handbag of white plastic in one hand, in the other a small canvas traveling bag. She wore white socks and white wedgie sandals, the kind his younger sister said only the cheap girls wore.

He repeated his question, a little impatiently because he didn't like this situation at all, his car stopped here on the road, the girl standing outside looking in at him. At any moment a car from Indio might overtake them, or one appear from the eastern crest of the road. A chill sense of apprehension came on him and he wished to hell he hadn't stopped. This could be the initial step in some kind of shakedown, although how, with nothing or no one in sight for unlimited miles, he couldn't figure.

He spoke up more sharply than was his wont. "Well, do you want a ride or don't you?"

"I guess so." As if in speaking she'd made her decision, she opened the door and piled in.

He set the car in motion again, picking up speed until he hit the sixty-five-mile maximum for this highway. He didn't look at her or say anything more to her. From the periphery of his eye, he saw her set her traveling bag on the floor mat, away from him, close to the door. Her soiled sandal touched it protectively, as if it were filled with gold and precious gems. For no particular reason, he was relieved that his suitcases and his medical bag were locked in the trunk of the car.

Far ahead on the road, he saw the shape of an oncoming car as it lifted itself over a culvert. He switched on his lights. The sky was still pale, the pale lavender of twilight, but the sand world had darkened. It was difficult enough to drive at this hour, the lights would identify the presence of his car to the one approaching. When the other car passed his, headed toward Indio, he saw it was yet another jalopy filled with kids. It was hopped up; it zoomed by, with only scraps of voices shrilling above the sound of the motor.

In his rear-view mirror, he watched until it disappeared in the distance. Just for a moment, he had known fear. It might have been the same group which had hectored him in town. The trap might be sprung by his picking up the girl; they might swing about and come after him. Only when the car had disappeared from sight, did he relax and immediately feel the fool. It was surprising what old experiences remembered could do to a presumedly educated, civilized man.

If the girl had recognized the group, she gave no indication. She was slumped down in the seat, her eyes fixed on the long road ahead.

He held the wheel steady, and lighted another cigarette. He asked then, "How did you get there?"

"Where?" She was defiant.

"On the road. Where I stopped for you."

"I got a ride that far."

"How could you get a ride that far and no further? There are no ranches around."

She considered her answer. "I got a ride that far and then I didn't like—I didn't like it—so I got out."

It could have been true. "Where are you going?"

"Phoenix."

"Hitching?"

"How else could I get there?" The defiance heightened. "I haven't got a big Cadillac and money."

He was going to ignore her remark, but because of his uneasiness, he didn't. He said, "It's a borrowed car." He didn't say borrowed from his mother. He spoke placidly, wanting to diminish her tension. "Does your family know you're hitching to Phoenix?"

"My family doesn't care what I do," she flung at him. She'd have told him it was none of his business but for the fact that, having accepted this ride, she didn't want to take any chances on losing it. "I'm not running away," she said. "I'm going to Phoenix to visit—my aunt."

There had been a perceptible hesitation, his ear was certain. Just as sure as he was that no family, how little they cared for this unappealing girl, would knowingly permit her to hitchhike to another state, so he was sure she'd invented the aunt. Most likely, her family had given her bus fare for the trip and she'd spent it. She wasn't going to tell him whom she would visit and he didn't care.

"What about school?" he asked.

"We got a holiday until Monday. Some teachers' meeting or something."

She didn't hesitate on that, and it explained the number of young people running free in Indio.

"How old are you?" he asked suddenly.

She was angry at the question, but she answered. "I'm— eighteen."

She couldn't have been more than sixteen, possibly no more than fourteen or fifteen. One thing certain, she wasn't any eighteen. She hadn't the maturity which came imperceptibly at that age. His younger sister, Allegra, at fifteen, no matter what she thought, was still a child. Celeste, the older, coming up eighteen, no longer was. This one was a child, telling her whoppers, expecting them to be believed. He knew now he would not drive her all the way to Phoenix. Not across the state line.

He asked, "Where are you from? Indio?"

"No, I'm from Banning." She spoke too fast, lying again. Even she knew she was caught out; she raced on to ask him, "Where you from?"

"Los Angeles."

"What do you do?" The Cadillac was still on her mind.

"I'm a doctor—an intern."

"Really?" She stretched the word, like a credulous child. Yet the answer had somehow taken away her uneasiness, even her resentment. She half turned in the seat to look over at him.

"Really," he said good-naturedly. The response didn't disturb him. "I'm at the Med Center—UCLA."

"Did you go to UCLA?"

"I did my pre-med there and finished at Northwestern. UCLA didn't have a full medical program at the time. Then I did my Army stint and now I'm interning." He was talking with purpose, to keep her relaxed, with a hope of her becoming friendly. If he could get her to that point, possibly he could find out the truth about this trip of hers, perhaps help her. A young girl hitchhiking to Phoenix needed all the help she could find. "Are you in high school?"

"Yeah, I'm a junior." She said it with pride. But if she was a junior, she was older than he thought she was and brighter.

"Do you want to go to college?"

"I don't know. I don't like school much."

Again she was retreating, and he made conversation quickly. "I have a sister, a freshman in college. UCLA. She'll be eighteen this summer. She's a brain, I guess you'd call it. Not that she's always in a book, she's a babe. My other sister, she's fifteen, is a sophomore at L.A. High. She's not so much on books but she's knocking herself out to get college grades so that she can go to UCLA too. She doesn't want to miss the fun."

She said, "If I was going to college, I'd go to UCLA. They have the best teams."

"They usually do," he admitted.

"Did you play football?"

"No. I played some basketball."

"How tall are you?"

He smiled. "Only six and a point. Not tall enough to be a star."

"There's a boy on our team is six seven. All the schools are after him. He's good."

"Where does he want to go?"

"UCLA, of course. If he can get in. You have to have awful good grades to get in there."

"Don't I know it? Doesn't Allegra know it—that's my younger sister."

"Allegra. That's a funny name."

" 'Brave Alice and laughing Allegra—' "

She was lost.

"Don't you know 'The Children's Hour'?"

"I never watched that."

He said gently, "It's a poem. By Longfellow."

"I guess we haven't had that in school yet."

He guessed she didn't read anything out of school but comics and lurid romance magazines. He said, "My mother said Allegra was laughing as soon as she was born. My mother learned the poem in school when she was a girl."

The girl asked then, "What's your name?"

"Hugh Densmore. What's yours?"

She hesitated rather too long. "Iris Croom." It might be. The hesitation could mean only that she didn't want him to know her name. Without warning, she asked, "What kind of a doctor are you?"

He didn't quite understand her meaning. He began, "At the moment, I'm not practicing. I'm interning. That means working at a hospital before actual practice."

"I know." She flounced. On television they learned all manner of bits and pieces. "But what are you going to be? A brain surgeon? Or a baby doctor? Or just plain."

"I want to do research," he said. "Cancer research. That's why

I'm lucky to get in at Med Center. They're doing exciting things about cancer."

He didn't know if she understood what he was talking about. She was abruptly silent, watching the road ahead. Then again she turned suddenly to him. "I'm hungry."

"I'm sorry," he said. "I don't even have a candy bar. Didn't you eat before you left Indio?"

"I had a malt. But I'm starved now."

She wasn't hinting, there was not so much as a service station in sight. There'd be no place to get food until they reached Blythe. Nor would he stop if there were one, not until he got to Blythe, where he could put her off at the bus depot. "I have some gum." He felt in his pocket and found the package.

"Maybe it'll help." She extracted a stick and handed the package back to him. He unwrapped a piece for himself.

"This'll keep me from smoking so much," he said.

After a moment, she stated, "I guess I'll put up my hair." She rooted in her handbag, found bobby pins and a man's black pocket comb. She pulled off her scarf and ran the comb through her hair. She looked even younger with the lank, badly bleached hair hanging around her face.

"Don't you need a mirror?"

"I have one." She showed him, inset in the lid of her box purse. But she could wind the pin curls without it, there wasn't enough light from the dashboard for her to see in the mirror. By now it was quite dark outside the car. Johnny Mathis was singing from the radio; she hummed with the song.

He wondered again just whom she was meeting in Phoenix in the morning. Or was it simply habit that she put up her hair at night. He asked, "Do you have a boy friend in Phoenix?"

She was immediately suspicious. "Why'd you ask me that?"

"Putting up your hair—"

"I don't want to get to Phoenix looking a mess. It got all wet this afternoon when I was swimming."

He didn't say anything, but it must have been quite a day. From Banning to Indio to the desert highway. Swimming where?

"Are you going to Phoenix?" she asked.

"I am." He was ready for the question, he had been expecting it. "But I'm not going through tonight. I'm stopping over in Blythe."

"Do you have friends in Blythe?"

"No, but I'm too tired to drive through." Actually it was true. "I've been on night duty." Although he'd wanted to walk in on the family tonight, it would be just as well to have some rest and be ready for tomorrow.

"I wish you were driving through." She tied the scarf around her head again, and put on the heavy school jacket. "I'm going to sleep," she announced.

"It's only eight o'clock."

She gave a small but knowing smirk. "I didn't get much sleep last night."

"Do you want to move in back where you can stretch out?"

She considered it, pushing onto her knees and leaning over for a careful investigation. There was nothing on the back seat but his folded jacket. On the floor was a Thermos jug of water. He disliked, from taking family trips as a boy, no doubt, a cluttered car when touring.

She decided, "I guess not. It's warmer up front. I'm used to sleeping in cars." She giggled a little at that, as if it were funny. She turned her back on him, curled herself into the corner, and rested her head against the cushioned seat. She went to sleep almost at once, he could tell by her slightly nasal breathing.

He drove on through the night. The road was good; he hadn't seen half a dozen cars since leaving Indio. He should reach Blythe by around nine o'clock. He began to wonder about the bus schedule to Phoenix. He couldn't simply drop this girl on a street corner. If there was no bus out tonight, he'd probably have to give her the price of a room. In a motel as far as possible from the one where he would stop. He was quite sure she wouldn't have enough money to get one for herself. He didn't have much with him; he never had much money, not on an intern's allowance. Again he wondered if the girl had ever had bus money.

If he had to, he'd lend her what she needed. The aunt could repay him, if there was an aunt in Phoenix. If not, perhaps her family would some day. By now he was in his own mind certain that Iris was a runaway. The sooner he could be shed of her, the safer he'd be. If there was a teletype out for her by now, his position could be more precarious than he wanted to think about.

Worrying about it was pointless. Nothing was going to call attention to them until they reached Blythe. At Blythe he'd see that she was taken care of, and that would end it. And he'd never pick up another hitchhiker, never. Not even a ninety-year-old grandfather or the chief of police.

※

She wakened when a gargantuan oil truck thundered by, rocking the car. She made a word sound and then for a moment her sleep-dulled eyes looked at him in fear. But she came more fully awake and said, "Oh, it's you. Where are we?"

"About ten miles out of Blythe."

"You're still going to stop there?"

"That's right. But I'll see about your bus first."

"I'm not going on the bus," she said sullenly. "Don't worry about me. I'll get another ride."

He was sharp with her. "What's the matter with you? You can't pick up a ride with strangers in the middle of the night. It isn't safe."

She looked at him for a moment, a level, too-old look. It said she'd let him pick her up and that she was safe with him. Or was she wondering why she'd done it. She said finally, "I can't go on the bus. I don't have any money."

Anger came to his voice. "Now look here, Iris, or whatever your name is, you can't tell me your family let you set off for Phoenix without a bus ticket."

"You don't know my family." Her voice was brittle.

"I don't know your family but I know my family. I know lots of families. There isn't a one that would let a fifteen-year-old kid hitchhike—"

"I told you I was eighteen."

"You've told me plenty of things. You haven't made me believe them. You're not more than sixteen. And unless you're running away from home, you started out with a bus ticket." He calmed down, losing his temper wouldn't help matters. "I'd like to help you. Why don't you level with me? Are you running away?"

"No, I'm not," she flared. "I told my father I was going to Phoenix and he didn't care. He told me to go on and go."

"What did your mother say?"

"My mother ditched us six years ago. She was a tramp."

His hand clenched to keep from striking her. "Don't say that!"

"My father says she was. He ought to know better than you, hadn't he?" she asked insolently.

"Don't you say it," he repeated. "You don't know her side of it. You respect your mother until you know better." It occurred to him, "Is your mother in Phoenix?"

"We don't know where she is. My aunt's in Phoenix."

"Your father's sister? Or your mother's?"

"My mother's."

"And that's where you're going."

"That's where."

"Your father gave you the money to go."

"He didn't give me nothing."

"How did he expect you to get there?"

She said, "I knew he wouldn't give me the money. When he asked me how I was getting there, I told him I'd saved up from baby-sitting."

"You hitchhiked to Indio?"

"I didn't have to. I rode down there with some of the kids."

He was trying to form the truth. "It was the kids who dropped you there on the desert. And drove back again to see if you had a ride. That car we passed—"

"You think you're pretty smart, don't you?"

"No, I don't. I'm trying to find out what happened. That's the way it was, wasn't it?"

She didn't answer him.

"But why? Why didn't you try to get a ride in Indio? You're from Indio, aren't you, not Banning? You were afraid someone might see you trying to hitch a ride there, tell your father."

"That wasn't it," she denied. "It was Guppy's idea. He hitched to Phoenix once. He said they're more apt to stop for you out on the desert than in town. They're sorry for you. In town they think like you do—'take a bus.'"

It disturbed him too much to keep silent, although he didn't want to know, actually was afraid to know. "You were one of the kids in the beat-up car at the drive-in, weren't you?"

She was furtive. "I don't know what you're talking about."

"It was the same car passed us going back to Indio." He demanded fiercely, "Did you have my car staked out from the beginning? Were you waiting for me?"

"I should say not!" she denied with emphasis. "That's not the way it was at all. I wouldn't have—" She broke off. "It wasn't that way," she started again. "I was expecting to get a ride with a family. Not many women would pass up a girl on the highway."

More of Guppy's wisdom, no doubt. With some rancor, he said, "You were willing enough to get in my car."

"It was turning dark and I was getting sort of scared. I didn't want to have to go home and start all over again. My aunt's expecting me. I wrote her I'd be there in the morning."

"And she thinks you're coming by bus."

"That's right. But I didn't tell her which one because I didn't know what time I'd get there."

He studied it. It could be the truth; it could be a pack of lies. It didn't make much difference to him now. He said, "Well, I can't take you on to Phoenix. But I won't just desert you in Blythe. I'll see about a bus and I'll lend you the money for a ticket. You can pay me back tomorrow when I get to Phoenix."

"With what?" she sneered.

He was patient. "I'm sure your aunt will lend you the money. What's her address?"

She made a quick gesture of her head that might have been panic, and again he decided there was no aunt. "Don't you come bothering her," she said. "You give me your address. I'll bring the money to you."

He had no intention of giving her an address. He said, "Never mind that. Just give me your aunt's number. I'll phone before I come, to make sure I'm not bothering her."

His sarcasm was lost on her. She didn't care what he said,

she was too involved in putting on fresh lipstick by the dash light. They were coming into Blythe. It was just a small town of the sort you passed through on any highway but for some reason it was, to Hugh, a singularly pleasant one. The wide main street managed to give the impression that it was a main street in spite of being also a state highway. The business section was no more than a few blocks with the usual small-town businesses, the usual wealth of gas stations which cluttered all highway towns, and an abundance of motels, good-looking modern motels. Neon lights were rainbow above the latter, otherwise most of the town was dark.

The bus depot was on the other side of the highway at the western end of town. Hugh pulled around the corner of a side street and stopped the car. "You stay here," he directed Iris. "I'll see what I can find out." He reached for his jacket and put it on.

She was gazing into her purse mirror although there was not even reflected light there. "Hurry up will you? I'm hungry."

He took the keys from the ignition. "I'll hurry." He couldn't make it fast enough to be rid of her, to be solitary and safe again.

He waited on the side of the darkened road for passing cars—it seemed a long time—then cut half on a run across to the depot. A dumpy woman in a yellow cotton dress was behind the ticket counter. She was talking in a desultory fashion with three workmen seated at a table in the lunch section. All of them became silent at Hugh's entrance.

He walked over to the woman. "Are there any buses to Phoenix tonight?"

"They run all night." Unsmiling, she indicated the posted schedule.

He didn't let his expression change as he studied it. But inside, his smile of relief was so broad, he put his hand to his face in fear it might break through. There was an eastbound bus at ten fifty-five. Time for Iris to get something to eat, not too much time to wait after. He had no doubt but that the ticket woman would make certain everyone was aboard when the bus pulled out.

"How much?" he asked her.

"One way or round trip?"

"One way."

"Six thirty-eight."

He took a ten-dollar bill from his wallet. The woman pushed the small bit of cardboard and his change across the counter. He said, "Thanks," and left the place. Again he had to wait to cut across the highway, hoping that those inside the depot weren't watching to see where he was headed. They couldn't see Iris from here, he'd parked the car far enough around the opposite corner to make sure of that.

He wasn't certain she'd be waiting but she was there. As he opened the car door, she greeted him with the complaint, "Didn't you bring nothing to eat?"

He got into the car and closed the door. He said, "There's a bus to Phoenix at ten fifty-five. Here's your ticket."

She took the pasteboard as if it were dirty.

"Put it in your purse so you won't lose it."

"I won't lose it," she said unpleasantly. But she complied, unearthing a red plastic wallet from the handbag, and putting the ticket into the zipper compartment. "Now what am I supposed to do, starve?"

He consulted his watch in the dash light. "It's nine-thirty. You have plenty of time to eat something."

She continued unpleasant. "What do I use for money?"

"How much do you have?"

She emptied the change compartment into her hand. "Seventeen cents."

"That's all?"

She opened all of the wallet compartments. "That's all." She pulled out the pockets of her slacks. "You want to look in my jacket?" She shoved it at him but he didn't touch it. "You can't even buy a hamburger with seventeen lousy cents."

From his pocket, he took the change from the ten. Anything to be rid of her before the local law or a busybody wondered why they were parked here. He said, "Here's three dollars and sixty-two cents. The ticket was six thirty-eight. That's ten dollars you owe me."

Her fingers clutched the three bills and she held her hand palm up for the change. Ungraciously she said, "Thanks."

"There's a café a few doors from the depot. It looks better than their lunch stand."

She was gathering up her belongings.

"Whatever you do, don't miss that bus."

She didn't say anything. She opened the door of the car and backed out, holding the handbag and traveling case against her. She pushed the door shut with her foot. She looked in at him and again said, "Thanks," as if she hated to say it.

He watched until she had darted across the highway and was headed toward the restaurant he'd pointed out to her. He then drove on, and only then did he remember that he'd failed to get the address or phone number of her aunt. He shrugged. Good-bye to ten bucks, ten hard-earned bucks. He couldn't regret too much; he'd have paid out more than twice that to be free of Iris Croom.

He followed the dark country street to its intersection, rounded the block, and returned to the highway. Now that he was rid of her, there was no reason why he shouldn't go on to Phoenix. No reason save that reaction had set in and he knew he was too tired for the long drive. He'd been on night duty for the past month. Last night he'd doubled his job with duty today, a trade to get away early this afternoon. He wouldn't be a safe risk on the road.

He drove the few blocks through the town. There was a large chain motel near the eastern end. He'd stayed there before. He hoped there'd be a vacancy tonight, you never knew. Sometimes even when the sign said there was one, the last unit had been rented just before you arrived.

The vacancy sign was lighted. He turned the car down the circular driveway. Although it was almost three years since he'd been here, he recognized the young woman inside the office. There was nothing distinctive about her. On the street he wouldn't have known her, but in her own setting she was remembered. He was relieved to see her on duty. She'd been a pleasant hostess before, he didn't expect her to be changed.

She wasn't. There was a vacancy and she didn't up the price for him. Five dollars. After he'd taken his kit bag into the room, he was just too tired to drive back downtown and try to find a place where he could eat. It could have been that he was less tired than he was afraid he might come upon Iris again. He settled for an aspirin. Hunger would not keep him awake. He was trained to fall asleep when his head was put to a pillow.

He woke at seven when a loud-mouthed man and woman took off from the next-door unit. He wasn't exactly rested but he couldn't get back to sleep. There was a compulsion to be on his way before any more trouble could develop. And by now he was ravening for food. He shaved, showered, put on fresh linen, replaced his kit in the car trunk, and was ready to leave.

The morning air was cool. Later the sun would be intense but at this hour there was only golden warmth, the color of summer wheat. He drove out to the highway and headed back toward the town to find a restaurant. He changed his mind when he saw the supermarket. Swinging the car into the lot, he went in and bought a quart of milk and a package of six cinnamon rolls. He could have breakfast while he rolled along. It could be better than greasy-spoon food.

He had the car serviced at a nearby station and was on his way. He was as hungry as his passenger had been last night. Before he reached the old bridge that spanned the Colorado, he'd finished a couple of rolls and half the milk. The river was full and lush and green, from green-white winter snow of northern mountains, from spring rains that never fell on this parched earth. Even this early, there were little sunbrowned, near-naked boys splashing along the green banks.

He rolled the car down the other side of the bridge and across the state line to the Arizona inspection station. There were a couple of cars ahead of his under the long sheds. He pulled up. Not until he inched under the roof did he see Iris. She was waiting at the side of the road, just beyond the inspection tables. If possible she looked shabbier than she had last night, unwashed, her hair done up in pin curlers under the dirty scarf, the oversized jacket draped on her shoulders. Her dirty sandal rested against the small traveling bag; the white plastic handbag was clutched to her.

He knew why she was waiting. She thought she could force him to take her along to Phoenix. He wondered if she'd cashed in the ticket and spent the money or if she was saving it to spend in Phoenix. He wondered where she'd spent the night.

He heard the usual questions, "Any fruit? Citrus? Plants?"

"None," he said.

The inspector considered the answer suspiciously. "Let me see in your trunk." He was a fat, sour-looking man, the kind who'd like to make something of Hugh's picking up a dirty blond teen-ager. He'd resented the big white Cadillac the moment that Hugh drove up in it. A second inspector lounged in the doorway of the station.

"Certainly," Hugh said. He got out of the car, not looking toward the girl, and went around to the rear. He opened the trunk. It was as neat as the interior of the car, the way he liked it. His large suitcase, the car case, the kit bag, his doctor's bag, his father's golf clubs. Tools at the side by the spare tire. If he ignored Iris, she might not have the nerve to approach him. Not after pocketing the bus ticket and not using it.

"What's in that one?" the inspector snapped.

"I'm a doctor." Hugh unlatched it. "It's my medical bag."

"Any dope?"

"No, none." Because he'd thought of this inspection when he was packing, he had removed emergency packets for which he had registrations, permits, the works. He was aware that such legalities could make little or no difference to a small-town official bent on trouble.

"Open the other bags." Not please, not even in intonation.

Seething inwardly, Hugh complied. If this big wart-hog threw his clothes around, Hugh decided he would find a way to carry his complaint up to the governor's office.

The man didn't. He snorted at the neatly packed cases and said, "Okay."

Hugh closed the trunk and started around again to the driver's seat. He hadn't quite reached it when he heard the call.

"Dr. Densmore!" Iris was hurrying over to the car. "Dr. Densmore," she shrilled. "I thought I recognized you." On her face was a sickly-sweet innocent smile.

The inspector stopped in his tracks and turned to watch.

"Oh, Dr. Densmore"—she was deliberately speaking too loud—"would you give me a lift to Wickenberg, oh, please? I must have missed my ride and if I don't get there this morning I'll lose my job and I don't know what my mother will say."

Both inspectors were watching, listening; suspicion like hoods over their faces. There was absolutely nothing Hugh could do to escape her. To refuse would have been worse than to accede. He couldn't say he was not going to Wickenberg, there was no way to miss it in this direction.

He spoke politely but aloofly, as if she were the daughter of a man he'd known not well, possibly in a business way. "Why, certainly, Iris. Get in."

Smug triumph flashed in her eyes but the inspectors couldn't see that. She climbed in the car with her belongings and he set it in motion, conscious of the officials following the license plate out of sight. When they were on the road, he asked her, "Why didn't you take the bus?"

"Waste all that money when I could hitch?"

"What did you do with the ticket?"

"Turned it in. I told the lady my plans were changed."

"I suppose you told her I was your chauffeur."

She giggled. "I didn't say nothing about you. I just said I was visiting friends and had decided not to leave yet."

"You're a practiced liar, aren't you?"

"I manage."

"What did you do with the money?"

"Don't worry." She yawned. "You'll get it back. From my aunt, remember?"

"I'll get it back if I have to tell her the whole story. Where did you sleep last night?"

She giggled again. "I didn't. I met up with some kids who knew some of the Indio kids I know. We just kicked around." Her laugh was nasty. "First we spotted your car at that snazzy motel where you stayed. So I knew you hadn't lied to me about staying in Blythe and that I could get a ride to Phoenix with you this morning."

"And if I'd said no?"

"You couldn't. I fixed it so you couldn't." She knew what she'd done, could boast of it. She was an evil little girl. She went on slyly, "I knew why you wouldn't take me on to Phoenix last night. You didn't want to cross the state line with me. So the kids took me out there this morning and I walked across. You got nothing to worry about."

She hadn't known last night. Some of the "kids" must have put her wise.

"What about those inspection officers? What do you think they thought?"

"They thought I was waiting for some friends to give me a ride to work. Then when you came along—you heard me."

"Do you think they believed you?"

"Who cares? Blobs they were. Both of them. Blobs. I'll never see them again."

But I will, Hugh said silently. Every time I visit the Phoenix relatives. And every time I pass this station, I'll be suspect. He didn't say it to her. Whether she spoke it or not, her reaction would be: Who cares? She was interested only in her own affairs. He took another bun from the package and began to eat it.

"Food!" she cried. "Can I have some?"

"Didn't you eat last night?"

"I didn't eat nothing this morning. I'm starved."

She didn't deserve it but he handed the rest of the rolls to her. "You can have these but you can't have my milk. I didn't get any dinner."

"Why not? Didn't you have any more money?"

"By the time I'd taken care of you and found myself a room, I was too tired to do anything but fall in bed."

"At least you got to sleep." She munched on the bun sloppily. "Maybe I ought to sleep now but I'm not a bit sleepy."

"You will be later. Or did you take a pep pill?"

"Of course I didn't." she retorted indignantly. "Where would I get one of those?"

"I thought maybe one of your new friends might have given you one."

She licked one finger. "You're teed off at me, aren't you?"

"Don't I have a right to be?" He drank what was left of the milk.

"I don't know why. I didn't do nothing to you. Unless it's the bus ticket that's bugging you. You'll get your money. Just relax. You'll get it."

"I'll get it," he repeated firmly.

She looked at the carton in his hand. "Is there any of that milk left?"

"None at all." He dropped the container on the seat. "There's some water in the Thermos. It may be a bit stale, I didn't refill it this morning. But if you're thirsty enough, you can drink it."

She scrambled to her knees, leaned over the back seat and lifted the Thermos from the floor. "You want some?"

"No, thank you. You'll find a glass in the glove compartment."

She punched the compartment open, took out the glass and poured it full of water, slopping some of it on her and some on the floor mat. "It's not very good," she said, wiping her mouth with her hand. "I wish you had more milk."

"If I'd known I was having a guest for breakfast, I'd have bought two bottles. When you're through, put the jug back where you found it."

"You're so funny," she said sarcastically. "Ha ha." She finished the water, replaced the glass, banged the compartment shut, and with another scramble swung the Thermos in place. "Maybe we could stop for a Coke in Wickenberg."

"Barring car trouble—God forbid—our first stop will be the bus station at Phoenix."

She said cheekily, "Suppose I have to make a stop."

"I'll pull off the road where there's a bush," he stated. "And no Coke machine."

"I honestly think you would."

"I would," he confirmed.

She believed him and settled back. "Mind if I turn on the radio?"

"No, I don't mind."

She played with the finder until she had a station, there weren't many in this neighborhood. As she had last night, she hummed with the music. When the announcer broke in with an ad spiel, she said, "I wish they'd play that new Johnny Mathis record. Do you like Johnny Mathis?"

"I like him."

"I go ape over Johnny Mathis."

"Personally I prefer Sinatra." He wondered if that dated him, as his mother was dated with Bing Crosby.

At least the music kept her quiet and he could enjoy the morning ride. He'd always had a quickening of the heart when he crossed into Arizona and beheld the cactus country. This was as the desert should be, this was the desert of the picture books, with the land unrolled to the farthest distant horizon hills, with saguaro standing sentinel in their strange chessboard pattern, towering supinely above the fans of ocotillo and the brushy mesquite. Because there had been some winter rain, the desert was in bloom. The saguaro wore creamy crowns on their tall heads, the ocotillo spikes were tipped with vermilion, and the brush bloomed yellow as forsythia.

There was little traffic, never much on this span, and the road was well built. They rolled through Quartzsite and Hope and within an hour were in sight of the weathered curio café and new resort motel of Salome-Where-She-Danced.

Iris sat up brightly. "We could get a Coke here."

"You can get a Coke at Phoenix." He kept his face expressionless, set ahead on the road, driving with care at the reduced town speed. He must attract no attention from country constables or curious tourists while the girl was in his car.

She wailed, "But that's ages!"

They were already out of the town and approaching the shining span of the railway bridge.

"Two hours. One to Wickenberg. Another to the city limits. Maybe another half hour to get across town to the bus station."

"I can't wait. I got to have a Coke, I'm dying."

He made evident his disinterest. "Drink water."

"That stuff! It tastes like you took a bath in it."

"If you're really thirsty, you'll drink it."

"You're revolting." She sulked for a mile, then asked, "You got any more of that gum?"

He put his hand in his pocket, found one stick and handed it to her. She settled down, still sulky but at least near-noiselessly so. She chomped gum. He ignored her. This was his special part of the countryside, the prime of desert and far mountain landscape. The sun was lifting higher and hotter; it was a good thing he'd made an early start.

The hour passed and they were coming into Wickenberg. It meant reduced speed again, and he didn't like it. At this crawl, the people in passing cars, the people on the downtown main street, couldn't help but notice Iris. But at least she didn't open up on her Coke bit. Once free of the outskirts traffic, he pushed up to the sixty Arizona limit. There'd be traffic between here and Phoenix, but the closer he drew to Phoenix, the less he cared. Phoenix was a city. In a city, people were too busy with their own affairs to wonder about a strangely assorted couple.

They wound through the canyon and emerged into the hot flat desert area. There must have been some familiarity with this final stretch which put the excitement in Iris' voice. "I guess I'd better fix my hair." Not for the aunt. There was a boy friend somewhere in the visit. At her age it was strange that she hadn't been babbling about him. She untied the scarf, laid it over her knees and began taking the bobby pins out of her hair.

He was curious. "Did you leave it up all evening?"

"Are you nuts? I took it down in the little girls' room at the café before I met the kids. Then I put it up again before I went to sleep."

"You said you didn't sleep."

She didn't like being called to account. "Not in a bed. I took a little nap in Rocky's car, that's all." She pulled the dirty comb out of her purse and combed out the lank curls. She peered into the inset mirror. "I wish I'd left it up longer. Darn it. Does it look too awful?"

He didn't know how it was supposed to look. He said, "I wouldn't worry about it. Your aunt won't care, will she?" He was holding her to her story.

She tied the scarf under her chin. "No, she won't care. But I want to look nice when I get there just the same."

"A bath and some clean clothes would help."

"I know," she said unhappily. For once she wasn't putting on an act. And he realized what he should have before, she didn't have any clean clothes with her. There wasn't room for them in the small bag.

"Maybe you can borrow from your aunt," he suggested.

"Sure I can. She has lots of clothes, beautiful clothes." She was lying again. "She doesn't care if I wear her clothes. We're the same size. She's real young for an aunt. She'll fix my hair too. She's a beauty operator, she has her own shop."

Poor kid. Poor, poor kid. He was a little ashamed of the ire he'd had toward her. But not enough to forget the lies and the perhaps lies. "You haven't given me her address."

"I don't have a pencil."

"I have a pen." He removed the ball-point from his jacket pocket. By now it was too hot for the jacket but he wouldn't slow the car to take it off.

"I don't have any paper."

He had the letter from his mother which had come yesterday. He slid it out and handed her the envelope. "Write it on the back."

Slowly she inscribed an address.

"Put her name on it. And phone number."

"I don't have her phone number." Reluctantly she wrote a name. He let his eyes touch it when she returned the envelope. Mayble Carney. She couldn't have invented Mayble. No one could.

"My pen?"

She pushed it at him.

"You tell her about the loan right away. Don't make up a big story, just tell her the truth."

She said huffily, "You're sure worried about your money. You'd think it was a hundred dollars."

"Do you know what an intern's pay is?"

"No, I don't."

"It isn't enough to cover bus tickets for strangers," he said.

They reached the city limits of Glendale. Oleanders were a magic wall of rose and white hiding the railroad tracks. Traffic was heavy from now on in; he didn't make conversation. She too was silent, shimmering with anticipation. She kept her head turned to the window, looking out at the buildings and streets. He followed Van Buren into the heart of town.

He said, "Keep your eyes open for the bus station. It's on the left. We'll probably have to go around the block to get to it." Even if a left turn were permitted, the unending line of cars would prohibit it.

They saw the sign at the same time. She cried, "There it is. Just let me off at the corner." Her hand was on the door.

"No, thanks. I'm taking you to the entrance. And you go right inside and telephone your aunt that you've arrived." He'd do that much to get her settled before she looked for more kids to kick around with.

The light changed as he pulled up to the corner and he turned right before she could get out. He circled the block to First Street, drove across Van Buren, and double-parked.

She was out of the car the moment it stopped. She didn't say good-bye or thank you and she didn't look back. But he saw her walk into the station before he rolled away.

The bad dream was over. He was rid of her. He might or might not get in touch with the alleged aunt. She might or might not be told of the loan. He'd rather write off the ten dollars as enforced charity than take a chance on having Iris move into his life again.

2

HIS GRANDPARENTS' HOME was a large old frame house on Jefferson, freshly painted white each spring. Pink and red roses were climbing the trellises against the porch. The oleanders were a glory of white in the dark glossy green of the tall hedge. He'd spent so many summers here as a child, it was like coming home. He'd never noticed the heat then.

He ran up the steps, across the broad porch, and pushed open the screen door. The air conditioning was welcome. "Anybody home?"

From the dining room he heard the clamor of voices, his grandmother's treble piercing through with excitement. "It's Hughie!"

They were around the big dining-room table, like a scene which never changed no matter how many years he was away from it. His grandmother was smaller and grayer but his grandfather stood tall despite his years. His mother was there; the family had flown to Phoenix earlier in the week. And to his delight, his sister Stacy and her doctor husband, Edward, had dropped in. It seemed impossible that Stacy was old enough to be the mother of a bride. Yet Clytie was twenty, older by two years than Stacy had been when she married.

"The house looks as if it knows there's to be a wedding in it. Where is the bride?"

"The girls had a luncheon at the university," his mother said. "I thought you might be in last night, Hugh."

"I stayed over in Blythe. It was late when I got off." He wouldn't tell her the story, he wouldn't worry her. "Where's Dad?"

"Playing golf. He wanted to escape wedding chitchat for a time."

"Whose clubs? I have his in the car."

Edward said, "Mine. I wish I were with them but I have to get back to the office." With mock woe he added, "Doctors can't take time off, right, Hugh? I'll see you at dinner."

Stacy went to the door with him. By the time she returned, Gram had Hugh plied with more food than he'd seen in years.

Stacy sat down beside him. "We've come up with a housing problem, Hugh. I hope you won't mind too much. We're putting you up at The Palms."

Gram interrupted. "I still say that's foolishness, Stacy. I can make up a nice bed for Hughie on the back porch—"

"And he'd be waked at dawn with the kitchen racket, Gram. You know what Edward said. An intern needs every bit of rest he can get while he's free of the hospital. You don't mind, Hugh?"

Gram tossed her head. "I am not rackety in my kitchen."

"I don't mind at all." Actually he was pleased, though he couldn't say it in front of his grandmother. There wouldn't be much chance to sleep here, not with wedding preparations underfoot. Clytie had chosen to be married in the ancestral home, to walk down the long front stairway as her mother and her mother's mother had before her. With Grandfather to marry her. He was retired now, but once a minister of the Lord, always a minister.

"I am not rackety," Gram said more loudly.

"Of course you're not," Hugh's mother said. "Stacy didn't mean it that way. But Hugh will get more rest at a motel. It's only a few blocks away."

Hugh grinned. "I can be over here before you get that rackety breakfast cooked, Gram."

"You look thin," she accused. "You're working too hard." She said the same thing whenever she saw him. He'd always been her favorite.

"You see," Stacy continued explanation, "with Mother and Dad and the girls with me, and Ellen, Clytie's roommate from Washington—I don't have any more room. John and his parents and brother we put here. That still left a room for you. But at the last minute his grandparents decided to fly out. So there isn't a room."

Gram said, "Putting Hughie out for strangers. I don't hold with that."

"They aren't strangers, Gram," Stacy said with tired patience. She'd obviously been through this a dozen times. "They're almost in-laws. And John's grandfather is a minister just like Gramps. You'll like them."

"Hoity-toity New York people," Gram sniffed.

"Now, Gram, you know John's not hoity-toity. Why would you expect his family to be?" Grandfather asked.

"John's been in Arizona for two years. Time to get over it. They've never been West, John said so."

Gramps said gently, "We'll make them welcome, Stacy. Don't mind Mama. She's just feeling her pepper today."

It was all so homey and safe. Iris was only a small memory far back in Hugh's consciousness. She'd been out of it entirely until this matter of the motel came up, and with it, the strange sense of relief. When he analyzed it, he realized he had had a fear of her finding his car and turning up again. Making trouble. If she turned up at the motel, he could handle her. But she wouldn't. He was quite sure she'd take no chance of being held accountable for that ten dollars. She'd had what she wanted from him, the ride to Phoenix. She wouldn't want to see him again any more than he wanted to see her.

His grandmother had got up from the table and started to carry out the dishes to the kitchen. "I'll pepper you," she told her husband. "Hoity-toity," she muttered as she stomped away. "Hoity-toity."

She'd been born in the Territory of Arizona and was firmly convinced that only Arizonans were to be esteemed. She'd never quite forgiven Hugh's mother for marrying an Angeleno and moving to California. When Stacy married Dr. Edward and moved to Phoenix, Gram had considered it a judgment on her daughter for her own defection. Gram's other children had remained loyal; of the uncles and aunts, none was further away than Tucson.

Hugh said, "I guess I'd better go check in and get my things unpacked. What's the schedule for today, Stacy?"

"Edward has already checked you in, Hugh." She opened her purse. "Here's the key."

"Thanks." It was like Edward; he was always thoughtful about such things.

"The schedule? Tonight's a barbecue at Uncle Dan's. The whole tribe of course and members of the wedding party. Sports clothes."

Gram returned for more dishes. "Barbecue. Cooking outdoors like Indians." She didn't wait for rebuttal but trotted back to her kitchen.

"The Bents are flying in tomorrow morning from New York."

"Want me to meet them?"

"Thanks, but Edward believes we should do the honors. I suppose we should." She sighed. "There's too much to do. Clytie wants Mother and me to drop in on the party this afternoon. You can't imagine the entertainment she's had, Hugh. It seems as if every club on the campus has partied her. There are enough gifts already to furnish a mansion. I don't know where we'll store them until she and John return from Germany. He has European orders, you know."

He knew. It was the European orders which had pushed the wedding up from June to May. John's wing was leaving next week. Clytie would follow after graduation.

"Anything I can do to help—"

"There'll be plenty. Tomorrow is Ellen's bridal luncheon for Clytie. Then there's rehearsal in the afternoon and our bridal dinner at night. We're having it in the private banquet room at The Palms, where you're staying."

"And the main event?"

"Sunday afternoon. Four o'clock. We can't decorate until Sunday, we're using fresh flowers. Oh, we'll keep you busy, Hugh. You'll be run ragged like all of us. If you can get any rest today, make the most of it. You won't have another chance until after the wedding."

"Okay, Stacy. Count me in." He stood up. "When do you want your car, Mother?"

"You'll need it, staying at the motel. I'll ride with Stacy. You can bring the folks out to Daniel's tonight. Six-thirty."

"A pleasure." He stage-whispered to Gram, now folding the tablecloth, "You're going to be my girl at that Indian barbecue and you can so inform your husband."

She snorted, then regained her good humor and laughed.

"Whenever you do want the car, Mother, let me know. Bye, all. See you later."

He drove over to Van Buren and on east to the motor hotel. As he was registered, there was no reason to stop at the desk. He followed the circular drive around to 126, the number on his key. For once he had no rancor at being assigned to a rear unit. His car wouldn't be visible from the street, just in case Iris found some more kids to tour her about the town looking for him. Why on earth should she look for him? He was obsessed and it was nonsense. There was no reason for her to return to haunt him.

The Palms was one of the new luxury motels on the eastern extension of Van Buren. There were no second-rate units. He moved his bags into the bleached-wood elegance, cooled to proper temperature by the wall thermostat. Sliding glass lanai doors opened to a vast expanse of close-cropped green, bisected with bleached white walks. Across the green was a tropical blue pool with clusters of sky-tall palm trees bending over it. Hot-pink umbrellas shaded white tables and desk chairs, hot-pink chaises for sunbathers were grouped at the pool's tiled rim. A faint *plash* came across the lawn as a diver curved from the high board.

The large room with its two oversized beds was meticulously clean, the blue-tiled bath was stocked with good towels, the desk held hotel stationary and guidebooks, the television set worked. There was no reason to expect otherwise. Edward wouldn't select a place without standards of quality. But then you never knew. Remembering stories his mother told of traveling when she was a girl, personally recalling trips he'd taken as a child, he could believe that times had definitely changed.

He hung up his suits and slacks, put away his other clothes in the bureau drawers, laid open his toilet kit on the tiled dressing table. The medical bag he pushed to the back of the shelf. It was two o'clock. Enough of the pre-wedding excitement had entered him to cancel any ideas of sleep. He needed to unwind, but he was so unused to idleness these days, he didn't know how to begin.

Out of simple curiosity, he picked up the telephone directory from the desk and turned to the C's. No Mayble Carney was listed. It could be she lived in a rooming house or had one of those modern apartments with a switchboard. He flipped to the yellow pages, Beauty Parlors. They bore cute names, not those of their owners.

He was just stubborn enough to try to find out if there was a Mayble. He asked the switchboard for Information. When that operator responded, he gave the name and address Iris had written. There was no such person listed at any address.

By now his stubbornness had solidified. There weren't too many beauty shops. He called them, one by one. It took a full hour. Not one had a Mayble Carney working there at present or in memory. He put away the phone and flung himself on the bed. So she'd got by with the lie, the one he hadn't believed could be a lie. He still didn't think she'd invented Mayble. But Mayble wasn't her aunt or didn't live in Phoenix. Possibly Mayble was one of the "kids" in Banning or Indio or Blythe, and Iris had been snickering to herself when she'd put across that whopper.

He'd written off the money, it wasn't that. It was being played for a sucker. He wouldn't suffer because he'd given away ten bucks, not like some of the poor guys who had nothing but their intern's pay. He'd been one of the lucky kids who never knew want, never knew the kind of deprivation which Iris, to look at her, must have lived with all her young years. His family wasn't wealthy but they were comfortable, had always been. He couldn't hold his anger against the girl, she was too miserable a creature. How could she help being what she was?

He got up from the bed. It was still too early to dress for the evening. He decided to go across to the newsstand and buy the Los Angeles papers. Just possibly there might be a report of a missing girl. He didn't have to believe that Iris' father and mother were what she said they were, although that too had had the ring of truth. Like the name of Mayble Carney.

He walked across the green to the motel office. The heat of the afternoon was a shock after the air-conditioned room. It was little wonder that the only guests in view were clustered by the pool. In the lobby the clerks and the bellboys were listless before the evening rush. At the desk he made arrangements for the car to be serviced and washed. With its cross-country dust, it was not fitting for wedding activities. He bought the *Times* and the *Herald-Examiner* at the newsstand. They were mail editions and most of the news would be old, yet the girl had left home yesterday. There could be a mention.

Returned to his room, he searched all the pages with care but there was no story of any missing person. Maybe she wasn't a runaway, maybe that denial had been honest. Leisurely he caught up on the sports and columns, on Gordo and Charlie Brown and Dick Tracy. By then it was time to shower and dress and go gather the grandparents. He wasn't worried any longer. He was actually relieved that there hadn't been an Aunt Mayble to find out who had given Iris a ride to Phoenix.

*

It was past midnight when he returned to the motel. It had been a singularly happy evening. Lieutenant John Bent was almost good enough for Clytie. As for Ellen Hamilton, Clytie's former roommate—why hadn't any of the family told him what to expect? She was the most beautiful girl he'd ever seen, he who came from a family of beauties.

Ellen carried herself like a model, tall and slender and prideful. Small nose, enormous black eyes slightly tilted, skin like golden sand. Smooth dark hair not worn in one of the silly modern French fashions but with a bang across her forehead, and brushed down to a slight curve just above her shoulders. He could almost believe his mother and Stacy had entered into a conspiracy of silence lest he shy away from her.

He hadn't had half a chance to make headway tonight. John's Air Force friends had surrounded her as if she were a shiny new spaceship. What Hugh had learned about her had been from his mother. Ellen had graduated *cum laude* from Vassar. She was taking special courses at George Washington, preparing for foreign diplomatic service. On that item, he had realized that her father was the Judge, that she was the Washington, D.C., Hamiltons.

It was just as well he hadn't had a chance to be alone with her, he might have fallen. A young doctor, not yet in practice, had nothing to offer an Ellen Hamilton. Moreover, he had no intention of getting involved with any girl until he had paid back the family for their backing him all these years, and was earning enough to support a wife on a decent economic level.

At this hour the cars were parked closely in their lanes at the rear of the units. Not that all the guests were in bed; there were lights behind most of the drawn curtains. The late, late TV show echoed from open lanai doors. He parked as close as possible to 126, locked the car, and walked over to his door. He let himself in, flipped the night latch to keep the maid out in the morning, and put on the lights. He'd left the air conditioning on when he went out; he turned it off now, the motor hum would be disturbing for sleep. It wasn't needed, the night had turned definitely cool. He checked the door screen, it was locked, and he drew the draperies across it, leaving the doors open.

He turned on the TV set, tuning until he found the one with the old movie. He removed his jacket and hung it in the wardrobe, loosened his tie, and stretched out on one of the beds. The soporific picture would relax him for sleeping.

The soft rap on the locked rear door came almost immediately. He didn't comprehend it at first, he took it for an extraneous sound, from the television set or the next-door unit. Only when it was repeated did he know it for what it was, a knocking at his door. His first thought was that it was a mistake, someone at the wrong unit; his second that it was, for some reason, the management. It couldn't be his family. If they'd wanted him for any purpose, they'd have telephoned before coming. He walked slowly back to the soft sound, unfastened the night latch, turned the knob. Only when he saw her standing outside, did he realize that he'd been afraid it might be Iris. She was wearing the same dirty outfit, even to the scarf hiding her hair.

He was furious but he kept his voice quiet. "What are you doing here?"

She spoke almost in a whisper. "I got to talk to you."

"No, you don't." He moved into the doorway, blocking it so that she couldn't push in. "There's nothing whatever you could have to say to me. You go on now. And don't ever come around here again."

"I won't stay but a minute," she protested. "Let me come in just a minute."

"I wouldn't think of it." He spoke with finality. He hoped she would recognize it as such. "Go on home. You could get in a lot of trouble coming here."

And get him into worse trouble. But he wouldn't say that to her, wouldn't put it in her head. She might not know how bad she could make it for him.

"I'm in a lot of trouble." Her head was turned and she spoke under her breath.

"Because you don't have an Aunt Mayble living here and you don't know what to do next?" But she had someone or she wouldn't be able to drive around and discover where he was staying. Or was it possible she had telephoned the motels until she found a Dr. Hugh Densmore registered?

"I do too have an Aunt Mayble. In Denver." She was peering beyond him into the lighted room. She said, "Please, let me in, just for a minute."

He stood firm. "No, you can't come in," he repeated. It was bad enough to have her outside on his doorstep. There was no way of knowing how many persons might be seeing her there. "I tried to help you on the road but I can't help you any more. Go to the Travelers' Aid. They'll see that you get home."

"I can't go home," she said dully. She looked up at him. She said it again with a muted emphasis, "I'm in trouble. Real trouble."

Somehow this had never occurred to him. It was a shock. "Is that why you came to Phoenix?"

She nodded dumbly. She looked sick. "I thought my boy friend would marry me. But he's already married. He didn't tell me that when we were going around together. He's married and got a couple of kids."

He didn't know what to say. Finally he told her, "I think

you'd better go to the police and tell them your story. They'll work out something for you." He didn't know what else to advise. Certainly there would be a welfare department in a city the size of Phoenix. Despite everything she was, he was sorry for her. "I can't do anything for you."

"Yes, you can," she said. The old familiar slyness had come into her face. "You're a doctor."

For a moment he couldn't speak. He was frozen with rage. When his voice returned, it didn't sound like his own. "I'm a doctor, yes. A doctor, not a quack. Now you get out of here before I call the police."

He shut the door on her before she could say anything more. He was shaken, he felt physically ill. That she'd had the brazen nerve to come to him for this. And her betrayer, had he been outside in one of those cars watching the scene, waiting to see if she brought it off? He must have driven her here after she had told him it was a doctor who gave her a ride to Phoenix.

If either of them returned, he would call the police. He realized the risk he would be taking, the lies she could tell, her word against his. But the police would check, they would find out that Hugh had never laid eyes on her before yesterday afternoon. He had the strength and the prestige of the University Medical Center behind him, if it came to that. But with that awful sickness of heart, he knew that she could say things which would ruin his hopes of remaining at the university, much less of being granted a research scholarship. There'd always be a residue of suspicion that the girl's inventions weren't all false. How could he prove otherwise? They had traveled together.

While the flickering screen unwound its meaningless story, while the sound track uttered its meaningless words, he waited for another knock on the door. He waited until the picture ended. But there was no more intrusion. She must have believed him when he said he'd call the police.

He undressed, turned out the light, and went to bed. It was a long time before sleep came. He knew how close he was to danger. When he heard the telephone ringing, he came awake at once as he was trained to wake, quietly, completely. He saw that it was morning. He was almost afraid to lift the phone from its cradle. When his mother's voice responded to his hello, he drew a deep breath.

"Did I wake you, Hugh?"

"That's all right. What time is it?" His watch was on the table.

"Ten o'clock. I wouldn't have called but I've an endless list of things Stacy wants done. She and Edward dropped me here at the folks' on their way to the airport."

"Hang on. I'll be there in ten minutes."

He almost made it in ten. Five minutes to shower and shave, five to dress—slacks, sport shirt, loafers. He'd learned in the hospital not to dawdle.

His mother was with his grandmother at the dining-room table, reading the morning paper. He had forgotten about the papers, what might be in them. His mother glanced at her watch. "I wouldn't have believed it possible of you."

Automatically he grinned at her. "Fooled you, eh? Want me to taxi you on the tour?"

"Not until you've had your breakfast," Gram declared. "Sit down, young man." She was off to the kitchen before he could deter her.

His mother said, "Would you? It would be such a help not to battle parking."

"It would be my pleasure." Casually, he picked up the section of the paper beside her plate. Sports section. She had the front page.

His grandmother reappeared with a platter of ham slices and three eggs.

"Gram! I'll be too fat to waddle."

"Nonsense. They've been starving you at that hospital." She skittered back to the kitchen, to reappear with a plate of hot baking-powder biscuits. "Now eat up. That's my own strawberry jam in the blue bowl. I'll pour your coffee."

He could ask it casually: Any news? He didn't.

But he wished his mother would comment on what she was reading. Surely she would if there were a missing-girl story. He couldn't ask for the paper, not with Gram visiting with him. Somewhere along the line of errands, he'd pick up the Los Angeles

Times. If a California girl were missing, the report would be more complete than in a Phoenix newspaper.

He put aside his napkin. "Sorry to eat and run, ma'am, but that's the way it is when you're a doctor." He kissed his grandmother's dry cheek. "That's the best breakfast I've had since I was a boy. Remind me to marry you when you get a divorce from Gramps. Where is he this morning?"

"I sent him to the barber shop to get prettied up for the wedding tomorrow." She gave him a wicked smile. "And to keep him from underfoot while I did my baking. I'm making the wedding cake, did you know that? Clytie didn't want a boughten cake, she wanted old Gram to make it."

"Clytie's a smart kid," he said. "Come on, Mother. Let's get with it."

They left the cool house for the blaze of the street. As they went down the steps, automatically he scanned the neighborhood. There was no one of the size and shape of Iris in sight. He helped his mother into the car and took the wheel. "Where first?"

"The florist's. To order the corsages for tonight." She gave him directions. She couldn't have been more casual when she asked, "How did you like Ellen?"

"So-so."

"Hugh!"

Her outraged exclamation made him shout with laughter, the first decent laughter he'd had since yesterday afternoon. "You're too transparent, Mother. She's gorgeous, absolutely gorgeous, as you darn well know."

"She's been dying to meet you."

"Sure. And now her dreams are shattered."

"They are not. She likes you."

"Me and the Air Force."

She didn't have an opportunity for rebuttal. They were at the florist's. He let her out and found a place to park further up the block. Ellen Hamilton didn't have to come to Arizona manhunting. She would have the pick of the lot in Washington and Philadelphia and New York. His family was good, but it wasn't one of the old eastern families whose status went back to Revolutionary days. Except for his grandmother and one branch of the Densmores, none of the lines was more than three generations out of the South. No, he wasn't going to start dreaming any dreams of Ellen. He'd settle for one of Celeste's sorority sisters. By the time he could afford to marry, it would more likely be one of Allegra's.

His mother returned. "Now the stationer's. With John's grandparents coming, we need more place cards for tonight. I hope I can find the same pattern." She touched her temples with her handkerchief. "When I'm in Phoenix, I wish we had air conditioning in the car like the Phoenicians."

"John seems a good guy."

"He is. A real darling. Clytie's a lucky girl."

"What about his luck?"

His mother pretended to sigh. "You're always too quick for me, Hugh. But you might start doing a little shopping around yourself. When your niece gets married, it's high time you started to settle down."

"Don't you think I should wait until I'm earning a living?"

"Hugh, you know your father and I—"

"Okay, okay, lady." He touched her hand. "But you know how I feel about leaning. I've done enough of that. Don't worry, I'll pay you back in rubies some day." The words brought again the uneasiness of what Iris might be saying right now.

"We know you will. But you needn't. Right here, Hugh."

They were in the heart of downtown Phoenix, with no possible place to park. He said, "I'll drive around the block."

"It won't take me long. If they still have the pattern."

He circled several blocks, hoping there would be an opportunity to stop near one of the large newsstands, but there were no spaces anywhere. His mother was waiting on the walk when he returned.

It was the same in the half dozen or so stops. If he could park, there was no newsstand. If he couldn't, the racks were so near yet so far. After a time, he stopped bothering about it. He could buy the paper when he returned to the motel.

At noon his mother said, "I'll have to let the other things go for now if I'm to make the luncheon. Maybe I can get them later this afternoon, I don't have to attend the rehearsal. Do you want to drive me back to Stacy's or shall I drop you?"

"I'm your chauffeur. I shall even wait for you and deliver you to the luncheon party." And with luck, Ellen as well.

"I hate to take your time."

"It's your car and I haven't a blessed thing to do. As a matter of fact, it's fun—like old times."

"You're a charmer, Hugh. Now give me a cigarette and turn right at the next corner."

Stacy and Edward had built in the new section south of town. It was a neighborhood of attractive homes, some large, some not so large, comparable to any city's good suburban development. It took about twenty minutes from town to Stacy's door.

"You're going to have to hump it to make a one-o'clock luncheon, Mother. Where's the event taking place?" He matched her stride up the flagstone walk.

"All the way back to town. The Adams, private dining room. Stacy and the girls have probably gone on. You make yourself comfortable while I rush."

The girls had gone, worse luck. But the Phoenix paper was on the table. And the air of the house was revivifying. He leafed rapidly but thoroughly. There was nothing in the news about Iris. His mother had returned by the time he started to read the front page.

There was never a parking place near the Adams Hotel. He doubled to let her out near the entrance. "I'll be back for you at three and we'll finish off your errands fast. If you don't get some rest before tonight, you'll be on sedatives."

He drove away. He turned on the radio now. He hadn't earlier, preferring conversation with his mother. Since being in residence at the hospital, he hadn't had much time for visiting with her. There was no news coming from any station, nothing but music, not the kind of music he wanted to hear. He turned it off again. He didn't want to go back to the motel but he did want the Los Angeles newspaper. If he were in Los Angeles, there'd be a drugstore on every second corner where he could stop for it and a cold Coke. This was Phoenix. He passed only one drugstore on his drive to The Palms and it didn't look promising.

It was ridiculous to be chary of returning to his comfortable quarters. Iris wouldn't come again. She'd be afraid to. She'd known all right, by his voice and his face, that he meant what he said when he warned her last night. With no more debate, he turned in at the motel, circled to his unit and parked. He walked through the grounds to the lobby. Today's *Times* was on the newsstand. He bought it and the Phoenix paper, then went his room. The maid had already made it up. He turned the air conditioner to a higher notch, pulled aside the draperies and opened the lanai doors for the view across the green. The swimming pool was decked with sun-tanned lovelies, lobster-red hopefuls, and grub-white newcomers.

He covered both papers with the same thoroughness he had yesterday's and found nothing. Iris had perhaps had a rare moment of truth when she said her mother was gone and her father didn't care what she did. He presumed there could be such parents; he just hadn't ever happened to know any.

He put away the papers. He'd severed his connection with Iris; he didn't have to dwell on it any longer. But he couldn't help wondering what had happened after she'd left last night. The man who'd got her in this trouble would have had to come up with other plans. More likely than not, he'd put her on a bus and shipped her back to Indio. With whatever lies he could invent to fool an expert and make her willing to go. The promise of money. Of sending for her later. If he had a wife and two children, he couldn't have scuttled around trying to find an abortionist for her. Phoenix wasn't a large enough city for a man to be anonymous; he'd hardly risk word of such a search getting back to his wife.

Hugh wished he could have helped her last night. Not in the way which had occurred to her in her desperation, but helped her to get in touch with someone or some organization who would protect her. He had not dared take the risk. In his home town, yes, but not a stranger in a strange city.

At three he was again at the downtown hotel, hopeful for a glimpse of Ellen. She might have been one of the girls just driving off in John's car. His mother came out alone.

"It was a beautiful affair, I wish you could have seen the table, Hugh. Now if we can tick off these errands—"

It took close to another hour. In heat that was pushing the hundred mark. It was four o'clock when he returned her to Stacy's. "As your doctor I insist you lie down for an hour before you start any more activity. Say you will."

"I'll try." She didn't ask him to come in. "Dinner's at eight. Dad and I are picking up the folks tonight. You're escorting Ellen, did I tell you?" She didn't allow him to answer. She went on up the walk.

As he drove away, again he tried the radio, hoping for a news broadcast. Again it was the wrong hour; the same wailing music seemed to be coming over every station. He left it on, turning it down to a subdued murmur, just in case the news cut in.

There was no reason to go back to the lonely motel, to the vulnerable motel. He might as well drop by the grandparents'. Perhaps he could have a preview of the cake. He failed on that; no one, not even Hughie, was to view it until the wedding reception. But he spent a pleasant interlude with the elder Bents, not half as hoity-toity as Gram herself, and John's young mother, who was cooling herself with iced lemonade and his grandmother's palm-leaf fan. Dad and John's father were on the golf course; the heat couldn't deter avid golfers. While Hugh was there, John and his brother Paul, a younger but more serious edition, came in. They'd been swimming at the pool of one of Stacy's neighbors.

"Why didn't someone tell me about that?" Hugh moaned, covering the spurt of anger against Iris which erupted in him. If she hadn't intruded, he'd be having the carefree holiday he'd counted on, not contemplating dark corners of his soul. In his anger, he lost his fear of her. He rose to leave; it was past five. "Have to give myself plenty of time to dude up for the glamour girl."

Without prompting, Paul asked, "Ellen?"

"The line forms on the right," John announced.

"Do you know how many bids for the prom she had the year John graduated?" Paul queried. "Ten! Ten, no kidding."

"Who was the lucky man?"

"I was, who else?" John said. "But then I met Clytie and the other nine had a chance."

His mother said reprovingly, "Ellen's a lovely girl, John. Don't give Hugh the wrong impression of her."

"He's just showing off, Mum," his brother said. "His last blithe bachelor brag. Good luck, Hugh."

"I'll need it with John's winged cronies hovering. Later."

He didn't turn up the power on the radio when he drove away, he didn't think of it. He was almost to The Palms when the murmur came through to him: ". . . girl . . . this morning has not yet been identified . . ." That much, and the announcer launched into a coffee ad.

Hugh drove past the motel, on up Van Buren, flipping the stations but finding no other news. There was a cluster of shops near 36th Street; he remembered a combination variety and drugstore which carried the newspapers. He made a left turn across the road and into the sandy lot. The papers were stacked just inside the door. The black headline thundered at him: GIRL'S BODY FOUND IN CANAL.

The masthead was of the Phoenix afternoon paper. None of the others seemed to have the news. Somehow he managed to fumble a dime from his pocket and carry it to the woman at the cash register in the rear of the store. Somehow he managed to fold the paper under his arm and walk out of the place steadily, unhurried, untouched. Even before reading, he was certain the girl was Iris.

He didn't dare remain here. It was too public a place, he would attract attention. He drove further out on Van Buren toward Tempe, and turned off at a side street, deserted as a country lane. There he stopped the car and fearfully unfolded the paper. The fact that she was unidentified didn't mean that there might not be some mention of her appearance at The Palms, or of her arrival at the bus station in a white Cadillac with California plates. There was always the innocent bystander who noticed.

She was Iris. Wearing the same green slacks, the same soiled shirt, the same socks and sandals, even the gaudy scarf floating from her hair. There was no mention of the handbag or the traveling case. There was no mention of the high school jacket. The Zanjaros, who patrolled the canal, had discovered the body this morning, floating in the waters on Indian School Road in Scottsdale. The girl was believed to be about fifteen years old. An autopsy would be performed to determine the cause of death. Anyone knowing her identity was asked to come forward.

That was all.

It wasn't suicide. She was too resourceful to commit suicide. Hugh knew the cause of her death. That would be the next story. An illegal operation. A dirty, bungled operation. A murder. A murder committed by two unknowns, the man who had first betrayed her and then taken her to the abattoir, and the man or woman who'd killed her and her unborn child.

Hugh could come forward and identify her. But he dared not. Because he was a doctor, because he had brought her to Phoenix, and because he was so certain that death was the result of abortion, he could not risk telling the police he knew her. They would have to find out some other way. He could only hope they would also find out quickly why she was here and who her boy friend was. If they didn't and if the "kids" in Blythe and in Indio talked, Hugh would become the suspect. And, bitterly, he knew his truth would not be believed.

For long moments he sat there on the road, trying to arrange his thoughts. He couldn't leave town, not without telling the family why, not without spoiling Clytie's wedding. The wedding wasn't important only to Clytie, it encompassed the entire family, four generations of family.

Anyway, to flee in panic was not the answer. It was construed always as the act of a man bloodied with guilt, although in fact the innocent man involved beyond his depth might have more reason to run. Was there any possibility she had been seen at his door last night? He couldn't recall any cars driving up while he talked with her, nor had anyone in that period gone in or out of any of the units in his wing. No one could have been looking out of windows at her, the only windows at the rear were in the bathrooms and were of frosted glass. But he couldn't know how many persons might have seen her cross to his door. Nor could he know whether even now the Blythe inspectors might be hearing the story over the radio, and informing Phoenix of Hugh's license number and their version of yesterday morning's incident. He couldn't deny giving her a ride. Her fingerprints were all over the car.

If only there were someone he could tell his story to, someone who could advise him. There was no one, not here in Phoenix. At Med Center, yes; there were half a dozen colleagues. And there was the Dean, in whom he would have no hesitancy in confiding. But here, no one. Not his father or mother; he would not put this burden on them. At one time his grandfather would have been the perfect one, but he was too old to bear it now. His grandmother was too emotional and she was too old. Not his sister or her husband, not until after the wedding. After the wedding, if there were need, Edward would be the one. He was a respected doctor in town. Enough so to engender respect for his young brother-in-law? Hugh could hope. Perhaps enough so that Hugh's story would be understood and its truth accepted.

Nothing must happen until after the wedding. He would accept whatever ordeal there might be if only nothing were permitted to destroy the pride of the family, gathered together for this joyful moment of its continuance.

The sun was lowering in the sky. He looked at his watch. Six-thirty already, and he started the car. He turned up the radio; there was news coming in. He drove slowly, listening.

There was no new material. Results of the autopsy were not mentioned. Again there was a plea for identification of the girl. He had that much reprieve. His link with her had not been discovered. But fear leaped again. Undiscovered, or suppressed by the police for their own purposes? The police did not give out all their information to the press.

He had to return to the motel; he could postpone it no longer. As it was, he'd be late arriving for his first date with Ellen. He did not know how he could endure the long evening ahead. If only the bridal dinner were being held any place but in The Palms, somewhere private which the police could not know about. If only the police would not arrive until after the last toast had been lifted. If only they would not learn of him until after the benediction tomorrow. If only . . . If only he had never stopped to pick up Iris Croom.

✳

No one was waiting for him at the motel. No one stopped him at the door of his unit; he inserted his key and entered, locking the door behind him. For several seconds he stood there waiting, but no sharp knock sounded. And then he slapped some sense into his head. He was acting like an ass, acting as if he had some guilt in Iris' death. He stripped, started the shower. He had to snap out of it, not become the specter at the wedding feast.

He felt better after showering. He shaved and dressed, for Ellen Hamilton he didn't mind shaving twice in a day. It was seven-thirty when he surveyed himself in the mirror. He didn't look like a man wanted by the police.

What if the police did come to him? His story was straight and true, why should he think it wouldn't come across that way? He transferred wallet and keys, cigarettes and lighter to his pockets, remembered to fold a clean linen handkerchief for his white dinner jacket. He was ready to take off for Stacy's. But just before he opened the door he stopped and bent his head. He prayed silently, prayed as he often had when he was a little boy. *Please, God, don't let anything bad happen to me.*

No one approached him as he got in his car. No one stopped him from driving out of the grounds. His tension diminished and he drove with easy speed to his sister's home. There was no new radio news.

The afternoon heat had softened into balmy evening. The house was lively with light and the sounds of young laughter. He loped up to the door and walked in without knocking. Dr. Edward was adjusting Hale's tie. The youngest cousin was fifteen, this was his first dinner jacket. Ned Jr. at eighteen was an old hand.

Ned asked, "Shall I tell Ellen you're here? She's not half ready."

"I'm glad of that." Hugh sank into a cushioned chair. "I thought I'd be late."

His father emerged from the kitchen with a tray of martinis. "One round only. We don't want any accidents."

"One for me?" Hale quipped.

"When you're twenty-one," Edward said. He gave Hale a push. "Don't touch that tie again."

"But I get champagne at dinner, don't I? You have to let me have champagne," Hale insisted.

The argument must have been going for weeks. Hugh remembered himself at that age, someone's wedding. It couldn't have been Stacy's, he was ringbearer at that one in a velvet suit. It must have been Uncle Wood's, he married late.

"One glass, Edward," he put in his oar.

"One glass then. And sip it."

Hale winked at Hugh. Handsome and perfumed in her gray lace, Hugh's mother came from the bedroom corridor. Stacy followed, slim as a girl in her gold chiffon. And as nervous as if it were her own wedding, not that of her grown-up little girl. "We'd better get on our way. There are always last-minute things to do even with caterers."

"Just wait until I call Exchange, let them know where they can reach me." Edward finished his cocktail.

"Oh, Edward," she groaned. "Not at your daughter's bridal dinner."

He spoke as he dialed. "I'm a little worried about that hospital case. Besides, I have two little mothers waiting, none too patiently, for labor to commence. After nine months with me I don't think they'd settle for a substitute." He spoke briefly into the phone, then cradled it. "Just keep all of your fingers crossed that those babies don't decide to come out at four tomorrow afternoon."

The girls were approaching, the flutter of their voices preceding them. Hugh was surprised at himself; he awaited with the nervous excitement a boy was supposed to have only on his first date. Clytie came first, Celeste followed. Ellen was the last of the three, and Hugh's breath caught. With three sisters, he was usually up on female styles, but the honey-colored sheath which she wore, of some dull clinging material the exact color of her flesh, left him floundering. It could only be a French original, something the girls were always swooning over in the pages of *Vogue*, something you didn't find in L.A., only in Paris. Instead of the inevitable mink stole, Ellen carried a matching scarf, fully twelve feet long, lined in lynx. She told him it was lynx when he asked.

He helped her into the car and took the wheel. But he couldn't find words to entertain her. Once in the car his anxiety recurred. He'd been without news for too long. He wanted to turn up the muted radio but he was afraid of what might have developed in the past hour.

His anxiety heightened as he reached The Palms and turned into the driveway. The private dining room was on the side of the quadrangle furthest from his room. He didn't think the police would be waiting here, and they weren't. But he wondered how long it would take them to trace him to the dinner party. Particularly with the Cadillac parked outside the building.

He helped Ellen from the car. "You're very quiet tonight," she said.

Only then did he realize how withdrawn he'd been during the entire drive. He smiled and quoted lightly, "Problems. Always problems."

"Have I caused them?"

He touched her elbow. "You know, it must be awfully nice never to have to worry about that."

Her eyes slanted at him. "You don't know me very well."

"I don't know you at all." Her arm was satin, her perfume violets in cool rain. Cars were arriving in tiers. He saw no strangers among the wedding guests.

"Are you looking for someone?" Ellen questioned.

He didn't know he'd been that obvious. He must stop dwelling on it. There was no reason to think that the police would be searching for him tonight. Iris hadn't been identified. The last he'd heard she hadn't been identified. Until she was, it was a local story. Nothing to be reported in Blythe or Indio.

He smiled down at Ellen. "The Air Force," he told her. "I'm ready to take them all on tonight."

He doubted that she believed him, but she smiled in return. And they entered the safety of the private dining room. It was filled with guests and music and lifted voices. The long table was festooned with sweet white flowers. Spire white candles pointed their pale flames. Clusters of white camellias were at each setting. All of this for Clytie, secure, happy Clytie. And in a cold and dark place, a girl who'd never had anything lay unwanted, unknown; lay dead.

Hugh found their chairs and seated Ellen. "If I ever have a daughter I'll insist that she elope."

"My sister did. Mother was distraught but I must say Father bore up well."

Hugh didn't sit down until he heard Ellen's disturbed inflection.

"Are you sure you aren't expecting someone? You keep watching the door."

He laughed then and dropped into the chair beside her.

"I could disappear, you know," she said. "The Air Force is most accommodating."

He closed his fingers over her wrist. "Disappear with them at your own risk. I warned you what would happen if they moved in tonight." He could feel the throb of her pulse. "I didn't realize I was watching the door." He must guard himself. "It must be force of habit, expecting someone to rush in with 'Emergency, Dr. Densmore!' "

"It isn't a she?"

He made it definite. "It is not." Not a ghost.

She was laughing. "Or too many shes?"

"Don't believe Celeste. She's inclined to brag about big brother. Gets it from Gram—you know my Gram?"

"I know your Gram. She's in love with you."

"And I with her." And I could be with you. But his eyes jumped from her face to the opening door. It was only a uniformed hotel attendant with a salver of messages for Clytie.

Later he wondered how he ever got through the interminable dinner. He was there, laughing, listening, making the proper responses; eating without tasting, drinking too much champagne, falling in love with the charm of the girl beside him. But he wasn't there, he was in a fearful secret cave, waiting for approaching footsteps to sound, for the shape to emerge, the terrible voice to speak.

It was Ellen who had been speaking. Again he had to ask her what she had said. "I don't even know." She laughed. "Nothing important."

But he saw the puzzlement in her eyes and realized he'd been away once too often. He spoke softly. "I'm sorry. I'm truly sorry." He hesitated but he had to say it, to make her understand. "I do have a problem, a very serious problem."

"Would it help to talk?"

"It would. But not tonight." He recalled his earlier figure of speech. "There must be no specter at a wedding feast." He just touched her hand. "I won't go away again."

There was reassuring strength in her fingers as they clasped his. "Hold tight," she said.

After the dinner there was dancing and it was better then. There was no need for talk with her in his arms. When the Air Force took her away, he danced with Gram, then sat with her, not having to respond to her unending commentary.

At midnight the band played the plaintive bachelor song, "Good-bye, Girls, I'm Through," and the assembled voices were a choir serenading Clytie and John. The evening was over. Nothing had happened. Hugh's relief was so great that he felt lightheaded. He found Ellen in her usual encirclement. "Go home, little boys," he said blithely. "The party's over." He caught Ellen's hand, this time his had strength.

Her eyes were bright as jewels. "No more problems?"

"Not tonight. Shall we wait outside?"

She was demurely provocative. "Shall we?"

They skirted the crowd making farewells and slipped out the door into the night. The temperature had dropped to desert cold. They half ran to the parking area.

Before they reached the car, Hugh saw the two men, one large, one slighter, emerge from the shadow of the wall. They weren't in uniform but he knew them at once for what they were. He stopped, stood unmoving, dreading what was to come. Ellen gave him a quick, questioning look. There was no time to explain. The plainclothesmen were on either side of him.

The large one asked, "Hugh Densmore?"

"Yes, I'm Hugh Densmore."

"We've got some questions to ask you."

Hugh spoke courteously, no audible quaver in his voice. "Could they wait until I drive my friends home?"

The guests were spilling out through the doors. They didn't seem to notice what was happening. Perhaps they thought these men were California friends. Again he prayed secretly. *God, don't let the family come out yet. Don't let them know.*

The big man said brusquely, "We been waiting long enough."

If Ellen hadn't been there, Hugh could have questioned them as to their purpose, as an innocent man would. But she was there and he couldn't bear that she should hear their answers. Not until he could tell her the whole story.

He turned to her and handed her the car keys. He said, for her ears alone, "Don't let the family know. Whatever this is, I'm sure it's a mistake and can be cleared up easily."

She didn't say anything; her eyes were enormous with wonder but not with fear.

The big one grunted, "Let's go."

Hugh continued rapidly to her, "Make up something but don't let them know. Please. I don't want them to worry."

"I'll take care of it." She sounded competent. "Call me later."

"Come on," the other detective ordered impatiently.

He left her then, before the two laid hands on him. Their hands were restless. They walked, one on either side of him, rounding the building, moving toward the opposite area.

He asked, "Are you arresting me?"

"What for? You done something?"

"No, I haven't. I don't understand this."

"We just want you to answer us a few questions."

It was worth trying. "I have a room here."

"One twenty-six," the smaller man said. He had the weathered face of a cowboy.

Hugh wondered if they'd searched his room, without benefit

of warrant, while they waited for him. Even more he wondered why they'd waited this long. They must have staked out his car. But they wouldn't have known which guest he was if they'd come into the dining room. It might have been the hotel manager who'd kept them from invading the party. Such things were bad for business.

It was worth trying because the night was cold. If they weren't arresting him, it would be more comfortable for them to ask their questions in a warm, lighted room rather than in a cold police car.

He tried to phrase the idea so it would not be rejected. He wasn't afraid of the men although the big one looked surly and the little one mean. He didn't think they would start something without cause. In the past year there'd been too much national publicity about police brutality and the rights of all citizens.

"We could go to my room," he suggested. "It's over there." But of course they knew where it was, they'd been there.

The big one glowered, as if he'd reject the idea out of hand simply because it was Hugh's idea. But the cowboy said, "Come on, Ringle. We might as well go inside. It's too damn cold out here."

Hugh had been counting on him, the way he hunched his shoulders with his hands dug in his jacket pockets. Their rank was evidently equal, because he led off.

As if it had been his own idea, Ringle said to Hugh, "Come on. You got your key?"

"I have it." They had to walk the long open path, past the swimming pool, to reach his room. The way was out of sight of the cars departing from the dinner. They met no guests. There were the usual lighted draperies in many rooms but no one parted them to look out.

Hugh didn't have to direct the men through the arch to the rear, they knew the way. At the door, he took out his key, turned it, and touched the light switch just inside. He stepped back for them to precede him into the room. The small one scurried in but the big one growled, "Go on," as if he feared that Hugh might cut and run. Or perhaps it was routine.

If they'd been in the room before, they'd left no traces. It was unchanged. He walked ahead and turned on the table lamp. He pushed the switch on the wall heater. "The room heats up fast," he commented. The small man's face was peaked with cold. Hugh was thankful he had turned off the air conditioning before he went out tonight. They might have changed their minds about remaining here; they might have insisted on a warm squad room.

He didn't know the procedure for questioning. He didn't know what were his rights. If you'd never been in trouble, you didn't think of these things. Both detectives were still standing. Hugh indicated the comfortable chairs; he himself took the straight one by the desk, turning it to face the room. Ringle sat down in the big armchair, the other man remained standing close by the heater vent.

Hugh said politely, "I'd like to know what this is all about. You're from the police, I take it."

There was to be no violation of civil rights, at least not yet. Ringle took a folder from his pocket, leaned out of the chair, and held it open for Hugh to glimpse. He didn't let go of it. "Detective Ringle," he said. He pointed to his partner. "Detective Venner."

"And you want to ask me some questions." He was calm. Now that it had happened, his nervousness had diminished. He was also thankful that he'd taken on the champagne early in the evening. Most of it had dissipated while dancing, the last vestiges in the cold walk to this room.

"That's right. You know a girl named Bonnie Lee Crumb?"

He shook his head slowly.

"You sure of that?"

"I've never heard that name before in my life," he said with honesty. Crumb—Croom? And Iris? Something beautiful in her ugly Bonnie Lee life?

"Why'd you come to Phoenix?"

"My niece is being married tomorrow. Dr. Edward Willis' daughter." They'd know Edward. On many cases he was called in by the Phoenix police.

Ringle was suspicious. "You're Doc Willis'—"

"Brother-in-law. He is married to my older sister."

"When'd you get here?"

"Yesterday morning. Around eleven o'clock."

Ringle struck. "You come alone?"

"Yes." He saw the lurking triumph on both of the faces, waiting to spring the trap; the discouragement as Hugh continued, "I gave a lift to a girl outside Blythe. She was coming to Phoenix to visit her aunt. She wasn't with me, simply a passenger."

"Her name wasn't Bonnie Lee Crumb?"

"Her name was Iris Croom." It was too much to hope that the detectives wouldn't detect the Crumb-Croom similarity. "Her aunt's name was"—he pretended to search his memory—"was Carney, Mayble Carney. She owned a beauty parlor in Phoenix, the girl said." Let them look for her too.

"Did you take her to her aunt's house?"

"No, I let her off at the bus station downtown. She asked to be let off there." He explained as if it had all been true. "Her aunt had expected her to come by bus and was meeting her there."

Ringle's lips pursed. "This Iris Croom a white girl?"

"Yes."

"But she let you pick her up?"

He couldn't get angry. And he wouldn't tell the entire story to these two, it was too unbelievable.

Venner piped up. "She was looking at that big white Cadillac, not the driver."

Hugh had long learned to control his voice no matter what burned within him. He said, "I was at the inspection station when she came over to my car and asked for a lift. She said she'd missed her ride." Even as he spoke, he wondered if the inspection officers at Blythe had put the detectives on him. Would they have remembered the name she called out and her shrilled story, or only the white girl asking him for a ride, and the license number of his car? He waited for Ringle to pounce.

But Ringle was addressing his partner. "Ain't you warmed up yet, Ven? Whyn't you sit down?"

"I don't want to sit down." Venner continued to lean against the grill, letting the hot air blow against his thin, shoddy jacket.

Ringle turned back to Hugh. "You read the papers today?"

"I looked them over."

"Read about that girl we found in the canal?"

He couldn't deny it. No one could have missed that headline. "Yes, I read about it."

"Read how we asked folks to come in and identify her?"

He nodded. "Has she been identified?"

Ringle's permanent scowl deepened. "Some kids found her purse tonight. In a ditch about a half mile from where she was found. There was a school-activities card in her wallet with her name, Bonnie Lee Crumb. We put that on the ten-o'clock news."

Venner suggested, "I suppose you didn't hear that news."

"No, I didn't hear any radio reports tonight. I was at a bridal dinner for my niece." As they well knew. He would not suggest an alibi by giving the time of his arrival there.

"Bonnie Lee Crumb, Indio High School, Indio, California." Ringle punched out the syllables as if this information would shake Hugh. Hugh waited for him to continue. "Where was this —uh—Iris Croom from?"

"She said she was from Banning."

Venner insinuated, "How'd you like to look at the one we found in the canal? Maybe you could identify her."

Hugh feigned surprise. "You don't think it's the same girl?"

Ringle said with meaning, "We got a tip."

Venner smirked. "Why do you think we're asking you these questions?"

Hugh was careful. With just the right amount of indifference, he said, "I have wondered."

"Like Ringle says, we got a tip. Right after that report went out on the radio. This guy says a nigger doc driving a big white Cadillac brought Bonnie Lee to Phoenix."

Hugh took a long breath. "Who was your informant?"

Ringle answered diffidently, "The desk sergeant took the call didn't get his name." And Venner continued, "The guy said we'd find the doc at The Palms."

"He gave you my name?"

"Naw, but we didn't have no trouble getting that at the desk here." The implication was in his titter.

Hugh permitted Venner his moment of triumph. Then he spoke, with precision. "It seems to me that this informant is the one you should be looking for. The name Bonnie Lee Crumb was known to him. I never heard it until you mentioned it tonight. The girl to whom I gave a ride was Iris Croom."

"How old was she?" Ringle snapped.

"I don't know. Young. In her teens, I'd say."

"You better come down and have a look at this girl we found." He lumbered to his feet.

Hugh didn't move. "Why?"

Venner took an avid step forward. "You're refusing?"

Hugh said, "If she is Bonnie Lee Crumb, I can't identify her. I have never known anyone of that name."

"Maybe she ain't Bonnie Lee Crumb. Maybe she's Iris Croom. You gonna come or not?"

Ringle stopped his partner's advance. He blinked at Hugh. "You don't have to come. We don't force you. We do everything legal." He turned his scowl on Venner. "You remember the marshal says everything legal."

"I haven't forgot it yet," Venner sneered.

He hadn't forgotten because this was Hugh Densmore and not some poor shabby guy they'd picked off the street or out of a shack.

"I'll come with you," Hugh decided, "if you think it will be of any help." He didn't want to; he didn't trust either of them. No matter what some marshal had said. But he didn't know the legalities, whether he could rightly refuse. Nor did he know if his outright refusal might bring ethical forgetfulness. "Will you wait until I get a warmer coat?" He didn't delay for an answer. He went into the dressing room, turning on the light as he moved. Ringle came casually over to the entrance, where he could watch the change.

Hugh took off his dinner jacket and hung it in the wardrobe. He put on his gabardine topcoat. He looked like a musician at the end of a party, the soft dress shirt and black tie, the tuxedo trousers. It was past one o'clock; he was too tired to go anywhere. He wondered how long it would be before he was permitted to return. If he would be permitted to return.

He switched off the light and returned to the big room. Ringle stepped aside. Hugh remembered, "I don't have a car."

"You can ride with us," Venner said.

He didn't want to ask, "And you'll bring me back here?"

"Sure, we'll bring you back." His mouth was a sneer. "Everything legal."

Hugh continued to be apprehensive but it was too late to change his mind. Ringle was holding open the door. If everything was legal, they'd have to charge him to hold him. And what could they charge him with? Not murder. Not without some evidence. This wasn't the Deep South. It was Arizona.

3

THEY WALKED THROUGH the icy night to where they'd left the car —not a painted police car, a plain dark sedan. They put Hugh in the back seat. Ringle tuned in the police cycle while Venner drove. The radio wasn't like Los Angeles, with never-ending codes coming over. There seemed to be but one item at this hour, a highway accident.

Venner took westbound Washington across town. There were few other cars abroad. Even when they reached the downtown section. When they passed the courthouse without reducing speed, Hugh knew fear. He spoke up. "Where are we going?"

Venner snickered over his shoulder, "To see your girl friend. You didn't think we were keeping her in the office, did you?" After a moment he bared his small teeth. "The icebox isn't big enough." He was the only one who laughed.

They had reached the dead-end circle of the state capitol, and he swerved to the left. Hugh's fear was growing. They were cutting a south-and-west course through a shabby neighborhood he'd never seen before. He'd read of tactics such as this, where a man could be held incommunicado for days.

There were no passing cars to call out to. You couldn't call for help from a police car, anyway; he didn't think you could. When Venner turned down a dark and narrow country lane, panic came up into Hugh's throat. Only his pride kept him from crying out, demanding to know where they were taking him. Pride and the fear. He'd never known fear before, he'd only thought that he had. There were no handles on the rear doors.

Not more than a half mile down the lane, Venner turned a sharp left into an area of low-lying buildings. There was a small sign: COUNTY HOSPITAL. It did nothing to allay the fear.

The place could have been a reclaimed army barracks. The night lights showed faded green brick with darker green trim. There was no sign of life. There was no sound but of insects in the surrounding fields and a sudden scrap of song from a meadow lark awakened by the car's lights.

The car crawled past the buildings, following the driveway to the far rear. It stopped in front of a small blunt building whose night light revealed the legend: COUNTY MORTUARY. Hugh took a breath. Everything legal.

Venner cut the engine. He got out and opened the door for Hugh while Ringle was extracting his bulk from the front seat. "All out for the morgue," Venner chirruped. "Only we don't call it the morgue, the coroner don't like that name. The 'County Mortuary,'" he mimicked.

Hugh walked with the detectives across the recessed outer entrance to the back door. The knob turned under Ringle's heavy paw.

The attendant on duty was an old man. "You again?" he complained. He pushed up arthritically from his office chair. His voice scratched, "You want to see that same girl?"

"Yeah," Ringle said. "Anybody identify her yet?"

"Nary a soul come around. She must of been a floater."

Venner wheezed, "That's what she was all right, a floater!" Again no one else laughed.

The old man shuffled forward ahead of them and opened the door of the storage room. Venner stopped laughing and be-

gan to shiver. Hugh was glad he'd thought of the topcoat. The
detectives wouldn't get a chance to say that the suspect quaked
when he saw the body.

The old man didn't fumble, he knew the slot where she was
put away. He rolled out the drawer, folded back the covering.
They hadn't done an autopsy yet. That was Hugh's first thought,
and with it came a spasm of relief. Surely they wouldn't make an
arrest until they knew what caused her death.

He looked the body over carefully, Ringle and Venner and
the attendant watching him as if they believed the old fables
about Negroes and graveyards. They weren't bright or they'd
know that to become a doctor one must study both the quick
and the dead.

The girl was Iris—or Bonnie Lee—as he had been sure it
would be. No two girls matched the description the police had
issued. She hadn't been in the water long enough to be distorted.

Because of his medical familiarity with morgue procedure,
Hugh was without emotion. His tension had dissipated in the
routine of examination. He looked over at Ringle. "Yes, this is
the girl who called herself Iris Croom."

The attendant began covering her again, as he might a sleeping child. Venner left the room rapidly, shaking from the cold.
Probably chronic malaria. Hugh followed him, Ringle at his heels.
In the office outside, Hugh lighted a cigarette. He had to know
if they were calling it murder.

"What was the cause of death?" He doubted that it would
enter their heads that as a doctor he knew the autopsy had been
delayed. Down the corridor, the metal door banged and the
shuffle of the returning attendant could be heard.

Ringle said, "We won't know that until the autopsy."

"It hasn't been done?"

"The M.E. is out of town. Making a speech at the University
of Chicago," Ringle said with a blustering pride. Hugh suddenly
recalled the national reputation of the Phoenix medical examiner.
With a man of his distinction, there'd be no juggling of facts to
fit a possible suspect. "He'll be back Monday."

A delay in performing an autopsy wasn't unusual. This
one was for Hugh an answered prayer. They wouldn't know un-

til Monday what had killed Iris or if she had killed herself. By then Clytie's wedding would be over. He asked matter-of-factly, "Would you mind taking me back to The Palms now. I'm pretty tired."

Ringle's eyes rested coldly on his face. Hugh met them, unmoved. It was Ringle who shifted. "Will you sign a statement identifying her?"

Hugh gave it consideration. It wouldn't seem to incriminate him further. "I'll sign a statement identifying her as Iris Croom. I didn't know her by any other name."

Venner didn't cover a yawn. "Maybe she was carrying some other kid's school card."

Ringle was preparing a report, leaning on the old man's desk.

Hugh said, "If she was Bonnie Lee Crumb, that man who called you is the one to identify her."

"We told you we don't know who he is." Nor did Ringle care. "He hung up when the sarge tried to get his name." He thrust the paper at Hugh. "Sign this."

First he read it with care. The name of Bonnie Lee wasn't on it. There was a space where Hugh printed the name—Iris Croom. He signed his name where indicated and returned the form.

No one moved to leave. It would be a mistake to be insistent; they could keep him here all night asking questions if they so wanted. They could make it appear voluntary. Instead of saying anything more, he started moving toward the door. He counted on Venner as before, Venner who looked pinched with weariness. He had it figured right. Venner moved. "Come on, Ringle."

Ringle finished studying the form. He told the old man, "Thanks, Pop. You can go back to sleep now. We won't be bothering you again tonight." Catching up with Venner, he said, "Don't be in such a sweat."

As previously, they put Hugh in the rear of the car. He watched the dark streets out the window as they returned to town. There was no deviation; Venner retraced the route. They passed the courthouse without pause and wheeled over to Van Buren. Ringle said then, "You aren't planning to leave town?"

"Not until Monday. I'm due at the hospital Tuesday."

"Hospital?"

"I'm interning at the UCLA Medical Center."

"You ain't a real doc?" Somehow this was agreeable news to him.

Hugh explained, "I have my degree but I haven't completed my internship. I was given leave to attend the wedding."

Ringle warned, "You better not plan on going back Monday."

"Why not?"

"Might be we'd want to talk to you again. After the autopsy."

Ringle knew, or his suspicions were the same as Hugh's. Only as to her murderer did they differ. Hugh said, "I'll check with you before I leave."

They delivered him to his door, Venner releasing him from the car.

Hugh said, "Thank you" and "Good night."

Venner didn't bother to respond; Ringle made some sound. They had driven away before Hugh had his key in the lock. He went inside, hung the DO NOT DISTURB sign outside on the knob, locked and bolted the door. He'd forgotten about lights and heat when he went out with them; both were still on. The room was too hot but his reaction had set in. Like Venner, Hugh was shaking as if chilled to his bone marrow.

It was far too late to call Ellen, it was almost three-thirty in the morning. A call might disturb the entire household, this he couldn't risk. What was more deterring was the fact that the story was too involved to give over the telephone. He didn't have the strength now to go into it. A realization came suddenly: it might not be safe to talk over this phone. He didn't know how far or how deep the detectives' suspicions extended. They could have a monitor on the switchboard.

Hugh undressed. He couldn't solve his problems tonight. Perhaps in the morning he could figure out what he should do.

When he woke, it was not completely but in a blur. He wondered if he'd missed the bells, wondered at the lazy euphoria which seemed to engulf him. And then he came sharply awake and remembered he wasn't at the Med Center, he was in a Phoenix motel. This was the day of the wedding. And this was the day after the night of nightmare. The girl he'd known as Iris Croom was dead, irrevocably dead, and he was involved.

Innocently involved? No, he couldn't call it innocent. Rather, it was mindless. It was neither; it was a paper chain of circumstance, cut from sympathy and too much imagination. Imagination, yes—why else should he have thought that unless he picked up the girl she would be in danger? Another car would have come along, a family car for which she had said she was waiting, or even another man, a white man. Most travelers, like most men, were intrinsically decent. The end result for Iris would have been the same, cruelly the same. But he needn't have been involved. He was the wrong man to have played Samaritan, and he'd known it, known it there on the road and in every irreversible moment since.

The room was airless. He came out of bed and turned the conditioning to high. He parted the curtains and quickly closed them again, against the searing brightness of the sun. Only then did he look at his watch. He was dismayed at the lateness of the morning. He'd intended to go with the family to Sunday morning services at his grandfather's old church. He wasn't much on churchgoing these days, but when he weekended at home he always accompanied his mother to services on Sunday mornings. It pleased her. Would the eventual headlines read: MINISTER'S GRANDSON ACCUSED OF MURDER?

He shaped up brusquely. That kind of thinking was pure neuroticism. There was no reason to believe that he would become further involved in this death. He had never known Bonnie Lee Crumb. There was someone in Phoenix who had, someone who'd made an anonymous phone call. The police would be searching for him, not harassing an innocent bystander. Yet he was unreasonably relieved that the detectives hadn't returned this morning, that his sleep hadn't been disturbed by a telephone call from headquarters.

Why should they come back to him? He had told them the truth last night, if not all of the truth. For all of his rationalization, he decided he should get out of here and quickly. Before they did return. Before there were reporters and news photographers hammering at the door. It occurred to him to wonder how it was that there were no newsmen last night at the mortuary. The police must be keeping this case well under cover. He didn't know if that was in his favor or not.

They had not put out a teletype with his name last night or as yet this morning. If they had, his sleep wouldn't have been undisturbed. It couldn't be that they would care about protecting Hugh's professional reputation. More likely it was because of the ramifications of the girl's double identity. They could be waiting to move until they made positive identification of Iris as Bonnie Lee Crumb.

He showered and dressed with his mind turning the maybe and if and perhaps and possible until he forced it to quiescence. If he were to emerge from this grim *geste* unharmed, he must walk through it the same man who walked into it. He, Dr. Hugh Densmore, product of his heredity and environment, sufficiently intelligent and well adjusted to his mind and body and color and ambition.

The services would be over, the family should be back at the grandparents', enjoying one of Gram's pioneer meals. He couldn't eat but he'd have a cup of coffee with them. This time he put on his sun glasses before parting the curtains. He slid open the lanai doors. It was another beautiful day, another hot day. There was no policeman on guard outside, no stranger at all. Far across the lawn by the pool, the sunbathers and the swimmers were again gala. He left the doors ajar, with the screen hooked; he liked fresh air with his air conditioning.

As he turned back to the room, he remembered his promise to call Ellen. His hand reached across the desk, then drew away. He wouldn't call her from this phone. He left the apartment, stepping out into the high blaze of noon heat. He'd forgotten he was without a car, he'd have to walk it. He didn't mind the walk, in a way he welcomed it. It would clear his head in a way that driving a car could not. There was no one on guard at this outside door, either.

He cut a rapid crosstown path toward Jefferson Street. Walking in one hundred-degree heat had little resemblance to walking on a Westwood campus. But he didn't diminish his pace even though he knew it to be compulsive. There was need to put as much distance as possible, and as quickly as possible, between himself and the motel. He wouldn't be hidden with the family. He had mentioned Dr. Edward last night. If Ringle and Venner didn't know, they could easily find out where to look for Hugh. His grandfather was as well known as the doctor.

Again the sick feeling overwhelmed him. Surely the police wouldn't interrupt the wedding. But having met Ringle and Venner, he knew that it would make no difference to them. They'd come for Hugh whenever they wanted him. It might even give them a twisted satisfaction to slur their black shadows over the shining white of the bridal ceremony.

When he reached his grandparents' house, he took the porch steps by twos as if Ringle's hand were outstretched to clamp his shoulder. He plunged into the living-room coolness. The voices led him to the dining room. They were at the table, not at one of his grandmother's Sunday chicken dinners, not on the wedding day. But the breakfast they were finishing was equally substantial. None of the young people was present, nor were the out-of-town guests. Only his father and mother and his grandparents.

His mother looked up, appalled. "You didn't walk over here, Hugh! Why didn't you call me?"

They hadn't heard of any trouble. They wouldn't be as normal if they had. He poured himself a glass of water and drank it slowly before answering the concerted hubbub.

"I'm a tenderfoot. Why didn't somebody remind me it would be a hundred and ten in the shade?" His voice sounded normal. He hoped his demeanor didn't belie it. He must remember to be supranormal all this day, not let an inflection or a glance betray the inner nerves.

"Have you had your lunch yet?" It was his grandmother, starting to rise.

Hugh put his hands on her shoulders. "I haven't had my breakfast yet. Don't move. There's enough here for all the starving Chinese." He sat down beside her.

"Those corn cakes are cold. And the bacon."

"You just brought them in, Mama." His father began to serve a plate.

"I'm not hungry," Hugh said quickly. "All I want is a cup of coffee." But he found himself eating; it was easier than arguing. "Where is everybody?"

His father said, "If by everybody you mean the girls, they've gone swimming."

"I thought you planned to go with them," his mother said.

"I planned a full day," Hugh told her. "I overslept." The Sunday papers must be in the front room. He should have thought about them when he first came into the house, before joining the family. Just for a quick look at the headlines. There could be nothing about him in them, not even implied, or his parents would be asking questions.

He heard his mother with his outer ear. "You needn't have sent the car back last night, Hugh. There are enough cars at Stacy's to take care of us."

This then had been Ellen's story. "It's your car."

"Maybe you thought you'd better not drive after the party," his father suggested.

"May be." His grin felt unforced. Ellen might have included such a suggestion. "Those magnums came around pretty often."

They were talking about the dinner and about this afternoon's reception and he tried to listen in case he should be called on for response. They didn't seem to notice his silence; as an excuse for it he kept eating. If he could get away from the table before they did, he could take a moment for the newspaper. The day's plans seemed to involve him; the girls would decorate the house but men were needed for the heavy work.

"Whenever you're ready," he heard his father saying. "You can give me a lift to Stacy's and bring the girls back here with you."

What he saw was his father taking the Sunday paper from the near chair. It had been invisible under the drape of the white tablecloth. Automatically his hand twitched out for it, even as he watched his father hand the folded sections to his mother. "I'm too old for heavy work," his father was continuing heartily. "Besides, after that champagne supper last night, I need a snooze. And once you clear the place of those babbling females, that's what I'm going to have."

Hugh could have asked her: May I have a quick look at the front section? But what answer could he give to her inevitable: Why, is there some particular story . . . ? And she would glance at the front page in passing, would see the headlines about the dead girl. Fear would squeeze her, the fear lying ever-dormant beneath the civilized front, beneath the normal life of a Los Angeles housewife whose husband's income was in near-five figures, whose children had been born and bred and coddled in serenity and security and status.

He did not ask. He rose from the table, made the proper good-bye sounds, and in a flurry of his mother's memoranda for Stacy, followed his father out to the car. He should have emerged with a reassurance granted by the untroubled respite of the dining table. But anxiety smote him as sharply as the sun glare when once he was in the open. He was not able to dismiss it until he was certain that there were no strangers loitering on the street, no unfamiliar cars standing at the curb.

"You drive," his father said. "I don't know whether it's the champagne or the weather, but I'm beat."

As Hugh took the wheel, the anxiety recurred. This was no longer his mother's white Cadillac, this was an item in police reports. He wondered how many eyes would be watching for it as it wheeled in and around the Phoenix streets.

It was important that he make a special effort to match his father's holiday mood. If anyone would sense something wrong in him, it would be Dad. "Anyone with no more sense than to play eighteen holes under an Arizona sun deserves what he feels," he said.

The radio had not come on at the turn of the ignition switch. Ellen must have turned it off manually last night. To protect him, just in case. He didn't turn it on. He couldn't risk it.

The inevitable question was being asked. "When do you have to be back at the hospital?"

"I can take a few days." He had to take at least one more day. If everything worked out right tomorrow, as it surely would, he could fly back in time for duty on Tuesday.

"I was hoping you might have a week, so you could drive

Mother home. She's going to stay on with Stacy and help her get rested up. The girls and I are flying out tonight."

How could it be possible to be comforted and fearful at one time? He echoed, "Tonight?"

"I must be in the office in the morning. Your sisters are bellowing to stay longer, but they've missed enough school this week."

Hugh said, "I wish I could stay." And he wished from the bottom of his heart that he could talk to his father about what had happened. But it wouldn't be fair. His father didn't get away often enough from his growing insurance business. Why should he have the vacation spoiled by Hugh's problems? Hugh was a man, not a child. Yet if it hadn't been that they were already in sight of Stacy's, he might not have been able to keep quiet. He'd always confided in his father, from the time he could talk. The dangerous moment passed. He parked in front of the house, and together, he and his father went up the walk.

Approaching the handsome suburban dwelling, for the first time Hugh's anxieties were truly allayed. The Densmores and the Willises weren't the kind of people you pushed around. The flurry of careless voices within the house increased his sense of security.

He called out, "All passengers for the fifty-cent tour to Phoenix, line up at the door. At once. This means now."

He was answered by protests and pleas from the bedroom corridor. The girls were obviously engaged in the multitudinous pre-preparations that were a part of partytime. In the midst of the clamor, Stacy sat on the living-room couch, turning the hem of her dress. "The girls said it was too long," she supplied.

Hugh didn't, couldn't, sit down to wait. He put out his cigarette in an ash tray and automatically lighted another. He was nervous about facing Ellen. He would have to give her an explanation for last night, and the only explanation there could be was the facts of the whole sordid mess. It wasn't something he wanted to tell her. Of all the many girls he'd known and liked and perhaps loved, she was one who might have developed into the real thing. If he hadn't met up with Iris Croom.

When Ellen emerged from the bedroom corridor, he knew

he hadn't been wrong in trusting her to handle things the night before. Her competence was implicit in the reassuring way her eyes met his in the moment before she put on her dark sun glasses. There might have been a flicker of relief that he was here, not held by the police. He attempted to move toward her, trying to make it unobtrusive, but his way was blocked by what seemed a roomful of sisters and cousins and nieces and nephews. She too made the attempt. But always before they could converge, the others, as in a ballet, had moved to thrust them apart again. He gave up and raised his voice, "Come on everybody who's going."

The rush through the door began. He watched Ellen approach. There was no chance to speak, for Clytie came pushing after her, calling back to Stacy, "But I have to go, Mother. I've always decorated the wedding arch. Besides, I'd go nuts sitting around here doing nothing until four o'clock."

When Hugh reached the car, the group was somehow mashed inside. With Ellen next to the driver's seat. He wondered if she had arranged it or if it were his sisters' matchmaking tendencies. He was sorry he would have to disappoint them. So sorry, but there was another girl . . . in another country, and the wench was dead.

Through his bitterness, he heard Ellen's voice, almost beneath her breath. "There's nothing about you in the morning paper or on the radio."

He said, as quietly, "It was too late to call you last night."

"I read by the phone until three. Is it—all right?"

He nodded. It wasn't a lie. Everything was all right as far as he knew. He said, "I'll tell you what it's about when there's a chance. Perhaps after the reception we can get away for a while."

"It's a date," she confirmed gravely.

Being able to postpone the recital somehow steadied his nerves. At the house, work, physical work, took over. He and the nephews put up the arch while the girls wrapped the white satin ribbon on the balusters and the handrail of the staircase. There was no time for brooding as they all raced against time to cover the whole with white oleanders and shining green leaves. His mother and Mrs. Bent were doing the dining room, the two grandmothers were stirring in the kitchen. It was near three o'clock

before all the groups were satisfied. And he must return to the
motel to dress.

He drew Ellen aside, ignoring the wise looks that followed
them. "Do you mind taking the crowd back to Stacy's? I'm going
to cut out."

"I'll drive you over."

"No," he said, too quickly, too sharply.

She must have known that everything wasn't right, but she
said only, "All right. You won't forget we have a date?"

"I won't forget," he told her, wishing that he could forget it,
or wishing that it was a date, no more than that. He waited for a
moment until attention had been diverted from him, then unhurriedly slipped out to the porch and ran down the steps to the
pavement. He struck out slantwise across the wide street, dodging
the Sunday afternoon traffic. The heat was no longer ablaze; by
now it was heavy, oppressive, as before a storm in the eastern part
of the country. In Arizona it didn't presage a storm, merely the
late afternoon. He walked as quickly as possible, but it was as
if he were walking through shifting sand.

He could have accepted Ellen's offer for a ride, but if Ringle
and Venner were waiting for him, he didn't want her exposed
to their scrutiny. Last night they had given her no attention,
they'd been too busy concentrating on him. Unless they saw
her again, they wouldn't remember her. They must not see her
again. He couldn't bear the thought of their ugliness touching her.

He was on the side street which led to the motel when he
first noticed the car. Noticed yet didn't notice the first time it
went by. It wasn't until it passed a second time, more slowly, that
he realized it was the same car which had been with him since
he'd crossed Washington. By then it was out of sight. He found
he could remember nothing, neither color nor shape nor make.
Just an old sedan with a man at the wheel. It could have been
a plainclothes police car; it wasn't so different from the one he'd
ridden in last night. But it hadn't been Ringle or Venner driving,
and there'd been only one man in it. The police usually worked
in pairs. For the first time it came to him that there would be
others besides the police interested in him. The unknown man Iris
had come to meet. The man who refused his name to the police.

The man because of whom the girl had met death. Three men or one.

The thought slowed his steps and the taste of fear was again in his mouth. Somehow he knew, knew with dreadful clarity, that this man had full intent to make Hugh the killer. He had begun last night with the anonymous call. No, before that he had shown his intent. The first shape had been when he brought Iris to Hugh's door on Friday night. It must have been he who brought her there.

Hugh half ran to the door of his unit. But he hesitated before turning the key and slipping inside. No messages, no persons waited for him. Having no radio, he turned on the television set, not expecting news but just in case. There wasn't any. He blanked out thought while he did what had to be done—another shower, a clean dress shirt, a cotton of lighter fluid to erase a spot of cigarette ashes from his white coat. When he was dressed in his wedding garments, he tried all the television channels but there was still no news. He said aloud, "No news is good news," but he knew he was lying as he said it. If only there were some way, some safe way, to make inquiries of the police. There wasn't. Not for him.

It was time to return to the grandparents' house, but he delayed. He was afraid, he admitted it, afraid to go outside. The fear was not now of the police but of a man without a face or name, a man who knew his face and name and where to find him.

He looked long at the phone. He didn't have to go back alone through the quiet, late afternoon side streets. He could call his sister's house; any one of a dozen cars would stop by for him. He had a good excuse, the wish to arrive for the wedding without passing through six or eight blocks of steam heat. He wouldn't let himself make the move toward the phone. He wouldn't give in to irrational fear. He turned off the air conditioner; the night's chill would have set in before he returned and he couldn't know but what he'd later need a warm room as he had last night. He could delay no longer. He took a last look at the television screen; it was advertising some children's remedy. He cut it off and was on his way.

It didn't seem so hot out now although the sun was still high above the horizon. In his white jacket, he was too visible. He wanted to cut and run but he made himself walk in normal fashion, paying no more attention to passing cars than he would have yesterday or the day before. If that one passed him again, he didn't recognize it. There were so many old dark sedans.

His spirits lifted when he reached the wide thoroughfare of Washington. Certainly nothing would happen here. It was a well-traveled street although there wasn't much traffic on a Sunday afternoon. He followed it to the side street which led over to the Jefferson house. On Jefferson he no longer had to fear. He joined the wedding guests making their way toward the house. He would be anonymous to strangers in the protection of the group.

Within the house, he took a place near the front door. He could step outside to meet them, if the detectives should come. Or if any uninvited guest intruded. But no strangers appeared.

✳

The wedding was quiet perfection. His grandfather pronounced the beautiful old words. The women wept and the men swallowed hard when Clytie's luminous face was turned to meet John's unaccountably solemn one. The bridesmaids were a frieze of summer-leaf chiffon; among them Hugh saw Ellen's flower face only. He wondered how much she had figured out. There was only one big story in the papers and she was not a stupid girl.

Because the wedding was in the home, the guest list was small—the family and a few old friends. But the reception which followed seemed to include the entire community. There was no segregation with Clytie's university friends and John's Air Force crowd on hand. In a way Hugh wished that Ringle and Venner could have been looking in. They might realize that poor shoddy little Iris couldn't have been the outworn cliché of sexual interest to Hugh.

During the reception, he couldn't remain on guard. He had to mingle with family and friends. With his fingers crossed against intrusion, he had to pretend the joy the others were feeling. Grandmother's towering white cake was cut, the toasts lifted. Hugh limited himself to one champagne cup. He would take no chance on a muddled head tonight.

At six o'clock Clytie tossed the bride's bouquet from high on the flowered staircase. Whatever arrangements John had made for their departure worked. The guests began to drift away. And at last he was free to go, to lift his dangerous shadow from the family's happiness.

If it had been possible, he would have gone alone, silently as shadow. But when he glanced across the room, Ellen's questioning eyes were on him, waiting for his signal. He had committed himself when he asked her help last night; there was no way to eliminate her now. He had to fill in the background for her, despite his reluctance. It was as if he knew that once the story was told, nothing could be withdrawn. From that moment, there must be a relentless march to an inevitable end.

He circled to her side. "Whenever you're ready." It was the first time he'd spoken to her since the beginning of the festivities.

"I'm ready."

"We can skip the good-byes. We'll be seeing the family at the airport later. I'm driving them."

She wasn't a girl who fussed. She retrieved an embroidered purse from somewhere and they left unnoticed among other departing guests.

In the car, he said, "We could go to my room at The Palms but I'd rather not."

She understood. "Whatever you say."

The only place where they could talk without danger of interruption would be a country lane. If the white car wasn't spotted—if he weren't being sought even now on a police call. He drove away, checking the mirror for a following car but there didn't seem to be any. At 24th Street he turned north as far as McDowell, then pointed east toward Scottsdale. The day's heat had softened, enough so in this before-twilight period, that the opened windows of the moving car gave an illusion of evening's cool. Raw green tract houses seemed to have taken over the countryside until they reached the cut. Here the troglodyte rocks and spire cactus were relics of what once had been.

The southern acres of Papago Park were unspoiled, although across the road the government area was newly scarred with a shiny wire fence. Had it been after dark, Hugh would have turned in at one of the sandy bypaths of Papago. But to park on the mesa was to induce attention; passing motorists couldn't fail to notice the big white car. He drove on to Scottsdale Road and turned north toward the village.

Until that moment it hadn't occurred to him that Scottsdale might be dangerous. Iris had been found in Scottsdale, not Phoenix. It was here the police might be watching for him. Or the anonymous man who had known the Scottsdale area well enough to choose a secluded section of the canal road to get rid of Iris. Having come this far, Hugh went on. He couldn't hope to hide, wherever he went. Phoenix and its environs hadn't grown that much.

He had remembered Scottsdale as surrounded by open country. He wasn't prepared for the startling growth the village had suffered, the gash of highway and the intricate, busy traffic pattern where little more than three years ago had been the quiet four corners. He turned off at Main Street and went north again at Miller Road, hoping that way might lead to what once had been. He was discouraged as he passed row after row of paint-clean doll houses.

"This was open fields the last time I was here," he said ruefully, but as he went on he was all at once off the pavement and onto a country lane. He might have been miles from the village, there were fields and an old tree somnolent against the water of a tiny stream.

He did not stop the car, it was too close to the little houses he'd passed. He continued north to the end of the lane and blundered upon the canal road. For a moment he was blunted with shock. It was as if he had entered a maze from which there was no escape whichever way he chose to move. But reason returned. At least he had found a place where it would be safe to talk. Iris had not been murdered here but on the other side of Scottsdale. He drove on, turning to the right away from town, and following the narrow, dusty contours of the road, where the unperturbed water was banked high on the left and on the right were the empty saffron fields. There was scarcely width enough for two cars to pass but there were no other cars, and any approaching from the east could be seen from far off with the whirl of dust to give warning. He pulled up against the side of the road and cut the engine. If any cars came from behind, the rear-view mirror would warn.

He offered Ellen a cigarette, took one himself, and lighted them. He didn't know how to begin, he didn't want to begin.

She spoke before he could. "It's that girl, isn't it?"

He turned and looked into her face. There was no distaste in it, no pity. "I thought you might know."

"What else would have brought the police last night? What else is there?"

He nodded slowly. What else? What else had happened here which could so affect him, a stranger in a strange town? It wasn't like Los Angeles or New York, where there were so many evil happenings.

She said, as if she'd made certain, "You had nothing to do with it but somehow you're involved."

"That's right," he said. "I'm afraid I'm involved."

Almost disinterestedly she asked, "How did it happen?"

He had intended to tell it only in part, but to his surprise he found himself starting on the road to Indio when the jalopy had cut in front of him.

She listened without interruptions. The only thing he didn't tell was the old insults the kids in the jalopy had shrilled at him. Insulated as her life may have been, she still would have heard them too many times. Nor did he mention the car which might have been pacing him this afternoon. By now he was ashamed of having let his imagination trick him into shying at what must have had some everyday meaning, someone looking for a house number or someone early for a rendezvous with a friend. Everything else he told her.

Twilight came down and turned into early evening before he had finished. Together they'd smoked almost a pack of cigarettes. When his ran out, she'd brought hers from her handbag. He concluded unhappily, "And that's it."

For a long moment she didn't speak and he wondered if he had quenched whatever spark of interest she might have had in him. By getting himself so stupidly involved in this affair.

And then she said, it wasn't a question, "You believe the girl was murdered."

"Yes." He was sure of it, as sure as if he'd done the autopsy himself and had proof. "She wouldn't have killed herself. She was too—tough." He explained, "I'm not using the word in the slang sense."

"I know." She nodded. She looked across at him. "Murdered by an abortion."

"Yes." He was reluctant to admit it, as if the admission were further self-involvement.

"And because of the chain of circumstance, you have been picked as the sacrificial goat?" She smiled, but only to soften the implication.

Without hesitation he admitted this as well. "Yes." He went on, "Of course I know I'm building it up. There's no reason why—"

She interrupted him. "There are many reasons why. You know them. I know them. I think you're in for real trouble, Hugh."

He didn't say anything, he couldn't. His hand holding the cigarette was as if a chill wind moved it.

"You need a lawyer."

"No." He rejected it utterly, violently. "What could a lawyer do? I haven't been accused of anything. I haven't done anything." He tried to make her see it. "Having a lawyer would make me look guilty. And I'm not."

She smiled wryly. "Most lawyers prefer an innocent client."

He tried to laugh. "The Judge's daughter."

"Perhaps. I've grown up under the law. And perhaps it's that I've seen too many cases involving innocent people, our people."

He said, "When I need one—if I need one—time enough then."

Without agreeing with him, she accepted his refusal. She asked, "You haven't told your father anything about this?"

"I couldn't. Don't you see? The wedding—"

"You should tell them." She was troubled. "You mustn't let them find out"—she hesitated, then concluded, but not what she'd been about to say—"another way."

He said, "Nothing's going to happen until after the autopsy." He'd convinced himself of this. "If the police had wanted a quick arrest, they could have held me last night when I identified her."

He wanted her to see it as he did. "If the autopsy proves she committed suicide, why put my family through all the agony of expecting the worst?"

"You know it isn't suicide, you've said that."

"I know, but only the autopsy can prove it. By then they may have the right man—"

"Don't dream," she said shortly. "You've also said they weren't interested in the unknown informant."

He pleaded his case. "By now they must have talked to her father. He can tell them I never saw the girl until I gave her a ride." Or could he, would he? Did the father know anything about Iris' private life?

Ellen said, almost impatiently, "They won't care who got her into trouble. All they'll want is the man, or woman, who committed an aborticide."

She was right, but he argued, "The boy friend will know who that was. He'll know I had nothing to do with it." And the fear was a knife in him. Because if the police looked for and found Iris' betrayer, that anonymous voice on the phone who must be the same, why would he be expected to tell the truth? He had given them Hugh.

Ellen didn't express her doubts. She only urged, "Tell your family, Hugh."

But he knew he couldn't. Not until it became essential. He couldn't bear it that they too should be in a vise of fear. Suddenly he remembered the time. He switched on the dash lights and looked at his watch. "It's almost eight. We'd better go if I'm to get Dad and the girls to the airport for Flight 305."

She knew he had rejected the idea. She protested no more, only said, "If I can help, Hugh, let me know."

"You've already helped." Like a child he touched her hand in gratefulness.

She smiled back at him but only with her lips. Her eyes remained somber.

The only turnaround was down a dusty bank into a field with a vertical pull up to the road again. The wheels made it. He drove back through Scottsdale and south toward his sister's home. They didn't talk on the drive. Only when they were nearing the house did he have a sudden, disastrous thought. "When are you leaving?"

She said, "I don't know. I think I'll stay on a few days and rest."

"Aren't you in school?"

"I'm taking some courses, without credit. I can catch up. I wasn't returning for another week, anyway. I'm going first to visit some friends in Los Angeles."

He couldn't have the arrogance to believe she was staying on here because of his troubles. But he said, trying to make it light, "I'm glad you'll be around for a few days. As long as I have to stay."

"Of course I'll move from your sister's tomorrow. The Palms looks pleasant."

"It is. But Stacy won't let you move out."

She smiled. "I can be very determined. She certainly needs to be free from company."

"My unit will be available. I'm checking in at my grandmother's tomorrow. She is also a very determined woman."

He didn't want to make the move. But it would hurt his grandparents if he refused without explanation. And he'd have to invent more explanations for borrowing the money from his mother to stay on at the motel.

There was little time to spare at Stacy's, he'd cut it fine. Somehow, while the girls' suitcases were being closed, Ellen managed to change from her bridesmaid's dress to a dark silk with jacket. It took Celeste longer than that to change the contents of her purse.

They made it to the airport close to eight-thirty, the check-in time. Hugh left the group and the luggage at the entrance and circled back to the parking lots. When he returned and entered the lobby, he saw Ringle. It was a large lobby and the big man was far across by the doors which led to the field. Yet he saw Hugh even as Hugh saw him. He didn't move. He stood there, a monolith, as if he were a passenger waiting for a flight announcement. Not a yard away from where Hugh's family was standing.

Ellen was waiting by the magazine racks. Perhaps she too had recognized the detective. Hugh joined her.

"Don't look now but that's Ringle over by the field exit. I'll go to the news counter and buy some cigarettes. Do you think you can get the family outside?"

"I can try."

"I don't believe he'll do anything if I explain. But in case—" He put the car keys in her hand.

She didn't waste time discussing it. She started out. He diverged to the counter and asked for two packs of Ellen's brand of cigarettes. The woman at the cash register passed them across to him and he put down the coins. He stayed there, taking time to open one of the packages while he watched Ellen move to the family. If anyone could manage, she could. The girls would be no problem but his parents might want to remain in the waiting room. She must have been persuasive, for in a moment they were all heading out the door.

He shoved the cigarette pack in his pocket and walked with quick steps across the room. He walked directly up to Ringle. "I'm not going anywhere," he said. "I'm seeing my father and sisters off for Los Angeles."

Ringle grunted. But when Hugh went outside, he followed, obtrusive in his unobtrusiveness. He watched Hugh join the group by the gate.

Dad said, "We decided to wait out here. There'll be a better chance for seats."

The sisters were both talking at once, giving and getting directions for the week ahead when their mother would be away. Hugh handed Ellen the unopened pack of cigarettes.

She smiled "Thanks" while her eyes questioned.

He said, "Thank you for the loan," and hoped his expression conveyed reassurance concerning the situation.

He circled to a position where he could keep an eye on the detective. He didn't think that Ringle would move in now, not unless Hugh started through the gate. But he couldn't be sure, and if it should happen, he was determined to be in a position where he could step up to meet it, not have it touch the family. It seemed an endless time before the plane was called and the passenger gate was opened. The family went on board, waving through the porthole windows to the three left behind. The motors roared, spitting flame, before the big ship taxied away for the take-off. And he had to stand there, still in Ringle's shadow, until his mother saw the flight airborne. After that, he didn't delay. He escorted her and Ellen into the lobby, across it to the outer door, and toward the parking area.

Ringle followed them. Not too close but not far enough for conversation to be unheard. He was by the parking meter when Hugh helped the women into the car. When Hugh drove away, he was still standing there. Perhaps by then it had percolated through his thick head that Hugh had meant what he said, that he wasn't leaving town.

Yet Hugh could not be certain that the car wasn't followed. There were lights at a reliable distance behind him on the road leaving the airport, lights behind him as he left-turned and continued over the country road south to his sister's. It wasn't unusual to be followed by headlights. Now that evening had come, there were plenty of cars on the road, returning from Sunday outings.

It was not until he reached Stacy's house that he was taken with a fear of returning alone to the motel, of being alone through the long evening. He said to his mother, "We won't come in with you. Ellen and I are going to get something to eat."

His mother scarcely covered her pleasure in having Hugh show an interest in Ellen. She opened her purse. "You'd better take my key, Ellen," she said. "I'm sure everyone here will be in bed before you get back." Ellen gave no indication that she hadn't been consulted on Hugh's plans.

Not until they had driven away did Ellen speak. "I'm not really hungry."

"I'm not either," he said. "But it won't hurt us to eat." He admitted frankly, "I didn't think you'd mind. And I didn't feel I could stand an evening of thinking about it."

"We won't talk about it at all," she decided. "At least not until after dinner."

He had turned east when they reached Van Buren. "You won't mind stopping at the motel while I change, will you? Maybe

I won't feel so vulnerable if I can get out of this white jacket."

"Why do you think I changed?" But she seemed relaxed, as if she had put the problem out of mind.

He pulled up at the door of the unit. "Will you come in?" She must come in, not wait in the car, not with the memory of that old sedan driving around and around the block. Not with Ringle hovering.

Before he ushered her through the door, he flicked on the overhead lights. Again he had that overwhelming sense of relief on viewing the room's pristine emptiness.

"Make yourself comfortable," he said. "I won't be long. I'm used to making a quick change."

He went into the dressing room. It wasn't until he reached for his sports jacket that he realized someone had been in the room while he was out. It was an occupational necessity that his personal things were kept in filing-cabinet order. The jacket was neat on the hanger but not where he had hung it. He turned to the dressing table and unzipped his shaving kit. Imperceptibly there was change. He pulled open the two drawers he had been using. His belongings had been searched.

Quickly he pulled his doctor's kit from the wardrobe shelf. This too had been opened and searched. His reaction was hot anger. If they'd wanted to search his things, couldn't they have asked, not sneaked in here while he was away?

They hadn't sneaked in. They didn't have to do it that way. They'd gone to the manager and been furnished a pass key. When the realization came, his rage turned to sickness of heart. Not for himself, but for those who would come after him asking for lodging at The Palms. They'd be measured against Hugh's status, against trouble with the police. *He looked all right but . . . That's what happens when you let them . . .* He could hear the reasonable, deprecating decisions. Or their anger. *I don't care what the law says, from now on . . .* And the tedious inching forward had become a long step back.

He returned slowly to the living room. Ellen was standing there by the coffee table, where he had left her. She said, "There's a message," and extended a slip of paper.

It was a memo from the motel office, a number, and the

notation: *Please call.* He twisted the paper in his fingers. He said, "My room's been searched."

She lifted her eyebrows. "You'd better return the call," was all she said. She sat down then in the big chair, the one Ringle had chosen last night.

He went to the telephone, and only after he had lifted it and heard the operator's metallic voice, did he remember that a call from this phone had to go through the switchboard. He was quite certain the message had not been from family or friend. He should have waited for an outside line, not compounded the damage done. But he went ahead, reading the number from the memo slip. The operator's voice repeated it to him, and he heard the sound of her dialing.

If the police had been private, the operator and The Palms' staff would not necessarily know of their visit to Hugh's rooms. Yet in any organization, there was a grapevine of communication which functioned without need of authoritative source or even a spoken word. He could be sure the management would curry discretion, having the police around wasn't good for a hotel's reputation. People were funny about the police. They gave lip praise to law and order, but its myrmidons brought an uneasy feeling even to the most innocent. You could taste it in the atmosphere of the receiving room even when the cops were on errands of mercy. Working in Night Emergency at the hospital had taken most of the unease away from Hugh.

On the other end of the wire a male voice stated, "Scottsdale Police Department."

The words somehow came as a shock. He swallowed and was able to respond. "This is Dr. Densmore."

The voice at the other end also seemed to have been surprised. There was a perceptible silence before it said, "Oh—hold on a minute."

Waiting, Hugh muffled the handset against his jacket sleeve. He said to Ellen, "It's Scottsdale. The police."

She put down the magazine she'd been holding and sat up tall, folding her hands into her lap like a schoolgirl. Her eyes were enormous.

Another voice came on. "Densmore? This is Marshal Hackaberry, Scottsdale. I'd like to talk to you." There was nothing menacing in the voice, it was as normal and hearty as if the man were suggesting a lunch date.

"Certainly," Hugh said. "When would it be convenient?"

"Can you come out here now?"

Hugh's hand tightened on the phone. This wasn't a friendly interview being set up. Did he dare say: *Not now, later. I have a dinner date.* He said, and the hesitancy was in his throat despite his efforts to eradicate it, "Well, yes, I can."

"You know how to get here?"

"Yes, I do." Surely a knowledge of Scottsdale didn't equate with guilt. Every visitor to Phoenix toured Scottsdale.

"I'll be expecting you."

Slowly Hugh replaced the phone. He didn't look at Ellen. "He wants to talk to me." She said nothing. "Now," and he looked into her eyes.

She rose from the chair. "We'd better go."

"Not you." His refusal was explosive.

She smiled as if at a child. "I didn't mean I was going to hold your hand at the interview. I mean I'll drive to Scottsdale with you and wait for you."

"No."

"I want to," she said flatly.

He shook his head and walked back to the dressing room. He didn't care how casually they dressed in Arizona, he needed all possible security. Such a small thing as the campus dress uniform of a white shirt and narrow dark tie was a part of it. He called out to Ellen, hoping she would be more amenable by now, "There'd be nothing for you to do while you waited."

"I'll find something. Or just stay in the car."

"No!" Again he was explosive. He strode back to the room, tying his necktie as he tried to explain. "They know the car. It's part of their—dossier, should I say? You can't stay in it, alone, at night, a girl—"

"So I won't stay in it," she said gravely, and continued, "I'm going with you, Hugh. And I'll find a place to wait, a safe place, where I'll cause you neither worry nor embarrassment."

They were standing too close together, their eyes meeting,

measuring their separate thoughts. He was the one who turned away. "All right. I should say thank you. I do need support—I expect you know that from the way I've been behaving."

Her smile was small but reassuring. "I'm not thinking of myself as a pillar. It's just—I couldn't stand the waiting anywhere else."

He understood and he appreciated but he didn't tell her so. Because he couldn't accept the intimacy which was rising between them. He couldn't endure the knowing it must lead to nothing, no more than the finality of a good-bye, it's been fun knowing you.

"I guess I'm as ready as I'm going to be," he said.

They left the room; he checked the door to be sure it was fast. Not that it made any difference. Locked doors didn't thwart the police. But at least he wouldn't be surprised by anyone else.

He couldn't make conversation on the drive to Scottsdale. He was afraid, he admitted to himself that he was afraid, while insisting there was no reason to be. If this were an arrest, the marshal wouldn't invite Hugh to come out for an interview, would he? He'd send the detectives with a warrant. This meeting would be less dangerous than the ordeal with Ringle and Venner last night. Yet Hugh's hands were icy and his heart leaden.

He turned off Scottsdale Road on East Main Street and found a parking place in front of the darkened windows of an Indian arts shop. He did not want to park by the police station; he didn't want Ellen to be seen there. Although this was one of the principal streets, Scottsdale was a village, and by night it was shadowed and quiet. It would have been safe enough for Ellen to remain in the car if it had not been this particular car.

He said again, "I don't know what you're going to do."

"Don't worry about me, please. We'll meet here when you're through. I'll check regularly."

"And if I don't come back?" He had to say it.

"Don't be absurd."

Before he could get out to open the door, she was out of the car. She walked away without turning her head for good-bye. If she hadn't been Ellen Hamilton, she might have been heading for the luxury restaurant near the corner. But she wouldn't try that, not alone, at night; not with him in trouble. She was doubt-less going to Luke's, the large lighted drugstore across Scottsdale Road. There'd be no lifted eyebrows much less outright rejection there, no better place at this hour to while away the time.

He removed the keys from the ignition, pushed them in his pocket. As he left the car, the swinging doors of the restaurant emitted a mottled blonde and her beefy tourist cowboy. She shrilled drunkenly into the quiet night. Hugh moved off in the opposite direction.

The pavement ended with this block of specialized shopping area. Beyond was a dusty country lane where the Town Hall, housing the police department, stood. He'd seen it many times, the small brick building which might once have been the village schoolhouse. Steps led up to its porch and it seemed there was always an Indian woman sitting there, a child's head pushing against her long draggled skirt. The reservation lay not far be-yond the town. The woman was here even at this hour of night, a toddler asleep in her arms, another child, scarcely older, sleep-ing against her knee. Waiting for her man who had been invited in for a little talk? No, it wouldn't be that. She'd go home if her man was in jail. The porch was no more than a place where she could wait undisturbed and in safety until her husband finished work or pleasure somewhere in town. It was better to wait for a ride than to trudge the miles with the tired children. She paid no attention to Hugh, she might not have seen him.

He moved to the steps on the right. They led down to the basement door with its sign designating this as the quarters of the Scottsdale police. The light over the door was a white glare. He had to will his feet to descend. If he could have run away, he would have. Facing the essential operation, the patient couldn't run. No matter his fright, he must submit, holding his tenuous courage to wavering hope.

✳

Without further thought, Hugh walked inside. He was in a low-ceilinged basement room. It was not a dank, gloomy dungeon. It was somehow bright and informal, it didn't have the look or smell of a police station. A young officer whose uniform was little different from that of a Scottsdale businessman—tan frontier pants, matching shirt, and black string tie—was in a railed-off sector at the left attending the stuttering police radio. A similar officer was at the water cooler. Beyond a casual glance, neither paid any attention to Hugh. They knew who he was; they must have known. He stood waiting, wishing he knew the protocol. Whether to speak or be spoken to.

Across the room was an open door leading to a private office. The entrance to it was blocked by a large desk of some light wood, the top cluttered with papers and office equipment like any businessman's desk. A third officer materialized in the door-way behind the desk.

"You Hugh Densmore?" he called out, not unfriendly. He was dressed like the others but his belt had handsome silver mountings, Indian silver work.

"Yes," Hugh said.

"Come on in."

He waited for Hugh to cross the room, edge past the desk, and follow into the inner office. Here there was another desk, more cluttered, and a couple of plain chairs which might have been borrowed from a school storehouse. There were two small windows, basement type, high on the far wall. The station was air-conditioned, as was every building in the Phoenix area, but it evidently didn't filter through to this smaller office. A revolving electric fan hummed on a shelf above the desk. The papers on the desk were weighted with desert rocks, a cigarette lighter, a pipe, and like makeshifts.

"I'm Marshal Hackaberry," the officer said. He might have been thirty years or fifty; he had the deceptive weathered face of Western outdoor men. His eyes were horizon-blue, his hair sandy. There was an Arizona twang in his voice. He wore low-heeled cowboy boots with his uniform, the embossed leather worn to a fine finish. He went around behind the littered desk and lowered himself into the revolving chair. He gestured to Hugh. "Sit down."

Hugh took the chair by the desk. All at once he was somehow at ease. He knew why, but only someone who knew the other side of the coin would understand. Hackaberry had looked at

Hugh, spoken to him, as to any man he might summon to his office.

"You know why I wanted to see you." It wasn't exactly a question.

"I think so," Hugh replied. "I think it's about the girl who was found in the canal."

Hackaberry nodded briefly. He lifted a thin sheaf of papers from beneath a piece of volcanic rock. "You identified the body."

"I identified Iris Croom."

His eyes shot up to Hugh's face as if expecting to find defiance there. There was none to find. Hugh had merely stated the fact. The marshal looked down again at the papers, tapping them with his forefinger. "I have here the reports of Ringle and Venner." He pushed back in his chair for comfort, and continued, "This is Scottsdale's case. At least for now it is. The girl was found over our line. Do you know anything about the way we work, Mr. Densmore—Doctor?"

"No, I don't."

"We're a marshal's department. Not county, although I'm also a county deputy as are most of my men. Two hats. If it turns out she was killed in the county, not Scottsdale, I'll still be in charge. If, however, the death occurred in Phoenix, the case will go to them."

The marshal had to wait for the autopsy before he could speak more plainly. But this was plain enough to Hugh. If aborticide had been committed in the neighborhood of the motel, the case belonged to Phoenix. If the murder was done by the canal where she'd been found, to Scottsdale. Hugh started to take his cigarettes from his pocket but thought better of it. The need to smoke might give an impression of nervousness.

"The autopsy may give us a lead. But maybe it won't. We may have to do some intensive investigation before we find out. Right now I'm bossman. That doesn't mean Phoenix isn't cooperating with me. We're a small department. When I took over the job a few years ago we had exactly three men on the force. We have fourteen now, but the way the town's growing, that's not enough for plain routine work. When we get a big one like this, we ask Phoenix to help us out. They've got the men and the labs and all the equipment. I'm telling you this so you won't get any ideas you're getting the treatment from both sides. Ringle and Venner are Phoenix Homicide but their chief has assigned them to me for this case. They're working for me."

"I understand," Hugh said.

"And another thing." He worried the papers, not looking at Hugh. "I don't want you getting any ideas that you're going to get a bad beef because you're a—because you're not a white man." He jutted his chin and met Hugh's eyes full with his own. His were like blue flint. "This isn't going to be any race affair. Get that straight. We're after a killer and we're going to get him. And when we get him, we're not going to have things messed up for us by a lot of bleeding hearts or snotty sociologists or NAACP legal eagles. I don't care what color you are, if you killed that girl you'll pay for it. If you didn't, I don't want you."

"I didn't," Hugh said flatly. Again he reached for cigarettes.

This time Marshal Hackaberry noted the move. "Go on, smoke if you like," he said. He himself fished one from a crumpled pack. "Now we understand each other, we can commence. I've got the reports but I want to hear this story myself. Personally. How you picked up this girl in Blythe and brought her into Phoenix."

Hugh took a deep pull at his cigarette. He had given Ringle and Venner no details last night. By now the border inspectors had probably communicated with Phoenix. But it was not this that caused Hugh to make his decision that he would tell the whole story to Hackaberry; it was something in the man himself. He could be wrong. Perhaps the marshal wasn't a straight shooter; it might be an act, so well practiced that it fit him like his old boots. Nevertheless it couldn't be wrong to tell the truth, the whole truth. Right or wrong, the decision was Hugh's. Only by the truth could his innocence be proved. Lies, evasions, suppression could only indicate a measure of guilt. And he was innocent. This was his shield, this his protection.

Hugh put ashes neatly in the glass tray at the side of the desk. "I'd like to start at the beginning," he said.

"That's the place to start." The marshal settled himself more comfortably. He must have been attuned to extraneous sound in the outer office, for he added at once, "Hold on a minute." He was around the desk and over to the doorway, calling out, "Those detectives here yet?" He leaned through the aperture. "Ringle! Venner! Come in here. Better bring another chair, we're short."

Hugh stiffened at the names. It had been too much to hope that he could talk alone to the marshal. Hackaberry had made it clear that the two were his men, their job to find the killer of Iris. They were not here by coincidence; he had sent for them. He must have known there was much more to learn from Hugh than what was in the report. And all the good-fellowship explanatory material was only to pass the time until their arrival?

Ringle came first, grunting what might have been a recognition of Hugh, and lowered his bulk onto the straight chair on the other side of the desk. Venner followed, carrying the extra chair. He placed it in the vicinity of Ringle's, sat down, and jockeyed its placement until he could tilt back against the partition separating this room from the main office. He acknowledged Hugh's presence by drawing back his lips in what might have been a sardonic smile.

Hackaberry was still in the doorway, talking to one of his deputies outside. His words did not carry. Hugh stubbed out his cigarette in the ash tray. He'd like another, but even if the detectives had sworn affidavits that Hugh chain-smoked on his breaks to make up for long work hours without tobacco, they would believe only that he smoked now because of anxiety. As if he could read Hugh's mind, Venner lit a fresh one from his own stub and sighed a deep satisfaction.

The marshal turned into the room again. "Where is your car, Mr.—Dr. Densmore?"

They'd checked. They knew it wasn't out front.

He said, "I parked in the next block. By that Indian shop."

"You wouldn't mind if my men go over it while we're talking? It'll save time for you and for us too."

He did mind. Ellen might have gone back to it in spite of his warning. Or she might look for it before the police had time to replace it. Ellen could cope, that had been made clear to him long before now. And a police request was only the initial polite form of a demand. He knew his hesitancy, although fleeting, had given the wrong impression. He could not help how they misconstrued, he would not mention Ellen. He drew his keys from his pocket and carried them over to the marshal. "She rode to Phoenix with me. You know you'll find her fingerprints all over the car."

"The back seat?" Venner smirked.

"She was never in the back seat!" Only Venner had the power to send him into these quick rages. Perhaps that was the runt detective's function. He controlled the anger before repeating to Hackaberry, "She was never in the back seat. She reached across from the front to get the water jug off the floor. That's the only contact she had with it."

The marshal said, "Let me get this going and you can fill in the whole picture." His boots clacked as he crossed to the door and the keys jangled a counter rhythm.

As he disappeared, the eyes of Venner and Ringle, as if they were iron bars, moved to contain Hugh. He couldn't take it; he looked away, focusing on the blank wall as he returned to his chair.

Venner said to Ringle conversationally, "Maybe I was wrong. Maybe he didn't wait to get in the back."

Ringle's noncommittal grunt could have been a warning. At least he changed the topic. "Did you see Crumb?"

"Yeah. I just come from that."

"How's he taking it?"

"How would you expect him to take a nigger messing with his daughter?"

Hugh forced his eyes to stay on the wall.

But Ringle exploded, "You didn't tell him—"

Venner was laughing so hard that for a moment he couldn't reply. Then he cackled, "Naw, I never mentioned black boy here." Disgustedly he spat. "I told him just what Hackaberry said to tell him—nothing. But when he finds out—" He made an uncouth clicking sound in his throat. "He's not going to like it."

The last words were near-whispered as the marshal burst in, calling over his shoulder, "Don't interrupt me for anything." This

time he closed the door soundly before returning to his comfortable chair. Briefly he fingered the papers in front of him,
anchoring them with a larger-size rock. He took his pipe from
another stack, shifting his ash tray to hold it down. He used his
elbow on another segment while he removed the tobacco tin
from them to pack his pipe. There was no sound in the room but
the measured drone of the fan and the sibilant riff of the flimsies.
In the next room, the spluttering police radio could be heard distinctly.

Venner watched the checkerboard maneuvers with his cus-
tomary sardonic smirk. Ringle appeared lost in his own glum
thoughts. Hugh also watched, wondering how much of the business was for effect, how much a habit of makeshift convenience.

Hackaberry puffed the pipe into a waft of smoke and spoke
through the stem. "With your permission, Doctor, I think I'll tape
this meeting." He yanked open a drawer of his desk, indicated
the recording machine which was fitted into it. "That way none
of us will have to worry about misremembering."

Again Hugh had no choice. He inclined his head as permission.

Hackaberry set the machine into operation. He stated time,
place, those present, and continued, "All present understand this
is an informal session. Dr. Densmore volunteered to come here
to tell us what he knows of Bonnie Lee Crumb, known to him as
Iris Croom. Dr. Densmore is not represented by an attorney, nor
is he charged with anything. This is clearly understood?"

There it was, for later introduction in court, if permitted.
Ringle growled his response, "Yeah." You could tell he didn't
believe in informal questioning. Venner slurred, "Oh, sure." His
methods wouldn't be influenced by legalities, not if he could
help it.

The marshal repeated to Hugh, "You have no objections to
taping?" He needed audible response for the record.

"I have none," Hugh said. Not that tapes couldn't be edited.

"Thank you." Hackaberry stopped the machine, played back
what had just been recorded. He was satisfied. The voices were
distinct. "Okay." He set the machine again. "You can start in,

Doctor. Right at the beginning, when she asked you for a ride at the check station."

Hugh said, "I'd like to start before that. When I first saw the girl."

He had expected, even welcomed, the sensation his words would arouse. In a small way, it would expend some of his hostility to the detectives. But when the response came, the quick ugly anger in Ringle's face, the pitiless narrowing of Venner's lips, it would have been frightening had not Marshal Hackaberry been present. Hackaberry took the statement without any noticeable reaction. He puffed his pipe and asked matter-of-factly, "So you had met up with her before?"

At that moment all three of them were convinced that their suspicions of Hugh were well grounded. Would the full story uproot them? He didn't know, he could only tell them the truth. The truth must be self-evident. He had nothing else to offer, no corroborating witnesses.

He answered the marshal, "Yes. I first saw her the previous afternoon, on the road out of Indio." He kept his attention on the marshal while he told of that initial meeting, his reason for giving her a lift, his growing distrust of her story as they traveled toward Blythe, his decision to put her on a bus there.

When he stopped at the end of that day's story, taking time to light a cigarette, Ringle accused at once, "You didn't tell us none of this."

Hugh took a draught of the cigarette before answering, "I thought that what you wanted from me was simply an identification." He hoped he sounded as innocent as he tried to sound.

Ringle glowered but he said no more.

Hugh took another pull of the cigarette before beginning the events of the next morning. He had left her at the Phoenix bus station, where, allegedly, she would telephone her aunt.

Hackaberry had put down his cold pipe. He was doodling on a pad of paper. "You have that envelope where she wrote down the name and address of her aunt?"

"I have it somewhere at the motel. But there's no such address and no such person here. I called every beauty shop in town. Iris told me later that she did have an aunt of that name who lived in Denver."

"You saw her later." Venner's drawl was pornographic.

Hugh clipped the monosyllables. "Yes. Once."

This was the hard part, this was the part they must believe or his position was hopeless. If they rejected its truth, they would look no further for the abortionist. The marshal, for all his seeming open mind, would have Hugh, as Ringle and Venner already had, fit the role.

Hugh's cigarette had burned to a tip as he talked. He took his time pressing it out in the ash tray, arranging words and scene in his mind. The forthcoming passage must be given in exactly the right way. And he mustn't let a hint of fear or despair or reaction to their cynical disbelief filter through.

The brief pause was too long. The forelegs of Venner's chair came down on the floorboards with a jarring clatter. "While he's figuring out what to say, I'm going to get me a drink of water." He didn't ask, he told Hackaberry. "This is dry work." He hitched up his rumpled plaid trousers as he headed to the door.

"Tell one of the boys to bring in some water," the marshal called after him. "I'm sure Densmore could use some."

Hugh responded to the marshal's seemingly friendly smile. "I could."

Hackaberry pushed up from his chair. "Take a stretch if you want." He himself took a real one, arms upthrust, back arched.

Hugh stood, relaxing while moving away from the desk to the small windows, then returning to his chair.

Ringle didn't get up. "I'd like a can of beer."

"Make it two," Hackaberry said, and smiling again at Hugh, "Three."

A deputy came through the door, not with the water but with several sheets of paper which he carried to the marshal. As he started away, Hackaberry said, "What about that water?"

"We're looking for something to put it in, Hack," the deputy explained on his way out.

"Use a milk bottle," Hackaberry shouted after him. To Hugh, he laughed, "We're not as fancy here as you are in Los Angeles, are we?"

Bemused, Hugh said, "I wouldn't know. This is the first time I've been in a police station." He'd never thought of it before; stations were so familiar from movies and television.

Ringle snorted, "You never got a traffic ticket?"

He mustn't antagonize the buffalo further. He tried a smile at him. "Oh yes. I've had my share of those. But I always pay through the Auto Club." And realized at once that he'd done it again. Not for using the service but by taking for granted the use. Ringle's reaction was visible on his face. Such conveniences were for white people; Negroes shuffled in line before a judge.

Venner returned before the moment developed. He carried the milk bottle of water, handed it, snickering, to the marshall, as if remembering a dirty joke. His eyes touched Hugh with malice, but he spoke to Ringle. "Did I miss anything?"

Ringle didn't bother to answer. Hugh accepted the glass of water from the marshal and drank it gratefully. All three were waiting for him to continue the story. Again he addressed himself to Hackaberry, as if the detectives were not in the room. Hackaberry alone might recognize the truth when it was spoken. He told the story of that night, told also his reaction to Iris' suggestion; it was part of the whole truth. He concluded, "I never saw her again, not until these detectives—as a result of an anonymous tip—took me to the County Mortuary last night to identify her body." He stressed the anonymous tip. Perhaps the marshal would realize that the important thing was not to question Hugh but to find that man.

Venner slurred, "All strictly legal, Marshal. He came voluntary."

Ringle slashed in, "And when you identified her, you didn't think none of this stuff was pertinent?" He quoted the word savagely.

"I didn't know the cause of her death," Hugh said. "I only knew I wasn't involved in it."

The marshal was deceptively mild. "Didn't it occur to you when you read the story in the paper Saturday, that the girl in the canal might be the girl you knew?"

Hugh had known this question must come. He also knew that he could not lie, he could only dissemble. He didn't answer too quickly, nor did he hesitate over it. "I don't believe it did. It may have come into my mind fleetingly but there was nothing to support it. I was convinced the girl who drowned herself was a local girl."

"Why?"

"Because of the canal. A visitor wouldn't know about your canal system."

"How'd you know about it?" Ringle asked quickly.

"As a boy I visited my grandfather here every summer."

The marshal's voice expressed doubt. "You mean when you read the story you thought the girl was a suicide?"

"In the story I read, there was no reason to think anything else."

Ringle pounded, "But you didn't come forward to see if you could identify her."

Hugh made himself speak evenly. "That never occurred to me. I thought the girl's family would have identified her as soon as the story was published."

The marshal nodded, as if Hugh's story was credible whether he believed it or not.

And Venner insinuated, "You didn't want it to be your girl, did you?"

Anger rushed into Hugh. At the implication in the question which he could not deny without feeding it. "Did I want it to be the girl I gave a ride to? Certainly not!" He managed to control himself and again direct his words to the marshal. "I hoped she had taken my advice and asked help from an organization which could help her."

"She sure didn't come to the police," Ringle said.

Venner snapped his gum, happy at Hugh's outburst.

The marshal sucked his cold pipe, then suddenly pointed it at Hugh. "We don't know this is murder. The medical examiner won't be back until tomorrow. She could have been bunged up in the water. But one thing we do know—unofficially. She was aborted before her death." He stood up. "We may want to talk to you again after the autopsy. I'll have to ask you not to leave town without checking with me."

The interview was over. Hugh rose. He said, "I'll be mov-

ing from The Palms tomorrow to my grandparents' home." Un-
asked, he gave the address. He wanted to plead: *Don't disturb
them, they're old,* but he was afraid it would stimulate the detectives to do just that. Rather, he added the telephone number,
suggesting, "You can call me there, if you want to see me again."
And hoped he could explain the call if his grandmother or grandfather should receive it. Ringle was stubbing the information into
his notebook.

"You'll find your car where you left it," the marshal said.
"Thanks for coming in." As Hugh started to leave, he added,
"We've borrowed the tools temporarily."

Hugh spun about. Could they believe, could it be possible,
that car tools were used on Iris? He was sickened at the thought.
The three of them were watching him; to them his shock would
be more indication of his guilt.

"You don't mind?" the marshal asked.

He managed to say, "Not at all," and turning again, walked
away, aware of the silent eyes following him. He walked on
through the main office; the two deputies merely glanced at him,
uncuriously, not interrupting their conversation. He opened the
door and stepped into the cool night air. Now that it was over,
he was trembling.

The Indian woman and her children were no longer on the
porch. He looked at his watch. It was close to midnight. And
where had Ellen spent the hours? Anxiety for her safety quieted
his personal tremors; he hurried away.

The moon was cold and white and high, giving a desert-
night brightness to the deserted streets. His car was in the exact
place where he had left it. You would not know it had been
moved. Ellen was nowhere in sight. The street slept, the village
slept. There was no sound, not even the murmur of a car passing
on Scottsdale Road. And then as he stood there, the door of the
elegant restaurant beyond was opened and a gash of sound
cleaved the night. Almost at once it was shut again, closing away
the intrusive piano and drunken singing and clamorous laughter.
The men who had come out moved raggedly in the opposite direction; nevertheless Hugh quickly got into his car.

He saw then the twist of paper protruding from the ash

tray. He turned on the dash light and read the note: "Am at Victor's." Although unsigned, it could only have been written by Ellen. The distinctive script did not belong to the world of Iris. He hoped it had not been in the car when the police were in possession.

He backed away from the curb and drove the block and a half to the large, bright ranch café at the intersection, whose neon beacon spelled Victor's. It wasn't one of the fancy restaurants of the area, it was a hamburger place. Not a dump, it was new, built like a great ranch house of redwood and stone. Despite the late hour, there was a goodly crowd inside. He found Ellen in a booth not far from the door. She gave him a quick, questing glance as he slid into the seat across from her.

He said, "I'm sorry it was so long."

"I haven't been here for long." There was hot coffee and the remnants of a sandwich plate in front of her.

A young waitress came to the table with a menu.

"It's not too late to order?" All at once he was hungry.

"We're open till one." She was neither friendly nor unfriendly.

He ordered; the waitress took Ellen's empty plate and went away.

Ellen said, "Your car was missing."

"They took it. To go over. Your note—"

"After they'd returned it." She studied his face. "Was it bad?"

"No. Not actually. Of course, they don't believe my story. Or rather, they believe it only up to the point where I say I never saw her again."

"What do they say?"

"They don't say anything. They look. Ringle and Venner—"

"They were there?"

"They're assigned to the case. From Phoenix. The marshal—" He broke off, said, "To be honest, the marshal seems to be trying to be as objective as he wants to be." He paraphrased, "He doesn't intend to have the case messed up with 'bleeding hearts.' So he looks objective. But he doesn't believe me any more than the others do." Might as well admit it, to himself as well as to Ellen.

The waitress brought his order. She didn't say anything. She put down the giant hamburger and the coffee without a word. She didn't care whether he was black, white, or mottled; she only wanted to be through with work.

Ellen took up her coffee cup. "Tell me the whole thing. All of it."

Hugh had started eating. "I will," he said, his mouth full. "I will in a minute. I didn't know I was this hungry." But he did know that an ordeal of mind and spirit could lower resistance as much as a physical workout. He finished the hamburger and lit a cigarette before he began to talk. He had enough energy now.

It didn't take as long to tell as it had to endure. Ellen already knew the story. She listened with her eyes on his face, more objective than Marshal Hackaberry. "Tonight wasn't bad," he repeated at the finish, "because they couldn't accuse me of killing her. Because they don't know officially how she died."

"It might not be abortion?" She was too hopeful.

"There was an abortion," he said flatly. "And they know it. They just can't say so until they get a medical report. Not for the record." He shook his head sadly. "It must have been a botched job for them to know." They had probably seen many botched jobs in their duty. The years of Ringle, the ugly years. No wonder he was devoid of sympathy. He continued, "They know there was an abortion but they won't know if that was the cause of her death until after the autopsy. She might have drowned herself, or have been drowned." And what possible reason could the killer have given her, in her pain, to climb with him the high bank of the canal to be put to death? "When they find out, they'll come for me."

"But, Hugh." She was still reaching out for the bent twig of hope. "If it wasn't an aborticide—"

Hugh said distinctly, "They'll come for me because there was an abortion whether it killed her or not." Savagely he asked, "Why should they look for the real abortionist? They've got me. A doctor—"

"A Negro doctor," she emended. "Go on, say it."

"No," he refused with violence. "I won't say it." But after a moment's thought, he admitted, "Perhaps I was beginning to sag into self-pity. I won't even think that way." He crossed his fingers, smiled a small smile. "I hope." Immediately he was grave. "I haven't time for that."

The clock on the wall pointed to one. There were yet a few booths occupied and no one seemed in a hurry, but Hugh picked up the bill. "We'd better get out of here." He hoped he had enough money with him to pay the tab; it would be the final ignominy if he had to borrow from Ellen on their first date. He made it; the cashier's weary mouth managed a "Thank you" as she returned the change.

The night was sharp with cold at this hour, the stars were broken glass patched against the dark sky. He helped Ellen into the car, unobtrusively noting that there was no police car about, nor a strange sedan. Instead of turning south through the sleeping village, out of some compulsion he followed Indian School Road. The shape of the canal rose on the right. Here, but one night ago —could it have been only then?—a living creature of hopes and dreams, joys and troubles, had mercilessly been given over to death.

It must have been appallingly easy to put her to death. Her cries, if she had warning to cry out, would have been heard only by the sleeping. She would not have been afraid until it was too late to be. She trusted the man, by whose act, if not deed, she had been delivered to death. Hugh remembered her childlike anticipatory delight as they drove into the city. She had known no qualms then, she had been sure of welcome. The man—boy—must have panicked to have killed her here on the Indian School Road. Or had she died here because the abortionist had done delayed murder? Or was it that she died on the table and was dumped by the man or woman who had killed her and what would have been a living child? In Los Angeles the victims were dumped more often than not. In an alley with the refuse cans, among the weeds of vacant lots; one had even been flung too late for care from a moving car onto a hospital lawn.

Ellen said, "It was back there she was killed."

"Or died."

She recognized the sadness in him, because she said with

emphasis, "You're not to blame yourself. You had nothing to do with it."

"But I did," he told her. "I had too much to do with it." Or not enough. "And everything I did was wrong." He drove on, turning south toward Edward's home. As if it were a sinuous snake, the Indian School Road seemed to follow him.

When they reached the safe suburbs, he and Ellen sat silently for a moment in the darkness of the car. She asked finally, "You don't think the police are through with you?"

She knew the answer, he'd already told her that. "I know they aren't." He broke out in savage frustration, "If I were a detective I wouldn't believe my story. Circumstantially, I fit." He put thoughts into words with crystal clarity. "I'll have to find the abortionist. No one else believes in his existence. I'll also have to find the man or boy she came to meet." There must be the two, to accuse each other, to prove the fact. Was it a plum tree or a peach?

"A good lawyer could help." She'd said it twice; the first time he hadn't heard, only her voice speaking from afar.

"Yes," he agreed. He could admit it now, it was essential to have a lawyer, to ward off arrest until he could find the two guilty ones. A lawyer meant confiding at least in Edward. Edward would know to whom he should go. He sighed his indecision; even after tonight the need didn't overbalance the more important need to keep the family out of this. He didn't know what he should do.

Ellen was waiting for him to continue. When he didn't, she said, "While you were with the police, I telephoned my father in Washington." She didn't apologize. She didn't seem to care whether he would or would not have consented to it. "He'll ring me in the morning with what he can find out." She smiled at his blank face. "You needn't worry. He knows everyone in law worth knowing. He'll find us the right man."

He couldn't help protesting, "Wouldn't it be a lot simpler if I asked Edward about it? He knows everyone worth knowing in Phoenix."

Her "No," was imperative, but she explained, "The police would expect our lawyers to believe your story. Or whether or not they believed it, to defend you as if they did. I told my father what you need." She had thought it out with care; she must have been thinking of little else all day. "A young man, not over forty, but top drawer in his profession; liberal, but not too liberal, no Civil Liberties lawyer, they're suspect from the beginning because they show up in any case involving minorities. As my father says, they're more interested in minorities than in the right or wrong of a case. I may be asking the impossible but I don't want this lawyer to be of any of the minority groups. I want a hundred-per-cent white American Protestant male. With wife and children, so we'll have them on our side too."

He found himself half laughing. "Is that all?"

She shook her head but she smiled too. "I know just the man in Washington but we're not in Washington."

"You don't think you'll find that kind of man here?"

"We just might. My father is quite a miracle man." She said, "I'll call you in the morning after I hear from him. It will be early—time difference, you know."

He helped her out of the car and together they went up the walk. At the door she said, "I wouldn't put off telling your family, Hugh. Maybe your luck will hold, yet—"

He said what she wouldn't. "I can't expect it to hold forever." The police couldn't keep the newspapers off him indefinitely. Reluctantly he said, "Perhaps I'll talk to Edward tomorrow." And, saying it, realized he must go to Edward. He was the only person who could give Hugh a lead to the abortionists in the vicinity. Doctors knew. He did not tell Ellen his decision. She might go legalistic on him, think it was the lawyer's business. But the lawyer's future life wasn't threatened. Hugh alone was in the realm of danger where the impossible could—must—be achieved. The two men he must find had had the time to cover themselves beyond finding.

Edward's car was gone from the port. For tonight he could continue to bear his own burden. Perhaps by morning there'd be no need for the fuss of a lawyer and the grief to his kinsman. Perhaps the marshal would ring up to acknowledge his mistake. Why not dream? Without dreaming there was no hope.

Ellen was saying, "Don't worry, Hugh. Go home and go to

sleep. It will all look better in the morning. I'm sure the lawyer will clear things up for you without any difficulty."

He said, "Yes, ma'am," and left her there, not even touching her hand in good-bye.

4

HE DROVE without incident to the motel; no news over the radio. There were lights beyond the drawn curtains, the voices of night-blooming young couples poolside lilted with the special heightening of sounds across water. He drove to the rear of his wing and parked. As he opened the door of his rooms, remembering to touch the light switch before entering, the small envelope was livid at his feet.

He took for granted it was a hotel note until he bent to pick it up and saw that it was pale pink, of cheap stationery. It was sealed; there was no name on it, only the room number. With foreboding, he opened it. The message was block-printed in pencil on ruled paper torn from a tablet. It said simply: NIGGER GET OUT OF TOWN.

If it had been meant to frighten or anger him, it failed. For he felt a wild surge of exultation as he read the words. His case was proven, if indeed he had needed this proof. He was the one threat which existed for the murderer or murderers, the only factor which stood between their anonymity and their apprehension.

Someone had had to come here, to his very threshold, to slide the envelope under the door. Someone guilty. How long a watchful waiting there would need to be to accomplish it unseen.

The comings and goings of a large motor hotel were constant. Or had the man dared make the move openly, fully aware that no one seeing him would ask questions or particularly notice his form and face. It must have been Iris' lover who wrote and delivered this; the abortionist would not creep that far out of concealment. He need not. He was too accustomed to being outside the law to worry, if he were found out, over one accusation with unsupported evidence. It must have been the man, or someone hired by him to deliver the envelope. Even better if he had hired a messenger; that would create a distinct link, after Iris' death, between him and Hugh.

His eyes were framing the five words, and in a quick decision, Hugh switched off the light and returned to his car. It was only half past one o'clock. Inactivity had suddenly become unbearable. The need to take the offensive at once was compulsive. He knew where Edward practiced—St. Hilary's, a large hospital across town near Thomas Road. He headed toward it. If Edward had finished with the birthing and returned home, there was no loss but a half hour's sleep. He was too keyed up at present for sleep.

Hospitals never slept. There was a middle-aged woman handling reception and switchboard. Behind her a nursing nun in white robe and headdress sat at a table, annotating the day's records. Hugh said to the woman, "Is Dr. Willis still here?"

She said, "I'll see," and checked a paper posted on the partition to her right. "He is," she told him.

"I'm Dr. Densmore from California." That had the sound of professional interest, not a family matter which could wait. "Could you tell him I'm here?"

"I'll see if I can locate him." She moved herself unhurriedly to the switchboard.

The sister came forward. Her smile was as fresh as if it were sun-up, not the weary hours. "Are you the brother interning at UCLA Medical Center?"

He was surprised she would know. "Yes, I am."

"Dr. Willis speaks often of you. That's a magnificent hospital, isn't it? I visited it last summer. I wish we had some of their equipment. Yes, Miss Deane?"

The receptionist was waiting. "Dr. Willis says he is to come upstairs, Sister Rose."

"You know the way?" The sister gave directions. "I hope that young woman delivers easily for Doctor. I'm sure he's tired after all the wedding excitement. It must have been beautiful."

"It was," Hugh told her. He moved off to the elevator. People were nice if you found the right ones. The trouble was there were so many of the wrong ones.

He pushed the button and the elevator rose slowly. Edward was waiting on the delivery floor as the automatic door opened. "I was just having a cup of coffee, Hugh. Join me?" He didn't ask questions, he didn't even seem surprised to have Hugh appear in the middle of the night. He could have heard rumors. Among doctors and nurses an abortion death would be the epicenter of conversation. "I've a room down this way for napping. It'll be a long night. Both of my mothers are in." He opened the door for Hugh, said, "I'll get another cup," and proceeded down the corridor.

Hugh waited on his feet. Now that he was here, it again seemed wrong to inflict this thing on Edward. Yet now it was essential.

Edward returned almost at once. He poured coffee for Hugh, refilled his own cup, and directed, "You take the easy chair. I'll be selfish and take the bed." He propped the pillows against the headboard and stretched out, his cup on the hospital table beside him. "Now what's happened to bring you here at this hour?" His face was cheerful; perhaps after all there had been no rumors yet.

Hugh stirred sugar into his coffee. "I'd rather take a beating than bother you with this. Especially tonight. I know you're too tired to take it. But I'm afraid to wait any longer."

From the intonation of Hugh's voice, Edward was already wary of what was to come. The fear of trouble was so close to the surface in even the most secure of them.

"You read in the paper yesterday about the girl found in the canal?" Hugh forced out the husky words, "I drove her to Phoenix."

"My God," Edward breathed. It might have been a prayer.

Hugh tried to speak without feeling, as if it had happened to someone else. "Last night when Ellen and I left the dinner party, two detectives were waiting for me. They'd had an anonymous tip that I could identify the girl. They took me to the County Mortuary and I identified her. Not under the name they had, under the name she'd given me."

He went back to the beginning, to the discovery of the girl on the road. He stripped the story to its bones; Edward might be called away any moment. But he told it all; it didn't come easy in repetition, it became more sickening. He concluded, "They'll do an autopsy on her tomorrow. I am certain they'll find she was murdered. By abortion or after abortion. And they'll come straight back to me."

Edward's voice was heavy. "There's no way to prove you didn't leave the motel that night?"

"No way. And I wouldn't have had to leave to be the abortionist."

Edward sighed. "We'd better get you a lawyer first thing in the morning. Before the autopsy results. Roger Hand is our most capable. And prominent. He's served in the legislature. You remember meeting him at the reception today?"

Hugh hated to say it. "Ellen wants a white lawyer."

Edward didn't believe the words.

"She called the Judge, her father, tonight to arrange it. She didn't tell me until after it was done."

Edward shook his head, not understanding. "What's wrong with our own?"

Hugh explained it. "Our own would believe me. She wants someone who would doubt."

Edward thought about it. "She could be right, she could be mistaken. Either way you're bound to come out all right. You've done nothing wrong."

"I wonder." Hugh walked to the window and looked out at the black green of the lawn. "I did something foolish. And that was wrong. I let my sympathy rule my judgment when I picked her up." He changed the subject abruptly, asking what he had to ask. "Have you ever been approached to do an abortion, Edward?"

"Of course I have." Anxiety had gone from Edward's voice; he was on familiar ground.

It hadn't been something in Hugh then, something a girl like Iris could discern.

"I suppose most doctors are asked at some time or other," Edward went on. "Certainly ours are. I doubt if any of them can escape that." His face was thoughtful. "One thing I'll say, Hugh, and it's God's truth. I've never been approached by any of our people. Only by the ofays."

The ugly word was incongruous on Edward's lips.

"Somehow they seem to think that a Negro doctor lacks morality. They become so surprised, almost affronted, when they're turned down. More coffee?"

Hugh said, "I'll get it," returning for his cup.

Edward poured for both of them, continuing, "You'd think they would realize that only a family of better than average economic status, Negro or white, can afford to educate a son medically. Which would rule out bribery."

Hugh lifted his shoulders. "You can't expect the kind of person who comes to you for that reason to be overly intelligent."

"Strangely enough some of them are. Some I've met up with. In their own world, that is. It's only when they come to the dark side that their ignorance shows up."

"They've been taught," Hugh quoted without rancor.

"Yes." Edward smiled reassuringly at Hugh. "Don't let it linger with you. I'm surprised you haven't been asked it before now; interns and students are always considered fair game." He put his head back on the pillows, remembering. "One of the fellows I knew at medical school, a white, although he could have been a Negro, no race has any lien on morality—anyhow, this fellow made enough for all his office equipment before he started practice. He's an important Chicago doctor today."

"I don't see how anyone educated in the meaning and purpose of medicine could."

"There are amoralists in any profession." Edward put down his cup and lit a cigarette. "I wish you'd told me about this when it happened. I would have reported it to our medical association."

"I couldn't. You see that, don't you? I couldn't spoil Clytie's wedding. Even now—" Hugh said desperately, "Only because I must have your help."

Edward's head lifted sharply.

"I must have the names of the abortionists in and around the city. I've got to find the man or woman who did it. The police won't. They have me."

For too long Edward didn't speak. Then he said, "I don't know that I've heard of any cases for some time now. I suppose Mahm Gitty is still at it. She's never been caught yet. She's an old crone who's been a registered midwife for some fifty years. She has a made-to-order alibi whenever she's brought in."

"How do I find her?"

"She's always lived in the Three Oaks district south of town. She hasn't any regular base, she moves from one cousin's shack to another. They're all *primos* in that neighborhood. I've heard the police say that the only way to find her is to poke around the district asking questions. But be careful. They don't like strangers asking questions in Three Oaks."

Hugh said, "There must be others."

"I'll try to get some other names tomorrow. It isn't an easy subject to approach, yet with this girl's death, there will doubtless be plenty of talk going around. I'll do what I can, Hugh."

Hugh moved to the door. All at once he was leaden-tired. Edward must be beyond exhaustion. "One more thing. Don't let the family know anything about this. Please."

Edward spoke quietly. "You may not be able to keep it much longer, Hugh."

"There's no need to worry them yet." Wishing he could hope, he insisted, "It might be they will never have to know."

"I hope so, Hugh. But if they do"—he smiled gently—"they can take it."

There was no opportunity for further words. A nurse rapped and flung open the door; in muted excitement she said, "Can you come now, Dr. Willis? Number One seems to be ready."

Hugh took himself down in the elevator. The nun was no longer at the desk. The receptionist didn't speak to him.

When he was nearing the motel, he passed a police cruiser headed in the opposite direction. For a moment he thought it was

Ringle at the wheel. But the car continued east; in his rear-view mirror he watched it disappear.

No further messages had been insinuated under his door. He was asleep when his head touched the pillow.

✳

Ellen's voice on the telephone was as bright as the slant of the sun dividing the drapes on the lanai windows. "I let you sleep as long as I could." His watch hands read quarter to ten. She was speaking with an eager carelessness, girl to boy, in case anyone was listening. "Do you want to come out and get me? I'm moving to The Palms."

"I'll be there as soon as I check out." He tried to shunt his voice out of sleep. "Do we have an appointment in town?"

"Noon. So don't be too long."

"I won't." He groaned out of bed, showered and dressed before packing his suitcases. After the shower, he was awake. When he was ready to leave, he called the desk. "This is Dr. Densmore in 126. Will you have my bill ready? I'm checking out."

He loaded the car and drove over to the office. He hoped there would be no difficulty about a check, he didn't have fifty cents in his pocket.

The clerk on duty was an attractive woman with prematurely gray hair. "I caused you an unnecessary trip, Dr. Densmore. When I looked up your bill, I realized that you were Dr. Willis' guest. I'm sorry."

He'd settle with Edward later—Edward, who thought of everything, even the possible financial status of an intern. Edward, who must by some miracle come up with the right name. He thanked the woman and went out to the car. He didn't leave a forwarding address. Temporarily, the unknown man would be balked in his harassment.

As he waited for traffic to subside in order to wheel into Van Buren, he wondered if the woman had spoken the truth or had purposely created a delay to give her time to report his departure to the police. Well, they already knew. He decided he believed her words. It wasn't a good habit to be suspicious of all motives.

Time was passing too quickly. He could move in on the grandparents later, right now he'd better get Ellen. He anticipated conversation with his mother and Stacy but Ellen was alone, her two small cases in the hallway. She was wearing the same dark silk she'd changed to last night.

"Where is everybody?"

"They went to town to see the Bents off." She pulled on a frost-white glove. "I left the big suitcase for you. It's in Clytie's bedroom."

He fetched it and locked all the luggage in the trunk. With her beside him, he started back to The Palms. "What excuse did you give for staying on in Phoenix?"

She shrugged slightly. "Only that I'd decided to rest up for a few days." She was a direct girl. "They think it's because you're staying over."

"It is," he said bluntly. But not what they thought. His anger, at her being held here by his trouble, was near the surface.

She sensed it and diverted the subject. "I had a battle to move to the motel. But I'm firm."

He managed a smile. "You're an army with banners flying." He didn't want to talk about the trouble, but after all that was the only reason they were together this morning. "I take it we have an appointment with a lawyer at noon."

"Yes, he's giving up his lunch hour to see us. My father had spoken to him before he called me. He seems to think it's a good sign that Mr. Houston would make that concession. Everyone Father questioned gave the same name as first choice, so it would seem he's the lawyer we're looking for. Skye Houston. Incidentally he pronounces it the proper old way, 'Howston.' His office is in that ancient bank building across from the courthouse."

Hugh acknowledged the information with an inclination of his head.

"Now if we can only convince him he should take your case."

"It's not settled?" In his alarm, Hugh almost missed the turn into The Palms.

Ellen explained, "A lawyer doesn't take a case until he has first heard the facts, Hugh."

"I've plenty to learn," he acknowledged. "Do you want to go inside or register from the car?"

"I'll go in. And I think you should go with me. To make it quite normal and free from any indication of hanky-panky." She didn't have to explain that in a courtroom a prosecutor would utilize the meanest fact.

The same agreeable woman was at the registration desk. "Back again the same day?"

Hugh gave her what he hoped was a carefree smile. "Giving a lift to Miss Hamilton. She's been staying at my sister's."

The woman turned the registry card toward Ellen. "I know. Mrs. Willis called me about it."

Ellen's immaculately gloved hand filled in the card.

The woman glanced at it and handed over the key. "I'm afraid the room isn't made up yet, Miss Hamilton." She smiled her eyes at Hugh. "The previous guest just checked out. But we haven't any other space unreserved right now."

It was a lie and they all knew it was a lie, but there was no rancor among them. This clerk couldn't cancel the system; her genuine friendliness was her contribution toward eroding it. Five years ago she wouldn't have had a vacant unit; ten years ago she would have said, "We don't take Negroes," if any had had the courage or spunk to inquire.

She said, "I'll send a maid around right away."

Ellen told her, "There's no hurry. I have a luncheon date in town."

He drove Ellen around to the now familiar door. He carried in her bags and they continued on toward town.

There were no meter parkings open near the courthouse; he hadn't expected otherwise, not at high noon downtown. He drove on First Avenue until he found a parking lot. Until they started walking back, he hadn't actually felt the day's heat. It could have been more than the heat affecting him. His uneasiness over meeting the lawyer throbbed in his temples. He wondered if the Judge had mentioned that Hugh was a Negro, or if when you reached Judge Hamilton's position such subtleties wouldn't occur to you. And he wondered if Ellen had this latent fear when meeting someone new. With her background, it wouldn't seem to be something she had to face, yet how could she escape it entirely? The quickening in the eyes, the certain intonation of the voice, the unspoken awareness: you are black. Even if you were brown or beige or lightly sun-tanned.

The building they approached must surely have been a relic of territorial days. The red brick was weathered to rose, the stone facings were gray not white. There was a secure feeling about its age; it had endured. They entered through the First Avenue door. There was no elevator, only an old uncarpeted stairway leading up and up. Silently they climbed it to the fourth, the top, floor. It was three minutes to twelve when they reached the top, winded, and followed the worn boards of the corridor to the door whose frosted pane was lettered: SKYE HOUSTON, ATTY-AT-LAW. Beneath the legend was another in smaller letters: *Aqui, Se Habla Español.*

Ellen murmured, "*¿Inglés, también?*" as she opened the door. Somehow the absurdity relaxed him and he followed her inside as if he were sure of welcome.

The outer office was minuscule. It resembled a territorial government office, the kind you could see in old engravings. Against the wall was a battered black oak bench with spool back and narrow arms. Behind a low railing with swinging gate were two enormous golden-oak desks, staggered in placement to leave a narrow aisle leading to the interoffice door. There was no switchboard, only a phone on each desk. The surface of one was cluttered, the other neat, which must indicate the dispositions of the two secretaries. Neither of them was in the room. The sun blazed through two long, narrow windows, looking out on the courthouse across. There was an air-conditioning box on one window ledge, otherwise the cubicle would have been stifling. Even with the box, the room was too warm.

Hugh indicated the telephones. "Should we ring him?"

While he spoke, the twelve-o'clock whistle could be heard faintly through the windows. And the inner door was opened. The tall man in the doorway said, "Hamilton and Densmore?"

Ellen smiled, Hugh inclined his head.

"Come in." He'd known what they were, there'd been no flicker in his eyes. His face was without expression as he stood aside for them to pass through the doorway into his private office.

It was a corner room, looking out on both Washington and

First Avenue. It was of old-fashioned dimensions, spacious, particularly in contrast to the anteroom. It gave a comfortable impression, deep leather chairs and couch in dark brown leather,
worn in places to chestnut. Old documents rather than the ubiq-
uitous western paintings of this country were framed on the dark
paneled walls. The recessed bookshelves were crammed hap-
hazardly, not alone with law books. A large Navajo rug of browns
and grays and whites lay on the modern cork-tile flooring. The
massive desk, which might have been of walnut, was too old for
one to be sure. It must have been hand-hewn in the room, it would
never have gone through the narrow doorways. The chair behind the desk was oversize, cushioned in flaking leather. There
was no cooling system; overhead two old-fashioned ceiling fans
revolved slowly. Yet the room seemed cool.

Houston was a lean, broad-shouldered man, topping Hugh
by inches. He wore a dark summer suit, cut like a flannel, a
white shirt, and a neat dark tie. His close-cropped hair was sun-
bleached to pale lemon; he was tanned far darker than Ellen, almost as dark as Hugh. Against this brown skin his eyes were a
startling bright blue. He wore heavy horn-rimmed glasses; when
he removed them to gesture, a deliberately induced habit, he
looked older. He was probably in his late thirties. There was no
indication of what the inner man was like, if indeed there was
an inner man. He was as dispassionate as a photograph of himself.

He motioned to chairs. His voice was courteous but devoid
of any personal intonation. "Will you sit down? I'm sorry but I
must eat while we talk. I have to be in court at one o'clock." He
circled behind his desk, which was covered not only with papers
but with a white luncheon cloth. He was not a sandwich-and-cup
man. There was a steak, a decent green salad, a pot of coffee. He
resumed eating. "Your father spoke to me from Washington this
morning, Miss Hamilton. He seemed to think that Dr. Densmore
might need help and that I might be interested. That is all I
know. Do you care to tell me about it?"

He had addressed himself directly to Ellen, as if she were
an interpreter between him and Hugh. He was civilized; he accepted Ellen as of his own stature; he had no reason yet to accept
Hugh. Hugh didn't resent it, he himself was no different in meet-

ing strangers. Yet it left him unprepared when Ellen said, "It's Hugh's story. I'm merely *amicus curiae*."

Her gesture indicated to Hugh that he should take over. He wondered where to start. And because without the beginning it couldn't be fully explained, he began on the Indio Road. Because of time, he omitted unessential detail as he had for Edward, his own reactions, his thoughts. By now he could sum up the facts economically.

Skye Houston listened without evident reaction. He didn't miss a word, an inflection, although he completed his lunch during the recitation. He'd lighted a cigarette before Hugh was done. At the end he had one comment, "Interesting." As if it had been a piece of fiction. But he lifted his telephone, dialed a number. "Skye Houston here, put me through to the chief, if you please." While waiting he lit one cigarette from the glowing stub of another. "Bruce? Skye Houston. What are the results of the autopsy in that canal case?" He listened, his pencil touching a pad with repetitive marks. When the chief—of police?—had finished, he said casually, "I'm representing him. You may pass the word."

Ellen flashed silent triumph at Hugh. It helped the sick feeling which came over him at the certainty of his further involvement. His name must have been mentioned by the chief.

Skye was dialing another number. "Skye Houston. Have someone give me a buzz when His Honor gets there, will you? Thanks. See you." He rang off and dialed another number before he said to Hugh, "You're right. It's murder." He broke off when his party responded. He identified himself and asked, "Hack in?" While waiting, he broke a long ash carefully into a silver bowl. "Hack? I just talked to Bruce about the canal murder. Are you planning to question Dr. Densmore again?" He gesticulated with his cigarette impatiently. "Why do I want to know? I'm representing him." After a short moment, he asked, "Can you make it tomorrow at three? I'm in court this afternoon." Briefly he listened again, cutting in sharply, "Certainly you can talk to him whenever you like, with or without me. Just remember, I'm representing him." He was more agreeable when he cut in again, "I'll ring you in the morning, Hack. Thanks a lot."

He hung up and set the phone aside. "All right. This is it.

There was an abortion. She didn't die of it, although it might have caused death later. It was badly bungled. But she died of a knock on the head. With a wrench or some such tool." He took off his horn-rims and made of them a pendulum. "I'm taking your case. I haven't any business taking it, I've twice as much as I can handle now. But it interests me. I don't get a chance at interesting cases too often, not in Phoenix."

To be uneasy because to the lawyer it was no more than a technical problem, wasn't justified. Why should he have a personal interest in a stranger?

There was a tap on his door, the office had no intercom system. Houston lifted his voice slightly. "Come in."

A head came in, a young, pretty, blond, curly head. A glance touched Ellen and Hugh but with no curiosity.

"What is it, Meg?" Impatience was on the surface.

"You told me to let you know when it was time to go to court, Mr. Houston."

"Let me know when we get a buzz from the clerk. That billy-goat judge has kept me waiting often enough."

The head disappeared quickly.

"Where was I? Oh yes. I'll slough off some of my routine stuff on the needy." He recapitulated, "Yes, I'll take your case. I'm expensive. You may as well know that right now."

Before Hugh could speak, Ellen said something like, "It doesn't matter." He agreed.

"I intend to be governor of this state. My target is four years from now." He spoke coolly, agreeably, but there was an underlying hint of power in him that hadn't surfaced before. It was somehow exciting and strangely reassuring. "I'm going there on your shoulders. This I tell to all my clients. They have a right to know they're building my war chest. Moreover, they have a right to know that without the cases they bring me to win, I wouldn't be tall enough to reach the chair." He began to gather his papers. "I don't say this to worry you. Your credit is good, Dr. Densmore. When I've cleared you, we'll figure out what's fair. Expensive, but fair."

Again the girl tapped and poked in her head. "He's coming."

"Thank you, I'll time it."

She had disappeared before he finished the sentence. Still talking, Houston fastened his briefcase and pushed back his chair. Hugh and Ellen came to their feet. "We must discuss this more thoroughly and make a plan of action. We can't afford delay. What about dinner? Do you mind coming out to my place? It's in the book, Mockingbird Lane. You know, Scottsdale." He came around the desk and shook hands with Ellen. "You, too." It was a directive, not courtesy. "About six-thirty?" He gripped Hugh's hand. "Bring your suits if you want a swim. I find it relaxing after the heat of the day." Briefly he seemed human as he realized, "You must be feeling the heat. You aren't used to it. You won't mind letting yourselves out?" His private door closed behind him; they could hear his tread striking down the corridor.

Hugh looked, bewildered, at Ellen. "You approve?"

"We couldn't have done better. Not even in Washington."

He was surprised at her enthusiasm, he'd never seen her excited before. He was ashamed of his fleeting thought that it was because there had been chemistry between her and Houston; it had been there, he'd sensed it. She was too knowledgeable to let that count. But he didn't express his own doubts as to this lawyer being the right one for him. Perhaps a cold, emotionless legalist who took a case as a hieroglyphic rather than out of conviction was what he needed.

They returned to the outer office. The curly Meg was at the first desk, the cluttered one; a slant-eyed brunette was speed-typing at the other. Meg looked up and said, "Good-bye. Let me know if I can be of any help. Call in any time." She wasn't curious, nor was the brunette who smiled at them as she changed carbons.

Hugh thanked them and opened the door for Ellen. They walked in silence the length of corridor and began their descent of the narrow staircase. What could Hack, who must be Marshal Hackaberry, have said that so annoyed Houston? Why hadn't Houston told them?

Over her shoulder, Ellen said, "He gives you confidence."

"Yes, he has it," Hugh responded. He didn't tell her that he was more afraid than ever.

✳

He had to get away from her; he was unable to contain his impatience to go to Three Oaks and look for Mahm Gitty. He'd forgotten he had had nothing to eat until Ellen said, "Where will we go for your breakfast and my lunch?"

There was no excuse he could give for postponing food; it was past one o'clock and she knew he'd had nothing this morning. He remembered, "There's a bakery cafeteria a couple of blocks from here. Not elegant but friendly and the food used to be good. Will that do?"

"It sounds just right." She was a different girl since Houston, as light of heart as Allegra or Celeste. "Air-conditioned, I hope?" The sun burned down, the sidewalks pushed the descending heat up again into your face.

"Everything's air-conditioned in Phoenix." Deliberately he matched her mood. "Except Skye Houston's office."

They had come upon a newspaper stand; he bought both the Phoenix papers. And realized he couldn't take her to lunch, he couldn't even buy his own breakfast. Somehow he wasn't embarrassed; he could tell the new Ellen with amusement, "I hope you have enough money to feed us. There went my last dime. I haven't had a chance to get to the bank."

She said, "It will be a pleasure."

"A loan," he warned. "Positively a loan."

She laughed at him. "I wouldn't spoil a friendship for a dollar or two."

The cold of the cafeteria enveloped them like a snowfall. They loaded their trays and managed to find a separate table. Without apology, each took up a newspaper, reading as they ate, occasionally reciting a sentence or two aloud. They exchanged papers as they finished the only story.

The morning paper had a rehash of the original news but the early edition of the afternoon paper had headlines of the identification of Bonnie Lou Crumb by her father, Albert Crumb, a mechanic of Indio. There was a front-page news photo of Mr. Crumb's arrival at the airport. The picture showed an unimpressive average man, perhaps in his forties, wearing an open sports shirt and wrinkled slacks. There was no sob story. Mr. Crumb, "tight-lipped and obviously restraining his emotion," had identified his daughter and expressed the hope that "they'd get the punk who did this." If he could get his hands on the killer, "he'll never hurt any girl again." The only mention of the mother was the brief statement that she and Mr. Crumb were divorced when Bonnie Lou was a child. She had not come forward. Iris doubtless had spoken the truth when she had said they did not know where her mother was.

There was also front-paged a blown-up snapshot of Bonnie Lou, taken perhaps a year before, and a cabinet photograph at least two years old, all flaws removed, making her look quite pretty and very young. The paper had been printed before the autopsy results; there was announcement only that it was being conducted. There was no mention of Hugh.

He commented on it, and Ellen admitted, "I don't understand, either. I wonder—it could be they don't want to risk the loss of any sympathy for her. If they're building their case on a sweet, innocent little girl, that false-name business would wreck the impression."

"Or hitchhiking to Phoenix."

She repeated, "I don't understand. Where I come from the newspapers wouldn't defer that much to the police."

Nor would they in Los Angeles. The reporters must know more than they had written. It couldn't be possible that the case wasn't being tongued over in minute detail in both the Phoenix and the Scottsdale stations.

They had finished lunch. On leaving the cafeteria, the blast of the street temperature was unbearable. By the time they had walked back to the parking lot, Hugh felt as if he'd been in a steam bath. He wondered how Ellen managed to appear fresh; perhaps Washington weather was a conditioner. In Los Angeles the thermometer rarely reached these heights.

Not until they were at the car did he ask, "Do you mind driving yourself back to The Palms?"

She was instantly apprehensive. "No. But why?"

He put the keys in her gloved hand. "There's someone I want to talk to."

"Oh no!"

Did she think it was Mr. Crumb or that he'd found out where

to find Iris' friend? He couldn't and wouldn't say more. She would try to dissuade him, at least to wait until after tonight's conference. He knew it couldn't wait. Even now Ringle and Venner might be looking for him. That half-heard conversation between Houston and Hackaberry could only mean that the marshal wanted to have another interview with Hugh.

"Nothing to worry about. But I don't want the car." The most foolish thing he could do would be to drive into the Three Oaks district in the white Cadillac.

"In this heat?"

"There's the bus if I need it."

She had to accept his decision, she didn't know enough to countermand it. She opened her purse. "You can't ride the bus for free." She extended a handful of dollar bills. "Don't argue. I'll keep books if you insist."

He took the money. He'd forgotten that a few pennies were his only monetary supply. "Thanks, Ellen. And don't worry. I may ring you up for a lift later."

Her eyes studied him, curiously, thoughtfully. Then she gave her head a slight shake and got into the car. He watched her drive away. He hoped her faith in his innocence wouldn't falter under his refusal to explain. If it did, he could not blame her. She didn't know him well enough for blind faith.

When the car was out of sight, he left the lot. He removed his tie as he walked, folding it into his pocket. He slipped out of his jacket, folding it under his arm. With the collar open, the short-sleeved white sports shirt, wrinkled with dampness, lent an appearance of the kind of young man who might go seeking Mahm Gitty. He didn't remove his dark glasses; everyone wore dark glasses these days. They were no status symbol.

He walked to the nearest service station with Negro attendants. The younger was manning the pump, the older was in the small air-cooled office. Hugh went into the office. A radio was broadcasting a baseball game.

He lent his voice the cheerful informality of Phoenicians. "How's the best way to get to the Three Oaks district from here?"

The man cocked a wary eye. "The best way's to stay out of that district." When Hugh did not respond, he got up from his chair and moved over to the wall where a large map of the city was posted. "But if you got business there, let's see."

Hugh moved beside him.

"How well do you know Phoenix?"

As if he came to town now and again, Hugh said unconvincingly, "I know it pretty well."

The man accepted it as said. His finger pushed along the map. "I guess the easiest way's to go down here. Veer left here and keep going south until you get there."

Hugh asked, "Is there a bus goes that way?"

Again the man gave him a curious eye. "I wouldn't know. Only time I ever go down that way is when I get a call somebody's car is stuck." He must have decided that Hugh was what he appeared, a wayfaring stranger, for he explained, "It's not rightly a district. Just a collection of sharecroppers' shacks, mostly Mexicans. Folks call it Three Oaks because it's built around three old oak trees. When you see them, you're there."

Hugh looked out disheartenedly into the glare of sun. "Is it very far?"

"It's not too far," the man said cheerfully. He wasn't going to walk it. "Not more'n a mile maybe after you veer." As Hugh moved to the door, he added, "It's safe enough daytimes but I wouldn't be caught there alone at night."

"Thanks." Hugh matched the cheerfulness. It wasn't hard to do. He was on his way to something which had purpose.

It could have been no more than a mile, but it seemed ten times that as he moved, sweat-stained, through the heat. He was in the country once he'd veered left, but there was no difference between the heat of country and town save for the lack of shading buildings here. Eventually he saw ahead the three oak trees, tall, heavy-leafed oasis for the crazy-quilt of ramshackle flat-roofed shacks which angled about them. He made for the trees. There were several old wooden benches beneath them. On one, two wrinkled men in farmers' woven straw hats nodded over their knobby canes. On another, a young woman sprawled, surrounded by a bevy of dusty-footed children. The third bench was peopled only by two little boys, dripping ice cream sandwiches down their chins. Hugh sat down on the unoccupied end. The little boys gave him a solemn gaze, then ran off, giggling and gibbering in Spanish.

Hugh could have asked his question of the young woman, she appeared too tired to run away, but he saw then the lean-to grocery store fronting on the makeshift plaza. Surely there would be someone English-speaking there. He rested a little before crossing over to it.

It was insufferably hot inside the dusky store. Flies droned disinterestedly about a ragged bunch of overripe bananas. Behind the counter a stout woman in a housedress splashed with orange butterflies fanned herself with a newspaper.

Hugh removed his dark glasses and assumed the hangdog demeanor and accent the woman might expect from one of his color. "Scuse me," he singsonged, "would you happen to know where I could find Mahm Gitty?"

For a moment she stared at him, suspicious, then broke into furious gesticulating Spanish. He understood some Spanish, but she was speaking too rapidly for him to catch more than a few isolated words. It was probable she knew no English; however, she had recognized the name because it recurred in her torrent.

He didn't give up. When she had abruptly ceased talking and resumed her slow fan, he asked again, "Maybe somebody around here could tell me where Mahm Gitty lives?" This time he stressed the name, looking directly into her eyes and perceiving there the recognition of it.

Again she broke into galloping words, punctuated with Mahm Gittys, ending by raising her voice, "Pepita! *Pepita!*" with an epilogue which seemed to wash her hands of the whole subject.

Pepita appeared, an undersized girl of perhaps twelve years, her black hair, long and dank, hanging about her face. She might have been asleep; she was barefoot and wore only a crumpled wraparound dress. The woman spoke and the girl spoke. They shrugged shoulders at each other and they swiveled their eyes over and again at Hugh. Finally the girl said in heavily accented English, "She don' live here."

But they knew, they hadn't been discussing a grocery order. "I just want to know where she lives," Hugh said. "Where her house is."

The girl stared at him for long moments, not speaking, as if she hadn't understood his words. Then she turned to her mother and again the two were voluble. Hugh waited. Not knowing whether it was better to break into the conversation with demands, pleas, insistence, or hold his peace.

The girl gave a final shrug, shoulders, hands, head, and scuffed to the open doorway. "She live there." His eyes followed her thin brown forefinger to the row of windows and doors, each set in its own small frame box, to the rooftops beyond, any of which could be "there."

He wondered if he might ask her to guide him but knew at once that would but confirm their latent suspicion of him. Instead he asked, "Where the yellow dog is sleeping?"

"No, no. This one." The finger hadn't varied.

"Where the geraniums are on the window sill?"

"This one!" The finger stretched.

"The blue door." Next to the geraniums.

The girl smiled at his success. "The big one," she said. It was perhaps a yard taller than its neighbors.

He said, "Thank you very much," and to the mother, also smiling now, "Thank you, ma'am." Again he stepped into the plaza. He wanted like hell to buy a Coke but he was afraid to force his luck. It might be that only Spanish-speaking were served; it might be they learned North American prejudice after crossing the border. He sauntered past the three oaks and across to the house with the blue door. As he knocked, he glanced back at the grocery store. The girl in the doorway was watching him, the mother's head was shadowed over one shoulder.

He knocked again; there were women inside, he could hear their voices. Nor did the voices cease as the door was without warning opened by a little boy; it could have been one of the two who'd run away laughing at him. The boy was startled by the appearance of Hugh; he backed away, and without waiting for an invitation, Hugh went inside. He stepped directly into the front room. It seemed filled with women, ancient ones in black, rocking and fanning themselves; a young one, with child, sewing; a painted young one in a tall hairdress reading a movie magazine; a fat matron in a wilting pink sack, her puffy feet bare, who advanced on him. The room was suddenly silent. Her face like stone, she asked, "What you wan'?"

He retreated a step. "I'm looking for Mahm Gitty, ma'am."

"She ain' here."

She could have been one of the crones.

The woman's eyes were hostile. "What you wan' with her?"

There could only be one thing he'd want with her and the woman knew it. He said, "I just wanted to talk to her about something." He made his whine more servile. "You know where I could find her, ma'am?"

"I don' know no Mahm Gitty." Suddenly she padded toward him menacingly. "Get out of here, *gringo*."

He would have laughed but it was no place for laughter. He stayed in character. "Yes'm. I'm going." His departure was rapid. They knew where she was. The harridan knew and the girls and the old Mahm Gitty women. But he'd been afraid to persist. There was evil in the fat woman. He couldn't risk being involved in more trouble.

He walked back to the bench under the tree and sank on it. And now what? It didn't look as if he could go further on his own. He'd have to ask Houston for help. They'd be afraid not to answer Houston's questions. It rankled that he could not bring the same force to bear, that he had to forgo his own social position and become a caricature to ask a simple question. And receive no answer. Until the boy was at his knee, Hugh didn't see him.

"Ice cream?" the boy grimaced.

He sensed it was a trade. "Where is she?"

The round face grew solemn. "She is very sick. They take her to the hospital."

"Mahm Gitty?" He was incredulous.

The boy nodded solemnly. "She is in the hospital for a long time."

"How long?"

"It is two weeks. Two weeks on this Sunday."

Hugh wondered how a child could be sure. "How do you know it is two weeks? Not one week, or three weeks, or yesterday?"

"It is two weeks." The boy was firm. "It is the First Communion Sunday. She is in church and she feels sick. She tries to get up from her knees and she cannot." His eyes widened like dark flowers unfolding. "She falls down. There in the church. They carry her out and they take her to the hospital. She is very sick. Maybe she will die."

Hugh could no longer doubt. And Mahm Gitty was absolved of any present evil.

The boy was standing there. "Ice cream?"

"All you can eat."

The boy, grinning again, ran ahead to the grocery doorway. Hugh followed. The girl and the woman were both waiting inside. Hugh didn't play the old part. He ordered, "A Coke for me and ice cream for my friend."

There was no trouble. The girl uncapped the Coke bottle and handed it to him. The boy was removing from the ice chest a precarious pile of assorted ice cream sandwiches. He shouted, "Thank you, mister," and scuttled away.

The Coke was icy. Hugh drank it in grateful gulps. He tendered one of Ellen's dollars and received the change. Only when he was leaving, did he ask of the girl, "Why didn't you tell me Mahm Gitty was in the hospital?"

"You did not ask me that. You ask me where her house is."

It was factual and he accepted it. The way back to town didn't seem so far as when he'd traversed it looking for the three oaks. When he reached Jefferson, he used a public telephone booth on the lot of another service station. He called Edward's office. Edward was in, but engaged with patients. "If you'd leave your number," the nurse suggested.

"This is his brother-in-law," Hugh told her. "I'll see him later."

It was close to five o'clock. If he were to make Houston's by six-thirty there was no time to waste. He walked over to Van Buren and caught an eastbound bus to The Palms. He didn't enter the grounds until he was near the unit. The car was there. He knocked at the door.

Ellen hadn't yet dressed; she was in tennis shorts and a white blouse. "You didn't phone."

"I took a bus up from town. Anyone asking for me?"

"No, it's been quiet." She led him to the table by the window. "I made daiquiris." She'd even frosted the glasses.

He sank into the blessedly cool chair and accepted the drink. "I may revive." He knew she was waiting for him to tell her where he'd been but she didn't ask.

"We've only time for one," she said. "I don't want to miss the swim. I didn't go in this afternoon because I was afraid I might miss your call."

He was casual. "You were going in the pool here?"

"Didn't you?"

"I didn't have the guts," he admitted frankly. "I'm no crusader."

"Nor I. But I like to swim. I don't think many of the guests will leave in high indignation if I do. Most of them are darker than I." She smiled slightly. "And somehow I don't believe the management will drain the pool afterwards. It's too expensive a job." Her smile widened. "They may add a bit more chlorine."

He sipped the good drink comfortably. "If you were Lilymay Johnson in for the night you wouldn't dare it."

"I'm not Lilymay Johnson, I'm Ellen Hamilton," she stated coolly. "And if I swim here, that much sooner Lilymay will swim here."

"Of course you're right," he agreed. "It's legal, now it must become custom." He finished the drink too quickly but there wasn't time to dally. "I'll run over to Gram's and change. I'll try to make it back by quarter after. I wonder if Houston is as much a stickler for time with his dinner guests as with his office clients."

"We may find out," she commented.

She followed him to the door, her eyes still asking the question he could not yet answer. He said, "If anything goes wrong, I'll call you."

5

THE FAMILY WAS GATHERED in the living room. Waiting for him. For a moment, he felt sick, certain the police had been here. Then Gram spoke spicily, "It's about time." They hadn't.

He had somehow managed his load of luggage, the big suit-case and the small, the plastic car case for his suits, his doctor's kit. His grandfather came to help. "Why didn't you holler?"

He said, "It's all right," but the large suitcase was taken from him.

In the upstairs room which he always occupied here, his grandfather set down the suitcase and fumbled in his pocket. "You had a telephone call."

Hugh was afraid to speak.

"I wrote down the number." He found the fold of paper. "I didn't tell the ladies. They're too curious."

He chuckled a little while Hugh was reading blindly the Scottsdale number.

"You're not in any trouble, Hughie?" Either he had recognized the numerals or Hugh's face had given his turmoil away. "You can always come to me."

Hugh looked across at him, into the compassion and genera-tions of understanding. And he lied. He laughed and lied. "Not at all, sir. It's about the dinner tonight, a lawyer friend of Ellen's." He crumpled the paper and dropped it on the table. "She had the message earlier and passed it on to me."

At least for the moment, his grandfather accepted the state-ment. Hugh watched the anxiety fade out of the old eyes, the weight lift from the shoulders. And the question came softly, "White friends?"

Hugh said, "Yes. Her father is Judge Hamilton, you know," as if this were enough to explain.

His grandfather said, "You'd better get a move on or you'll be late," and went away.

He'd have to be late. He closed the door to the corridor. He wasn't going to get back to the hospital tomorrow. Not with the police again calling him. He could no longer delay writing to the Dean. The Dean had encouraged him since undergraduate days. He'd sponsored Hugh in Med School, been his mentor in good times and bad. If he could not be trusted with this trouble, whatever happened in the critical days ahead, there was no hope for Hugh's future. Hugh had to trust him.

There was paper in the desk, and envelopes; his grandfather used the room as a library when there were no guests in the house. The letter didn't take too long, he'd been over the story so often. The only personal note he permitted was his hope for an extension of leave. Although he knew the Dean would not betray his confidence, he felt impelled to add the warning: "My family knows nothing at all about this. I hope they will never have to know."

He sealed the letter and addressed it. If he got it off special delivery, it would be delivered to the university in the morning. He put it into his jacket pocket and, unbuttoning his shirt as he moved, went to the head of the stairs. He called down, "Hey, Mother. Please call Ellen I'll be a little late." He didn't wait for her response. He stopped at the bathroom on his way back and started the shower. While he stripped, bathed, and dressed, he refused thought. He transferred the necessary billfold, empty of all but identification, his car keys and addenda. At the last moment, he remembered the crumpled memo and shoved it into his pocket. It was possible that his grandmother or his mother might come upon it and identify the number.

He ran down the stairs to where they waited for him. His mother said, "Ellen said it was all right."

"Thanks. I'll see you tomorrow, Mother. With my dirty laundry." It was a weekend joke. He was half out the door when he called, "Bye, Gram, Gramps. Forgive the dash."

His grandmother snipped, "Ah, love!"

If it were only that. Not this suspended sword over his head. He drove the short distance to the airport, where there were stamp machines. After he'd posted the letter, he returned over 24th Street to Van Buren. It wasn't far to the motel. Ellen was ready, in white, a bright pink cashmere about her shoulders.

Hugh apologized, "I couldn't make it any faster. Should we call Houston that we'll be late?"

She was unperturbed. "I've already called."

She thought of everything, a well-ordered girl.

"Skye had just come in himself. He said not to hurry." This soon it was Skye. And doubtless Ellen. "Shall we go?"

Not until she'd lifted a small waterproof bag, flowered in matching pink and white, did he realize he'd forgotten his bathing trunks. And wondered if it had been a subconscious rejection of swimming in Houston's pool. Counter-bigotry. It wasn't fair to Houston. The lawyer was civilized, that had been apparent in the meeting today. He hadn't asked them to swim as a special treat to the deprived. He had accepted them as his own class and had issued the same invitation he would to such. It was too late for Hugh to change his mind now.

The heat of the day was still heavy over the town. Because of the crumpled slip of paper, a nettle in his pocket, he didn't turn off to cut through the Papago Pass, where the first breeze of evening might be stirring. He would skirt the town of Scottsdale as far as was possible; by now there could be a pickup order out for him, with the big white car for identification. Skirting meant the death road; he wasn't certain of locating Houston's home by way of Camelback. But having forced himself to take the road last night, he was no longer fearful of it. As he turned there, Ellen marked the signpost and became silent.

Last night it had been too dark to see how little the Indian School Road had been changed by time. He drove quite slowly; it wasn't a road for speed, it was no more than a winding, country lane. The canal wasn't visible behind the high banks. Opposite was the old canopy of leafy trees.

They came to the gates of the once serene acres of Brown-moor. Hugh remembered, from years ago, a Sunday afternoon drive with the family; remembered with a pang the dappled

walks, the deep shade of the tall trees, the voices of the school-
girls. Now the grounds stood sad and overgrown and shabby,
waiting the final destruction of subdivision. The stables were already gone. At one time, his grandfather had told him on that
long-ago day, every variety of native tree and plant had been
perpetuated here. It hurt to think that the poison of uncon-
trolled development, the money greed, if unchecked, would soon
reduce not only this oasis but the whole of the beautiful desert
valley to the sterility of the tract.

As they followed the road, past a remembered row of neat
bungalows with their grass aprons, there was no way to know
at what spot Iris' body had been found. All traces of police and
sheriff and laboratory activity had been removed. She wouldn't
have been visible from the road. Whoever had flung her away
had not known how thoroughly the canals were patrolled by
the Zanjaros.

In a matter of minutes they were in the town, at the intersection of Scottsdale Road. If it hadn't been for the heavy pattern
of traffic lights, and the widened pavement, it might still be
yesterday when there was no evil in his stars. He turned north
with the lights and drove as far as Lincoln, then cut back to
Tatum. It led to the other side of the mountain where the country was molded of golden sand in the setting sun. The homes lay
apart from each other, chameleon blurs against the desert earth
and sky. Mockingbird Lane wandered north and south and east
and west. He followed its contours to the mailbox where HOUS-
TON was painted in tall letters.

The house was perhaps a quarter mile from the road, long
and low, and from the front landscaped only with what was native to the barren land. Saguaro and ocotillo and yucca, and rose-
black volcanic rocks. A cedar rail fence surrounded the property.
Hugh got out, opened the gate, and after Ellen had driven
through, relatched it. He took the wheel again, following the
sandy burro path to the house. Ellen lifted the bronze knocker,
but before it fell, the door was opened by Houston himself. His
smile at Ellen was a welcome untouched by the rigidity of the
noon meeting. He was in a terry robe and zoris; he carried a highball glass.

"You'll excuse me for not waiting for you." He divided the smile with Hugh. "I was too damned hot." He closed the door after them and called, "Marcia?" giving the name the Spanish pronunciation.

From what must have been a kitchen wing, a middle-aged Mexican woman emerged. She was wiping her hands on her white apron.

"Marcia, this is Miss Hamilton. And Dr. Densmore. Marcia will show you where to change, Ellen." He explained, "My wife and daughter are on the Continent. I'm hoping to join them in June if I can ever clear my calendar." As Ellen followed Marcia into yet another wing, Houston said, "Hugh, you come with me." He didn't comment on using first names, he made it natural.

"I decided not to swim," Hugh told him.

Houston made no comment which might have induced an explanation, he merely said, "You'll have a drink then while we do?" and led across the huge Western living room to a lanai, and through it onto a patio. There was an outdoor fireplace where mammoth logs were already smoldering. A brazier hung from a spit over glowing coals, ready for the steaks. The long wrought-iron table was set only for the three, all at one end, a hurricane lamp at each place.

The patio was large but not too large to be uncomfortable. It was walled with whitewashed brick, against which the pink and red and snow of oleanders with their glistening dark leaves made a brilliant pattern. The tiled pool, lighted underwater to increase its cerulean blue, lay beyond the dining area.

Skye asked, "What will you drink?" There was no fancy bar, merely a white brick ledge where materials for mixing were set.

Hugh glanced over the bottles. "A light Scotch. I may need a clear head." He took the piece of paper from his pocket. "This call came for me this afternoon. My grandfather took it. I haven't yet called back. It was too late when I received it, if I was to get here in time."

Skye read the number and dismissed it. "Hack will be at home now. I'll ring him later. Don't worry about it." He stuffed the memo in his pocket and took off his robe. In his black wool swimming trunks with his brown skin, he was an even finer figure of a man.

He had seen Ellen coming through the lanai before Hugh did. Hugh said quickly, "I didn't mention it to Ellen." Skye's brief nod was acknowledgment.

She must have known from long experience the impact of her face and figure, for she wore both unselfconsciously. The enormous bright flowers of her suit seemed painted on her. She carried her towel over one shoulder and swung a plain white bathing cap from her forefinger.

Skye walked to meet her. There was an indefinable something which matched them as if they were meant to be a pair. Both were slim, long-limbed, sleek, expensive. Both were tanned, he darkly, she golden. Hugh watched them come together; he didn't hear what Skye said to her.

The first impact of seeing them thus together smote Hugh with the awful aloneness of a stranger in a strange place. He didn't belong where they were. He thrust away such megrims. He'd known from the beginning that Ellen wasn't for him. Nor was she for Skye Houston. This wasn't a social gathering.

He watched them go across to the pool, watched her cleave the air and water in one swift motion. At the splash, Skye seemed to emerge from his dream. He too ran to the tiled edge and shallow-dived into the water.

Hugh drank his Scotch slowly, admitting to himself his envy of them. They swam in long lazy strokes the length of the pool. They were arrows feathered from the high board. They floated with their laughter under the darkling sky and early yellow stars. And he could have held his own in the water with both of them. Being landlocked was his penance for envy.

The fireplace logs were blazing by now; they warmed away the first chill of the desert night. Marcia came and went, lighting the candles, bringing silver and china.

Ellen and Skye finally came out, glistening from the water. She wrapped herself in her towel and let her hair free of the cap before she sat down beside Hugh. "It was wonderful. You should have come in."

Skye said, "Yes." He put on his robe and poured drinks. "You'll have a fresh one, Hugh? Light."

He agreed. There was dinner to come. If he had to see the police later, the alcohol would be dissipated. He couldn't make an obsession of remaining apart from the two.

Skye said, "I'll put on the steaks. They'll be ready to turn when we've had the drinks." It seemed somehow out of character for him to preside over a cook-out but it made him more human. No one mentioned the case as they enjoyed the slow high-balls. The talk was cabbages and kings. When the steaks were turned, Skye said, "They'll be ready by the time we're dressed. You'll excuse us for a few minutes, Hugh?"

Hugh said, "Of course," and watched the two vanish into the house. As if it were their home and he the guest. He wondered what it would be like to have a house like this one. With Ellen. Perhaps by the time he could afford it, if ever such time came, it would be possible to build it wherever he wished. Even on Mockingbird Lane. But he wouldn't have Ellen to preside over it. An Ellen couldn't be kept waiting that long. He laughed silently at himself. By the time he had the house, she'd be marrying off her granddaughters.

Skye was the first to return; Marcia behind him brought the coffee container. She and Skye conferred at the brazier until Ellen appeared. This time Skye's smile for her was as if they'd known each other for years. "Your timing is perfect," he complimented. "Now if you'll both come to the table, we can eat."

He served the oversized plates. Marcia brought them to the table and she went away. There was little conversation while they dined. It was close to nine o'clock; the others were as hungry as Hugh was, it was a long time since noon. After eating they rolled chaises into the perimeter of the fireplace. In the flickering light, all of their faces were golden dark. The desert stars were brilliant in the black-blue sky overhead. It was too peaceful to prod with the sharp stick of Hugh's danger. But Skye hadn't forgotten the reason they were here.

He said, "Before I came home tonight, I talked to the marshal."

Hugh spoke without rancor. "He doesn't believe my story."

"Let's say he has a reasonable doubt of it. That's fair. On one side are the things in your favor, on the other the things against you. And some of them work both ways. It's in your favor that you're a doctor at UCLA. It's also against you that you're a doctor, a doctor knows how to abort."

"A doctor knows how to abort. He doesn't bungle it." He spoke with passion.

"He might. If he were in a hurry, without proper facilities. Or if he were doing it under pressure."

"Or if he were a Negro doctor." The words came out more harshly than Hugh intended.

Skye said, "It's in your favor that you're a Negro."

The absurdity of the idea curled Hugh's lips.

"It happens to be true," Skye stated. "In today's climate, no thinking man wants to turn a simple case into an international *cause célèbre.* Furthermore, if he's in politics, he can't risk being branded a bigot. Hackaberry's no different from any of the others. One of these days he's going to have to stand for re-election. So he's leaning over backwards."

"I don't doubt what you say. It's true in a good many cities these days," Hugh admitted. "But my color is also against me. If as a Negro I'm no longer the expendable scapegoat, I am a complication. You know the marshal would rather I was a white man."

"He would," Skye admitted freely. "He wouldn't have to walk on eggs. Possibly he'd be holding you right now as a material witness."

Ellen said, "You must also admit, Skye, that if a reputable white doctor had given Iris a lift, there wouldn't be this undercurrent to it."

"Maybe so, maybe not."

"At least a white doctor would be given the benefit of the doubt." Hugh tried to keep his voice empty of emotion. "It wouldn't be taken for granted that a quixotic act had a sexual base."

"I'm sure Hackaberry gives you that benefit. As sure as I can be about any man whom I know fairly well."

"That's not the way Ringle and Venner see it."

"Fortunately, it's Hack we have to convince. He knows that your story could be the way you've told it. But it's your unsupported story and it could be another way." He looked directly at Hugh. "How do we go about proving the truth?"

He knew how. He didn't want to divulge it lest somehow the sound of his words would filter through the night and give warning to the hidden men. But this was his lawyer, the man he'd retained to help him. This afternoon had proven he would need all the help he could find. He said, "We must find two men. The one she came to meet and the one who committed the abortion."

Skye thought about it before saying, "It won't be easy."

"I know that. But if we can find the first man, he can give us the second." The police would have ways of getting that information.

"We have no name, no description, no faint clue." Skye was thinking aloud. "How do we find him?"

Ellen spoke. "Her father might have an idea."

"From what he told the marshal, and the marshal believes him beyond doubt, this whole thing is entirely without comprehension to him. He had no idea that his daughter knew a man in Phoenix, much less that she'd been meeting him, shall we say, intimately?"

Hugh said morosely, "The way she lied about everything, as if lies were truth, it wouldn't have been difficult for her to keep it from him."

Ellen suggested, "She may have known her father would disapprove of this man. Perhaps he does know but isn't aware of it."

"That could be," Skye accepted. "But he was most certain that she didn't know anyone in Phoenix. According to him, she hadn't been in Phoenix since she was six years old."

"And that needn't be true," Hugh added. "She could have told her father she was spending the weekend with a girl friend in Banning or Beaumont, and come to Phoenix plenty of times."

Skye said, "If this man killed her to keep his wife from finding out, I don't believe he'd be seeing her in Phoenix."

"If that is the case"—Hugh was figuring out loud—"he met

her in Indio. Their affair was carried on in Indio. And he must have had some legitimate excuse to be in Indio. Either business or relatives."

"And some of her girl friends must know who he is." Ellen was suddenly touched with excitement. "I think we start there. With her friends. Girls confide in each other."

Hugh's heart quickened. If they could get a name, they could start moving. All three were silent, examining the idea.

At last Skye said, "I think you're right. We start there. I'll arrange to fly Meg to Indio in the morning. She's young enough to talk to teen-agers on their own level, she won't scare them off as I might." He interjected with some regret, "I wish we could have got to them before their mothers told them to say nothing, not get involved."

"Even so they'll talk," Ellen said, with certainty.

"As to the abortionist, don't think the police have settled on you, Hugh. That's the first action Hackaberry took, in concert with the Phoenix chief. The police have been out covering that ground since the autopsy results were announced."

"They won't find out anything," Hugh said.

Skye lifted his shoulders. "Perhaps not. The muck who are in that filthy business don't come out from under their rocks under average circumstances. With a murder, I doubt if anyone can lift enough rocks to find them. But it could be some informant will come up with something."

"That's why we have to find the boy friend," Hugh said. "He's the only one who can tell us who did it."

"Suppose he won't." Ellen spoke sharply. "How does one go about finding an abortionist? Let's say I wanted to find one. Where would I start?"

"It's an underground," Skye began. "All word of mouth. It isn't something the police have much documentation on, it's even too secret for that. But they figure it starts, and my apologies to Hugh, in the medical profession. A girl is in trouble. She goes to a legitimate doctor. He turns her down. She tries another one, and so on until she finds a medico who's on the ethical borderline, let us say. He's straight but he knows someone who isn't. Perhaps a surgeon barred for malpractice, or a nurse or student who

prefers money to ethics. Or it may be a doctor with criminal in-
clinations; there are such, as in any profession. Perhaps he's gone
over the line into illegal operations for quick money. At any
rate, she gets a name, and that's the beginning. The word is
then passed around. In the office, on the campus, in the bars—
God help us, wherever frail man and woman meet together. When
the next fellow gets a girl in trouble, he or she doesn't have to
go through the initial routine. They ask around and find a friend
who knows a friend who has the word." Skye took an angry breath.
"The police problem is that neither side will talk. Unless the case
becomes a murder, they don't ever hear of it."

"What I was wondering," Ellen said thoughtfully, "is how
this man found an abortionist so quickly, after Hugh refused."

"The police are wondering the same thing," Skye stated. "It's
not something you can discover in a hurry. It is most likely that
he was a previous customer or that he had it set up before the
girl came here. Certainly he knew where to go."

Hugh thought aloud. "Iris had told him she was coming to
Phoenix and when. She must have. She had none of the hesitancy
of a girl who doesn't know whether or not she'll find someone
waiting at the end of the journey."

"But you believed she was holding a secret joke," Ellen argued. "It could have been she meant to surprise him."

"No," Hugh denied. "She must have known he would be
waiting for her. She couldn't take a chance on not finding him.
She had no money."

"How could she write to him? He couldn't have let her know
where he lived."

"They had some way to communicate." Hugh was certain.

"By telephone," Skye suggested.

"I doubt that. She couldn't have made a long-distance call
from her father's without its showing up on the bill."

"Reverse the charges."

"Not to the man's home. The wife might have answered.
And not at his job, unless he has his own business."

It wasn't important now. Skye proceeded, "Somehow she
sent word she was coming. And why. And he got ready for her."

There was gall in Hugh's mouth. "He was ready, but when

she told him how she hitchhiked to Phoenix with a doctor, he saw a way to save money."

"But why did he kill her?" Ellen cried out. "Why go to the expense of an abortion if he meant to kill her?"

"Did he kill her?" Skye asked rhetorically. "Or did the abortionist kill her when he saw the operation was bungled? Right now that's the most important question for the police. Not the abortion, that problem is always at hand. When they catch one operator, there's a peculiar leniency in the laws that lets him free in no time. But murder's a different matter. It's the murderer they've got to find. They'll admit there may be a man she came to meet, as Hugh claims, but they aren't convinced that man killed her. The operation was a bad one, she was going to die—the logical killer is the abortionist."

Before she could name him. Yes, it was logical. But he wouldn't need a wrench or some other car tool to complete what he had begun. He could make sure she was dead more easily than that.

Hugh flared, "How can they not admit this man? Surely they don't think I made her pregnant?"

"No, they don't think that. But they do think her pregnancy may have come from one of the many boys she knew in her high school. She was a free and easy girl, that's implied in all the information on her. She couldn't do anything about her trouble in Indio, the town is too small. But someone knew where to go in Phoenix. And in Phoenix no one knew her."

"Or she had it arranged with me to take care of her between wedding parties?" The bitterness deepened.

"They don't go that far," Skye said. "They figure it was coincidence she met up with a doctor on the way."

"And the anonymous tip? What about the anonymous tip?"

"The marshal takes that seriously. Ringle and Venner think someone not connected at all with the murder could have recognized the description. Either an Indio boy visiting over here or a Phoenix boy who had met her over there. He wouldn't give his name because he didn't want to be involved in the mess. He was scared. Just like you were scared to identify her after you read that story in the paper. It's a normal reaction."

It could be that way, although Hugh could not admit it. For the identification hinged on what she was wearing. The one who called the police must have seen her in Phoenix.

"How much time do I have?" Hugh asked hopelessly.

"The police don't rush into a murder arrest, Hugh. They want enough solid evidence for the D.A. to go into court and get an indictment. It's true they're in a hurry on this case because they're on a spot. Whenever a young girl is violated and murdered, the citizenry and the newspapers are prone to get hysterical."

"They have enough facts right now for a case against me."

"Not for murder, Hugh. For abortion, yes, perhaps. But that's something the law moves on with exceeding caution. Particularly with a doctor involved. They know that once that accusation is made, the man will never be quite free of suspicion of guilt."

There was nothing more to be gained in worrying the perhaps and the ifs. It was past time to go. If he were to be keen tomorrow, to further his own investigations. The police might be looking into the local abortionists, but because they were police they'd get no answers. And didn't need them, they had enough material to fit the crime to Hugh.

Skye smiled, it was meant to be comfort. "I'm not worried, Hugh. I'm sure Meg will dig up what we need in Indio. We have an advantage just because we're not official."

"I hope so." He looked at Ellen. "We'd better go."

"Yes." She rose. "Just a moment while I get my things."

While she was out of the room, Skye said, "I called your number while I was dressing. Hackaberry wanted to see you but I got him to put it off until morning. Ten o'clock. At his headquarters."

"I'll be there."

"I'll try to make it too," Skye said. "But I may not be able to. My case was continued until tomorrow morning."

Ellen's steps were returning and Skye lowered his voice. "Don't be afraid of them, Hugh. If you're innocent you don't have to be afraid of questioning. But anything you don't want to answer, keep quiet on advice of counsel."

Hugh said again, "I am innocent." Even his lawyer had doubts. By now probably Ellen too.

She joined them at the door. Skye said confidently, "We have a right to believe that when Meg gets back from Indio tomorrow, your troubles will all be over."

"Let me go with her." It wasn't a sudden thought, Ellen must have been brooding about it all evening.

She and Skye looked long at each other. And he shook his head. "You'd better not." His voice was gentle. "You're too civilized."

And what he said was true. Ellen could no more meet in rapport with the inhabitants of a small western town than with the desert lizards. She was too far removed even for intuitive knowledge.

And yet had she been white, Skye could have risked it. All three of them knew it; it was in the trio of silence which held them for that long moment. There was no reproach in Hugh, nor would there be in Ellen, for Skye's rejection. As there was no personal rejection from the lawyer. The silence was recognition of an unalterable fact.

✳

There was little to say as Hugh and Ellen drove back to The Palms. It had all been said. He walked with her to her door.

She opened it and asked, "Will you come in for a stirrup cup, Hugh?" She didn't care much, her thoughts were miles away.

"Not tonight. I'm worn down."

"You are sleepy?"

"It's funny, but I am. Without a prescription." The want to take her in his arms was unbearable. He turned abruptly away. "Good night."

She misinterpreted the reason for his sudden mood, for her thoughts spilled from her. "There must be something I can do! Some way to help!"

He turned back. "You've helped unbelievably."

"There's so much to be done. I can't just stand aside—"

"How do you think I feel?" he cried. "But until we find—"

The ringing of the telephone in her living room was startling. For a moment equal alarm met in their eyes, then she whirled and rushed inside. He was on her heels, stopping only to close the door behind them. There was no logic in his following, undoubtedly it would be her family or friends calling. But it could be his family, with something so dire they would intrude on him here. Had Ringle and Venner come for him?

She had answered before he reached her side. He saw the expression on her face and snatched the instrument from her. A male slimy voice was speaking ". . . another babe shacked up with him . . ."

Hugh broke in harshly, "Who is this?"

"That you, Doc? Don't want to spoil your fun—"

Again Hugh interrupted, demanding, "Who is this? What do you want?"

The jeer went out of the voice. It became tough. Evil. "I'll tell you what I want. You better get out of town before something happens to you. Something real bad. You get the message? We don't like niggers mucking our—"

Hugh banged down the handset and started to the door. Before he was half across the room, Ellen caught him.

"No, Hugh, no!"

He tried to put away the hands clutching his arm, but her arms closed around him, holding him entangled.

"You mustn't go out there. You mustn't!"

He tried to force her away but she clung. Short of hurting her, he couldn't break loose.

"He isn't out there! He's on the telephone!"

The words came through and the fight went out of him. Not the rage which made fear nonexistent, but the will to action. His arms closed around her and for the moment he stood there holding her, as he'd wanted to hold her. He didn't kiss her, didn't caress her, he simply held her in his arms. After that moment, he released her.

"You shouldn't have stopped me." He pushed open the lanai doors to recover his breath, parting the draperies, gazing out on the peaceful moon-gilt greensward. No one at all was in sight. He closed the curtains before he turned. She had dropped into a chair. The flame of the lighter she held to her cigarette was shaking as in wind. He completed the operation for her, then took the other chair and lit a cigarette for himself. "It was the man we're looking for."

She too had no doubt. "Yes."

"He saw my car come in. He didn't know I'd moved out. He called the room, not my name. He was on a phone somewhere nearby." He was sure of it. Anger returned. "I might have caught him."

"You might have been killed." Her voice was pale. "You might have been lynched."

He said, "He's safe only as long as he's the invisible man. I'm going to have to come against him to find out who he is."

"You may be right." She was breathing more easily. "But rushing out at midnight to lay hands on a white man isn't going to help you. If he killed you, he could and would call it self-defense. He'd need only say you tried to kill him because he knew you'd murdered Iris."

"He'd have to involve himself to say that."

"I can think of a dozen ways he wouldn't have to. So can you. The simplest would be that she came to him, an old friend, with her trouble. That at her request he brought her to you, and that he never saw her again."

"He's not going to kill me," Hugh said. "He needs me to bear his crime."

She couldn't argue with that. She asked, "Would you like that drink now?"

"I don't need it. I'd rather not. He may try again."

"I doubt that. I think he's long gone. He may not have been around here, anyway."

"He had to be. To know I was here. He might have been calling from the lobby."

"That can be checked." She walked to the phone, lifted it, and when the office responded, she said, "This is Miss Hamilton in 126. That call you put through to me a few moments ago, can you tell me if it was from outside the hotel?" After listening to the response, she said, "I wondered. It wasn't for me. It was a mistake." She thanked the night operator and hung up. "It was from outside."

He said, "I think we should try to change your room. I'm afraid to have you stay in this one."

She considered it, then shook her head. "We couldn't ask it without letting too many people know you are concerned in this case. If he should call again, I'll simply say that you've checked out, that I'm the new occupant."

He wasn't thinking of a telephone call but of personal violence. However, if it were the white car that the man watched for, he wouldn't appear at Ellen's door unless it was parked outside. In which case Hugh would be there.

She said, "He must wonder why your name hasn't been in the papers. That must bother him."

He hadn't thought about that. "Yes. He may believe I've been cleared by the police. That would account for his warning me to get out of town, to make me look guilty." Excitement mounted. "He may be afraid I caught a glimpse of him that night, that I can identify him!" He said, "Ellen, he's got to call again! And when he does you'll have to keep him on the phone until I can find him."

She insisted, "He may be calling from Scottsdale. Or Tempe."

"It's the car," he reiterated. "He waited for the car. The timing isn't coincidental. From the time we drove in here tonight until your phone rang was just what it would take to put a call through at this hour, when the lines aren't busy."

She agreed with him but she didn't want to.

"There's that hamburger stand in the next block that stays open until midnight. There's an all-night dispensary right across from the hotel office. He could watch from either of them."

"And there are residential developments all around."

"He can't call from home. He has to have a phone booth or be somewhere with no one around to listen. Tomorrow I'll have a look at those late places."

"You'll be careful what questions you ask."

"I won't open my mouth unless the atmosphere is right. I'm not looking for trouble, I'm trying to get out of it. For all we know, he may work in one of those spots."

"You'd better let the police take care of the questioning."

"The police." As if they cared. But he suddenly said, "Do you think we should let them know about the call?"

"It's too late now. Let Skye do it tomorrow, he's your lawyer."

"Should we call Skye?" He didn't want to. Not at this hour.

She decided, "Tomorrow's soon enough. There's nothing he could do tonight."

"I'd better go." He didn't like leaving her alone, but fatigue had caught up again.

She said, "Let me look outside before you leave. I hate to have you drive alone at this time of night."

He said then what he had been thinking. "I don't like leaving you here alone."

"I won't open the door to anyone. Not without first checking with the office."

Before he could stop her, she had stepped outside onto the walk. He came close behind her and moved past to survey the silent rows of cars. There was no person stirring.

He said, "It's all right. You go back in now." He wanted to have her in his arms, not by accident this time, by design. He was falling in love with her as he'd never known love before, even with full realization of the hopelessness of the situation. Because of a moment of charity on a desert road, he would have to live with the taint of this case forever. That was cold truth. He could never sully an Ellen Hamilton with its ugliness.

"I'll wait until you get the car started." She managed a smile. "We'll synchronize. When the engine's running, I'll dash in and bolt the door."

He couldn't match her smile. It wasn't funny. She stood there framed in the doorway not only until he was under way but until he'd backed out and was turned toward the exit drive. He stopped then until she lifted her hand and shut herself behind the door.

As he drove away, he felt certain he was not followed, but nevertheless he circled several blocks. He wouldn't chance leading the man to his grandparents' home. When he was again on Van Buren, he covered it slowly in the area on either side of the motel. The hamburger stand was closed by now; in the dispensary a tired man stood behind the counter. But Hugh saw what he'd missed before, or seen without seeing, a lighted service station a block beyond the motel. A car parked in front of it could watch The Palms driveway. And there was at hand, on the corner of the lot, the total privacy of a public phone booth.

✳

He was late, six minutes late, the next morning, as he descended the steps of the Scottsdale station; seven minutes late as he stood in the doorway of the marshal's office.

They were waiting for him, the marshal moving the rocks on his paper reports, Ringle sucking a Coke bottle which looked like a toy in his heavy hand. Venner, wearing a damp plaid shirt of pink and yellow-green, was skitting about the small room as if he knew there was to be a pickup order soon.

An innocent man could apologize. Hugh said to Hackaberry, "I'm sorry. Traffic seemed slow-moving this morning." Nothing of how difficult it was to get away from the family without revealing his destination.

"Doesn't matter." Hackaberry waved the apology aside. "I'm running late myself. Have a chair."

Today there were extra chairs, empty ones aligned with Ringle's, two under the windows. Venner, his mouth snaked with disappointment at Hugh's entrance, blocked the latter.

Hugh said, "I'm sorry," and lifted one from Ringle's line, placing it near the marshal's desk. He sat down.

"We couldn't seem to find you yesterday." Hackaberry spoke genially, just as if it weren't important.

Hugh reacted the same way. "So I understand. I was out most of the day." If they wanted to know where he'd been, they would have to ask.

"You know the results of the autopsy?"

"I've read the reports in the newspapers. And I know what Mr. Houston was told."

Ringle rumbled, "Were you surprised?"

Hugh glanced at him briefly, then back to the marshal. "I don't believe I understand."

Venner said maliciously, "We been wondering how surprised you were to find out she'd had an abortion."

Hugh didn't let the insinuation disturb him. He continued to address himself to the marshal. "I hoped the autopsy would not show that she'd been aborted." It might not be wise to say more but he did. "Both as a doctor and as the person I am, I hoped she had been spared that."

Point-blank Ringle demanded, "Did you commit that abortion?"

"No, I did not!" His denial rang out, strong, true. There was no change in the attitude of the three men. They'd been conditioned to the guilty as well as the innocent forthright denials. He might just as well have saved his breath. He continued passionately, "I'm a doctor. I've sworn the Hippocratic oath. Under no circumstances that I can think of, would I violate that oath."

"But you weren't surprised," Ringle said flatly.

"No, I wasn't surprised. What did surprise me in the report was that her death was caused by concussion, not the operation."

The marshal asked, "Why did that surprise you?" He seemed interested.

He might be sticking his neck out, far out, to venture his opinions. But Houston wasn't here to advise him. He knew the interview was being taped and tape could be mutilated. Yet an innocent man would answer, frankly and freely. Hugh said, "Because if he was going to kill her, why would the man take her to an abortionist?"

"You don't think the abortionist killed her?"

"No, I don't," he returned. "I think she was killed by the man who got her in trouble and who found an abortionist for her after I turned her down."

"The mystery man." Venner sounded amused.

Hugh snapped the sentences, "The man she came to meet. The man who drove her to my motel Friday night. The man who telephoned an anonymous tip to the police." He brought out his wallet, removed the ugly scrap of paper and put it in front of the marshal. "The man who pushed that under the door of my room Sunday night. The man who telephoned the motel last night and warned me again to get out of town."

The marshal read the message and held it out to Ringle. The sedentary detective reached across for it, read it without expression, and waited for Venner to cross the room for his reading. Venner read it and tittered.

The marshal said, "You don't know who he is." He held out his hand to Venner for the return of the slip.

"I wish I did."

"He seems to know you."

"He knows my car. He knows my name. He knows the motel where I was staying." He might also know Hugh's appearance but he wasn't going to give Venner a chance for another titter.

Ringle said, "I thought you'd moved out of the motel."

"He doesn't know that; he asked for the room number, not for me by name." He had to go on with the explanation. "I happened to be there when the call came. A friend of my sister's has the room now, I had just brought her home from dinner at Skye Houston's." Deliberately he brought the lawyer's name in, a reminder that he was no longer without support. "Doubtless the man saw my car drive in and thought I was still staying at the motel."

While he was explaining, the marshal's phone had sounded and he had spoken unheard words into it. Now he said, "You can give us the full run-down on that telephone call later. Right now I've got another matter to take up."

One of his deputies was already at the door. With him was an undersized man, his face weathered from outdoor work, his thinning hair plastered with water, his eyes dull. He wore trousers needing a press, unshined shoes. For one wild moment of hope, Hugh believed they'd found the unknown man. And then he knew, from the deference in the deputy's manner, from the demeanor of Hackaberry, who this man must be.

The marshal spoke to the man, "I'm sorry to have to bother you at a time like this but I won't keep you long. Do you mind standing up, Hugh?"

Hugh came to his feet, without haste and without delay. As if he didn't mind. He looked down the room without expression, as if he were to identify the man, not the reverse. And he wondered what thoughts lay beneath the skull with the pasted hair, wondered what regrets would gnaw on a man whose daughter had died as Iris died.

The marshal was asking, "Do you know this man?"

He barely glanced at Hugh. "No."

"Have you ever seen him before?"

This time the man did peer at Hugh, as if to him all dark men looked alike and he was being asked to discover a birthmark to distinguish this one from the others.

"No, I never." The answer came flatly.

"You're sure of that?"

"If I'd seen him before I'd tell you."

The marshal didn't quite know how to phrase it. He asked hesitantly, "You never saw him with your daughter?"

"What you driving at?" Crumb's voice was no longer lackluster; it scraped. "What you trying to make out of her? My daughter wouldn't go with no niggers."

The marshal's voice clamored, "She rode to Phoenix with this man."

No one had told Crumb before. His face turned mottled with the shock. And then he lunged like a terrier toward Hugh. "You murdering bastard! You killed my little girl!"

The deputy caught his arm, held him.

"I didn't kill her," Hugh said. His sympathy for this shell of a man, distraught, bewildered, out of his depth, was stronger than any rancor. "I only tried to help her. She needed help."

Crumb wasn't heeding, he was struggling in the deputy's grasp, shouting obscenities.

The marshal passed Hugh, murmured, "You can sit down," and went to take the man's other arm. Together he and the deputy eased Crumb from the room. Venner began to cock about, his eyes little pointed rocks. Ringle gnawed his thumbnail phlegmatically. Hugh sat down and lit a cigarette. His hands were shaking.

The marshal returned, his boots clattering as he crossed to his desk. He took a last cigarette from a pack, wadded the paper and shot it toward a corner basket. It landed on the floor. "That was Albert Crumb," he said. "Her father." He needn't have said it, possibly it was for the tape.

Venner sauntered back to his chair. "He sure didn't like the idea of a nigger transporting his daughter to Phoenix." The word "transporting" had an ugly sound. If he were smarter than he seemed, he might have chosen it deliberately.

The marshal turned on him. "I don't want to tell you again, there's not going to be any color business in this case. I'm not going to have it messed up with Kluxers or with bleeding hearts."

"I keep forgetting," Venner drawled. But the ugly look he gave Hugh made it clear it hadn't been wise of the marshal to tongue-lash him in Hugh's presence.

Hackaberry went on as if he couldn't stop until he'd said it all. "You're going to handle this the way you'd handle it if Densmore weren't a Negro. That way we'll have a case which will stand up in court, not be sidetracked by a lot of loudmouths who don't care whether we got the guilty party or not, so long as they're in the headlines. You got that straight now?" He mashed out his limp cigarette. "Let's get back to that telephone call."

Hugh gave a full account of it, even to the final words. He said, "I hung up on him then."

Venner tilted his chair against the wall. "Didn't you want to hear what else he had to say?"

"I did not," Hugh said. To the marshal he continued, "I thought possibly I could catch him at it. There aren't many places near the motel where he could watch for me to arrive and get immediately to a telephone." He confessed, trying not to remember the moments with Ellen, "I was too late. Of course he'd be gone as soon as I hung up."

"Why?" Hackaberry didn't get it. None of them seemed to understand.

"He can't take a chance on being seen. Don't you see, once he's seen, once there's a description, you can find him? And once you find him, there'll be those who can identify him as being with Iris that night."

Ringle took out a notebook. Without interest, he asked, "Where could he be calling from?"

Hugh named the places.

Ringle wrote them down and put away the book. "Why didn't you report the call last night?"

"I didn't think of it until it was too late. He didn't wait around, I'm sure."

"We got things called prowl cars," Ringle said. "Just like you got in L.A. They get around pretty fast."

"I didn't think of that," Hugh said with honesty.

The marshal said, "Well, if you have any more trouble, let us know right away. Next day doesn't do much good."

"I will."

"We'll put a prowl car around the neighborhood tonight."

Hugh wanted to protest. A prowl car would scare off the man. The only chance to find him was to let him go on believing he was safe. He didn't speak up; it would do no good, only cast doubt on there having been a call.

The marshal turned to his detectives. "Do you have any more questions?"

"I got one," Venner said. His mouth was moist. "Did you beat that girl's head in because she wouldn't pay you for what you done?"

Hugh looked to the marshal. His voice was rigid. "I've said it and said it. I am absolutely innocent of any connection with her death."

Venner's chair clicked to the floor. "If you're so all-fired innocent, seems funny you'd hire that big-shot lawyer, Skye Houston, to defense you."

Hugh couldn't contain his anger. "I hired him to try to get a fair deal, not to be railroaded for a murder I know nothing about. Just because I'm convenient."

Venner snapped, "Don't get huffy with me, black boy. It don't pay." He said insolently to Hackaberry, "Black boy's got a temper, hasn't he?"

The marshal choked, "I warn you, Venner."

"Excuse me," Venner sneered. "I must of lost my temper too. I don't like black boys insulting my integrity." He walked out of the room without asking leave.

Ringle said, "Don't worry about him, Hack. I'll keep him in line. I need him on the investigation."

The marshal turned to Hugh. "Nobody's going to be railroaded. But nobody's going to go free who had anything to do with killing that girl." His voice was hard, and his jaw. Like the others, the so many others, he'd have a hard time believing that a Negro doctor had the ideals and ethics of a white doctor. "You are to remain in Phoenix for the time being."

"I've already written the hospital," Hugh said without inflection.

"Very well. You'll be hearing from me." It wasn't a warning, merely a temporary dismissal.

Hugh rose and left the room. He could feel the hostility follow him. Because of Venner, deliberately through Venner, the atmosphere had been changed.

In the outer office, Venner was leaning against the water fountain with the young deputy who had conducted Albert Crumb earlier. He looked at Hugh with spite and said something under his breath to the deputy. The young man laughed, and Venner, delighted with his success, began cackling with him. By then Hugh had reached the outer door, and he went out into the heavy noon. He was shaking with rage, for once the sun felt good. He got in his car and drove away, but only as far as the next block. He pulled in by the small white church. He was in no condition to drive a car until his nerves had calmed. He took off his jacket, laid it on the back seat to dry. He lit a cigarette; it was without taste.

If he were fighting only the routine means of inquiry, it would be hard enough to endure, but to be pitted against personal venom became in time intolerable. The possibility that it might be a deliberate plan, for every man must have a sensitive spot by which he could be broken, made it no less endurable.

The five minutes, ten minutes, he sat there in a square which the growing village had not yet eaten, gave him the tranquillity he needed to set out again. He must discover what Edward had found out, he should report the gravity of the morning's interview to Houston, he wanted to be with Ellen. On his way to Ellen's, he stopped at the Scottsdale branch of Edward's bank. He presented his credentials, gave local references, and had no difficulty in cashing a check. Because it was the closer way, he drove again over the Indian School Road. And for the first time it came to him that the abortionist must be in or near this area. It was highly improbable that the killer, whichever of the two he was, would have risked driving the suffering girl over a long route through town to reach that particular section where he struck. There would be too much danger of interference along the route. Phoenix was well patrolled by city and county police, there was scarcely a stretch of road where you didn't see one of the light blue or light tan official cars.

The murder hadn't been planned. It came out of the botched abortion. This seemed self-evident. There was no reason for the abortion if the man meant to kill. Why had he killed? And, remembering the girl, he knew. Because she had become a worse threat after the operation, because she threatened to tell. The abortionist hadn't killed her, he would have no need of the happenstance tool. It was the man she had come to meet, the man who had driven her to the motel, the man who had driven her to the abortionist's, the man who had driven her away after the operation and had listened to her threats. And that meant there was another car with more evidence in it than in Hugh's. It could mean that the abortionist could identify the man. Hugh was afraid to be hopeful. But it could mean the two would accuse each other.

He had reached the motel. There was no response to his knock at Ellen's door. He walked around to the front of the unit and saw her across the green, just lifting herself out of the pool. She raised an arm in greeting, she must have been watching for him. He remained there by her lanai door while she wrapped the bright beach towel about her and gathered her oddments into the flowered beach bag. Her swimming seemed to have caused no commotion. The sunbathers were somnolent under oiled brown skins, the pool was lively with young people. Under the umbrella tables, older men read newspapers and their women wrote postcards. For most of them Ellen was doubtless only a girl with an enviable tan. Those who may have wondered or known evidently accepted the changing face of society. He'd met with all the varying degrees of civility, of progression and regression as an intern. Unyielding bigots were a minority save in pockets of the Deep South. In today's climate, it was they who could do nothing but retreat behind their warped, sagging fences. No longer could they demand that the fences enclose the rest of the country.

Ellen pulled off her cap as she came across the lawn, shaking down her long, dark hair. When she reached his side, he said, "You needn't have come in. All I want is a private place to phone."

"That you may while I dress."

The sliding door opened at her touch. She hadn't left it locked. Common sense told him that she'd kept an eye on the room from the pool, that the maids were active all morning in every wing, that the anonymous man must hold a job by day, for his activities, save on Sunday, were all by night. Yet for the moment he was chilled at the thought of Ellen's entering the room to find evil waiting for her.

He said nothing now, unwilling to throw a shadow over the brightness of the morning. "And to invite you to lunch." He displayed his wallet, extracting a bill.

She said, "You don't owe me that much," and "I'd love to lunch but let's have it here. It's much more comfortable than a restaurant." She disappeared into the dressing room and bath. Before he was connected with Edward's office, he could hear the shower running.

Edward was out to lunch. Hugh left his name but no number, saying he would call back. Edward had enough to do without returning calls. Before he could look up Houston's number, Ellen returned, daisy-bright in a full-skirted summer dress. He couldn't tell her she was so beautiful it hurt; he substituted a dry question, "Just how much excess weight did you carry out here?"

She said, "I'm pleased you notice, sir."

"I have a mother and three sisters. I probably know more about femme finery than any male outside Don Loper."

"Then you must know that summer dresses don't weigh much. I didn't have any excess but I may going back. I miscalculated the heat of Phoenix in May. Most of the summer wardrobe I've acquired here." She suggested, "Why don't I call Room Service and order before you finish your phoning? There's a menu in the desk."

"I'd like something cool. Whatever you recommend. My grandmother keeps plying me with hearty meals. She thinks I need fattening." The morning paper was on the table. While she gave the order, he read more completely the front-page story.

The turnover brought him to the editorial page. The editor didn't call the police system inefficient, he merely insinuated it as he rang the bells of alarm concerning the safety of young girls in Phoenix. Hugh set the paper away. How long before he'd be thrown from the sleigh to appease the wolves of discontent?

Ellen had finished her call and settled in the wing chair, opening a portfolio and continuing a half-written letter. Hugh called Houston's office. The secretary who wasn't Meg answered, identifying herself. Houston was out, but she said, "I've been trying to reach you, Dr. Densmore. Mr. Houston would like you and Miss Hamilton to come to his house at eight-thirty tonight. Will that be convenient?"

He queried Ellen, and reported, "Yes, we'll be there."

At eight-thirty. That would be after Meg's return from Indio. Hugh's nerves began to quiver. The knock on the door made him start. He wondered if he would ever feel safe again, as safe as he had before Iris.

Ellen was admitting Room Service with the lunch trays. No delaying tactics here. The management was doubtless only too pleased that Ellen chose to eat in her room. The waiter, a gawky young fellow who looked as if he were outgrowing his uniform, arranged the silver and linen and iced food on the low coffee table. He said, "Give me a buzz if you want anything else, Miss Hamilton." He favored Hugh with a nod as he whistled away.

It was pleasant to be lunching here with Ellen, as if they were in their own elegant mansion, looking out over their close-cropped lawn and blue pool. The reason they were together spoiled it. "I hate to have you hanging around here, missing your vacation." He took a French roll from the basket.

"Am I that dull?"

"Ellen!"

"I'm not accustomed to such frankness from young men."

"You know what I mean." He wondered, "Will you still go on to Los Angeles?"

"Certainly. I'm considering driving there with you."

"Delighted." But the bleak prospects made him add, "I wonder if I'll remember how to drive when they let me go."

Her light mood had been surface, an attempt to take his

mind from his trouble. "You mustn't get depressed. We're on our way. Maybe you can't see daylight but it's just around the bend."

"I wish I could believe that." Deliberately he returned to unimportant conversation. "Do you know many people in L.A.?"

"Very few. Will you show me the town?"

He exaggerated a groan. "I'll introduce you to some great guys who'll show the town while I'm on duty. The only thing I'll have a chance to show you is the UCLA campus—an hour here, an hour there."

"I think I'll like the UCLA campus."

Without warning their eyes met and held, and in that moment, the game they were playing became real. He immediately turned back to his Russian salad, as if food were more important than furthering their relationship. He would not take advantage of whatever emotions propinquity and absorption in his troubles might have engendered in her. He said lightly, "I hear we have some fine courses in foreign diplomacy. Maybe you'll decide to transfer."

"I might at that." The dangerous moment was gone.

"What made you take up that field? It isn't a woman's."

"No, it isn't. But it could be. There's always need for office help and one needn't stay in that category."

"Okay, Madam Ambassador."

She smiled at him. "I didn't choose the field because I'm a feminist." Thoughtfully, she continued, "We've traveled abroad quite a bit. Because of my father's various assignments. I believe there's a definite need for what I call dark diplomats. A great part of the world is colored, you know."

"You'd rather live outside the United States?"

"Oh no!" She was quite honestly surprised at the suggestion.

"Isn't it easier?"

"To me, no," she said. "In our country, more often than not, we are what Ellison so well describes as invisible. It's just the opposite in Europe. Even in the Orient and northern Africa. As Americans, we are so conspicuous it makes me feel like a cockatoo in a cage. I've never been deep into Africa, I don't know what it would be like for me there, but I don't think I'd be at home. I've been an American for too many generations. Somehow I don't mind invisibility. I'd rather no one saw me as I walk down the street, or pretended they couldn't see me, than to have people nudging and pointing as if I were a freak. Even within its limitations, I like to live my life without comment."

"Then why are you training for foreign service?"

She laughed. "At heart I suppose I'm a crusader, like my father. I don't intend to spend my life in the foreign service, Hugh. I can spare a few years. After that I shall get married, raise a family, and point out proudly to them how much better their lot is than mine when I was a girl. Now tell me your story."

"I'd like to stay in research." He might have been talking about someone else. He couldn't speak of his own future when there was to be none. "However, as I have to earn a living, and want to make a damn good one, I'll doubtless end up in practice."

"You'll specialize?"

"You have to nowadays. Or so the doctors tell me. I'd be content to be a really good old-style family doctor like Edward. Not that I'd ever be the surgeon he is."

"Have you ever thought of a turn at Medico?"

The telephone rang. Neither one of them had actually been free of fear, despite their efforts. Both started at the sound. But she pretended as she went to answer. "We might find ourselves in the same neighborhood overseas," she said. After speaking, she turned, "It's for you," and before he could react, "I think it's your grandfather." She didn't know that increased the decibels of his fear.

The deep, soft voice said, "I'm sorry to bother you there, Hugh, but you've just received a telegram. I thought it might be too important to wait."

The Dean? Hugh said, "Thank you, Gramps. I'll be over in a little."

"We're going out but you know where the key is." Everyone knew where the key was kept. Under the rambler roses on the trellis. He wondered how he could suggest a change of hiding place for the present.

They said good-bye and he replaced the phone.

"Bad news?"

"I don't think it will be. A wire. It must be from the university. I mailed a special to the Dean last night." He sat down at the table. "Bad or good, I'm going to finish my lunch."

She poured more tea into his glass and her own. She'd led him to talk of this and that while they lunched as if there were no doom overshadowing him. Now that he would be leaving, she went directly to what must have been weighting her thoughts throughout the hour. "You were with the police this morning."

"How could you know that?" There was only one way. Skye must have told her.

She said, "You only have that particular face when you've been up against Ringle and Venner."

He admitted, "Yes, they were there. And the marshal. And Iris' father."

"And . . . ?"

"It wasn't good. When he didn't identify me, they told him I'd brought her to Phoenix. Then he called me the murderer."

"Are you afraid?"

"I'm almost past fear. Unless Houston's Meg gets the identity of that man, there's no hope. I'll be charged. Or unless I can find him."

"Did you tell the police about the call?"

"Yes. They're putting a prowl car in the neighborhood."

"That's good."

"It's not good," he denied. "It all but ruins my chance of finding him. He's not going to be active while they're in the neighborhood."

"It may keep you from being hurt." Her words went beyond the simple statement.

He hadn't thought before in terms of actual physical violence, only of facing up to the man, demanding the truth. He wasn't a fighter; he'd never had to be and never wanted to be. As a student doctor he had seen the results of the cruelty of man when reduced to animal viciousness. In particular the cruelty unleashed in today's juveniles, in the gang warfares of the city.

Although he and the police had used "man" as terminology for the killer, Hugh realized at this moment that his mental picture had always been of someone of Iris' generation, of the raucous, acned boys of the Indio experience. Teen marriages weren't unusual. Somehow he had believed that out of the experience of his maturity, he could handle this boy. He had not remembered that boys tended to run in packs. He might not be facing a single adversary.

And there was ever present the fact of color. If the man/boy attacked Hugh physically, after initial impact, he would be attacking the fact. The hatred of the fact, for him, would justify violence.

Hugh shook the thoughts out of his head. He would not be afraid. If he could find a way to confront the man, he would not hesitate, whatever might come. He didn't want the police there; he wanted it where he could force the truth. Alone, fact to fact. It was the only way he could hope to escape the net being woven by both the police and the killer.

He put out his cigarette. He said, "That wouldn't be very important if it saved my facing trial for abortion and murder." He moved to the door, not wanting to leave this oasis, not wanting to leave Ellen. But there were other things which must be done while he was yet free to do them.

He said, "I'll call you later."

✳

Hugh drove to the Jefferson Street house and climbed the porch steps. Venner was in the swing. Hugh turned to stone. "What do you want?"

The detective's lips were mocking. "I been waiting to see you, *Doctor* Densmore."

He couldn't have arrived while the grandparents were at home, he'd have been inside the house.

"Yes?" When you were arrested you were allowed to make one telephone call. To your lawyer? Houston couldn't be reached; he was in court. To a friend? Edward couldn't be reached. Again the burden would be Ellen's.

Venner gave the old wooden swing a backward push as he got out of it. "You going to ask me inside? I've always been curious as to how you folks live."

It was meant to be insulting but Hugh ignored it. He repeated, "What do you want?"

Venner ceased baiting. "I want your medicine bag." Before Hugh's outrage could become vocal, Venner fumbled a fold of paper from his back pocket. "I got the order here. Signed by the marshal. All perfectly legal."

Hugh accepted the paper. Perfectly legal. He returned it to the detective. The sharp little eyes watched as he took the key from under the roses. The place must be changed. Hugh opened the door. He must be rid of the man before his grandparents returned to face the malice.

Venner gawked around the living room. "Looks right nice." It looked exactly like the living room of anyone's grandparents.

Hugh said curtly, "I'll get the bag."

"Mind if I follow along? I wouldn't want you deciding to remove maybe a knife or a forceps."

Hugh said, "If I'd had any reason to remove anything from my kit, I'd scarcely have waited two days to do it." He started up the stairs, resenting the footfalls behind him.

The yellow envelope of Western Union was propped on the bureau in his room. He didn't touch it; it didn't matter if Venner did see it there. Venner was in the room as Hugh opened the closet door and reached down the black bag. He could not bring himself to pass it over to the detective. A doctor's bag was sacred to medicine, it didn't belong in lay hands.

He said, "My instruments are sterilized after every use. If I had used them, there'd be nothing to prove it."

"I don't know about that," Venner said. "We got a laboratory that can find a lot of things that aren't there." He held out his hand. "Might be you wouldn't have much of a chance to sterilize stuff, just being a visitor in Phoenix."

He sensed Hugh's resistance, he was enjoying it. He reached further and took hold of the handle. Hugh didn't relinquish it. For a moment they stood there, both clutching the small black kit. Hugh could have jerked it away from him, he was taller and younger and perhaps stronger than the detective. But he didn't dare worsen his position by force. Even if the idea of commandeering the bag had been initiated by Venner, the order was plain. It might be an extra-legal move, but it was legal.

Hugh released his hold, hating the smirk of triumph on Venner's mouth. "Now you got to sign the receipt." He pushed the bag under his arm, deliberately careless, while he pulled the paper from his pocket again. "Sign on the dotted line." He thrust it at Hugh. As Hugh took his pen from the desk, Venner continued, "We wouldn't want that high-toned lawyer of yours to say we done anything illegal."

Silently Hugh returned the signed paper. He started to lead out of his room but Venner didn't follow.

"You're forgetting your telegram," he said. He stood between Hugh and the bureau. He was greedy for the overt act, for one movement from Hugh which he could repulse out of pious legal violence. It had been a near thing when both clutched the black bag. If there had been more space, if they had not been penned in the small aperture between the bed table and the closet door, Venner might have created the excuse.

This was his last chance. When he saw Hugh would not advance, he dangled the kit carelessly from his fingers and with his other hand lifted the envelope. If he dared to open it, Hugh knew he would lose control. He waited, hoping his trembling rage was hidden.

"You haven't even opened it. Don't you want to know who's it from?" His eyes peered as if he could read through the protective cover. "You must be a mighty important boy to be getting telegrams you don't even open."

Hugh refused to speak.

"Catch," Venner said suddenly. He tossed it short toward Hugh. It fell on the rug between them.

Cautiously Hugh bent to pick it up. At once Venner thumped across the room, his heel coming dangerously close to Hugh's hand. But Hugh was quicker. He straightened with the envelope in his hand as Venner passed. He waited for the detective to precede him down the staircase.

Venner wasn't afraid of his rage. He moved lightly, not looking back. It could be he himself recognized how near he had come to his aim, and how damaging it could be to him as well as to Hugh. He had a last word as he went out the front door. "Fresh air sure smells good."

Hugh stood at the door until the car was driven away. Then

he moved quickly. He didn't even stop to read the wire. If his grandparents should see him now, they would know something was terribly wrong. He locked the house, replaced the key, and drove away. He didn't know where he was going, he only needed to get out of the neighborhood, to find a place where Venner could not reappear.

He was on North Central when he saw the big drive-in and remembered its objectiveness from previous visits. At this hour it was not crowded. He pulled in, and as soon as his order was taken, he opened the envelope.

It was from the Dean. A day letter in clipped telegram short-hand, but the expanded meaning was plain. There was disbelief that Hugh could be subjected to this misunderstanding, an offer to help in any way possible, and the Dean's assurance that he would arrange things at the hospital for Hugh to be absent as long as was necessary.

Hugh was moved. It was good to know that there was a friend who trusted him. When his Coke came, he drank it slowly and afterwards finished the ice. He was cooled in mind and body when he paid the tab and drove the few blocks to Edward's office. It was about three-thirty. The doctor would be in, and it might be possible to see him for a moment. With every new police move, Hugh knew how necessary it was for him to get on with the search. When he was arrested, there was no one he could ask to continue it. The abortionist would then be safe, not caring that an innocent man was in his stead.

Edward's office was off McDowell, a one-story yellow stucco building housing two doctors, a dentist, an architect, and a pharmacy. All Negro. The white tenants had moved out when the pioneer, the architect, moved in. He hadn't been a crusader; it wasn't easy then or now for a Negro to find good office space.

Hugh drove into the parking lot at the rear and entered the building by the back door. Edward's office was in the front. There were several patients waiting, idling over the magazines. Hugh had met the young secretary-nurse at the wedding reception, but he identified himself and said, "If it's possible to see the doctor for a half minute, I'll wait."

"I'll find out, Dr. Densmore." The patients wouldn't resent

a brief conference between doctors. The girl returned almost immediately. "If you'll go into his office, Dr. Densmore, he'll see you when he can. The far door."

He walked into the inner corridor, passed two closed doors, and entered the private office. He sat down across from the desk and waited. The air conditioning made waiting a pleasure. He was tense with hope. It wasn't long before Edward joined him.

"I'm sorry to barge in during office hours," Hugh told him. "But I haven't been able to reach you. Were you able to get any more names?"

Edward lighted a cigarette before taking a key ring from his pocket. "Only two and I must have talked to a dozen people." He fitted the key into the lock of a narrow desk drawer and opened it. He took out a folded prescription blank from his wallet and relocked the drawer. As secretly as if there were other persons in the room, he passed the paper to Hugh.

"The first is a number to call. No name. I had word of it from a nurse, a doctor, and an intern. All professed ignorance of the number; they'd heard of its existence, that was all. I won't tell you which one of them tucked a slip of paper into my hand just as I was leaving the hospital." He gave a muffled sigh. "Somehow I feel that no one I spoke to believed my cover story. They thought I personally wanted to know how to get in touch with an abortionist. My only solace is that I will be able to tell them the truth later. Or so I hope."

"I'm sorry." It didn't help to say it. It didn't relieve Edward's shame or Hugh's own disgust at involving his brother-in-law.

Edward's voice was more muted. "The second is old Doc. Jopher. He lost his medical license years ago, criminal negligence. Operated once too often when drunk. He was a natural to turn to illegal operation. He's served time twice for abortion, but as soon as he got out, he went back to work. No one seems to know if he's in the business currently, there have been no rumors that he is. He's getting pretty old. But somewhere he's finding the money to buy booze. He's usually drunk." Almost apologetically, Edward said, "I don't think he's your man. The police know all about him. He's always questioned if an abortion case is made public."

"And swears he's innocent," Hugh said. "A man like that won't tell the police anything."

"Do you think he'd tell you?"

Hugh shook his head. "But if he's the one, I'll have to find some way to get him to talk. Where does he live?"

"In a little farmhouse north of Scottsdale."

"Scottsdale?" Hugh reacted.

"Yes." Edward was aware of the pertinence. "The directions are on that paper. There's no telephone. But they say he's easy to find, he seldom leaves the place." He put out the cigarette, ready to resume practice. "What about Mahm Gitty?"

"She's out of it. She's been in the hospital for two weeks. I won't keep you longer. I want to get at these."

"Don't be disappointed if they lead nowhere. There may be others no one has mentioned. I may get more information."

"In Phoenix would there be more?"

"There might be dozens." Edward wasn't optimistic. "Destroy that paper when you've done with it. I wouldn't want it to be seen. Did you get a lawyer?"

He realized he hadn't seen Edward since. "Skye Houston."

Edward opened the door. "He's the top man here."

"Ellen's father arranged it."

Edward stopped in the doorway. "Understand one thing, Hugh. We'll all help on the fee. Your father won't have to shoulder all of it."

Hugh faced him firmly. "I'm going to pay every penny of that fee. I'll have to borrow the money but not you or my father or anyone else is going to be out one dime. I'm no longer little Hughie, Edward, this is my responsibility."

Together they walked the corridor, Edward leaving him at the first closed door. Hugh went out through the office, followed by the curiosity of the waiting patients. He'd kept Edward too long from his appointments; it would mean overtime again for an already overworked doctor. Some day he'd make it up to Edward, he didn't know how, but he would.

Again in the car, weighted by the immediate afternoon heat, he took time to reread the information on the prescription blank. Doc Jopher should be the one, but if the police had already questioned him, why should Hugh even dream that he could bring the man to confess? He'd start with the number. If it was so well known in town that three persons had mentioned it to Edward, it would seem the sort of information that Iris' friend could be expected to pick up.

It was not until he'd driven away that it occurred to him to wonder where it might be safe to make this telephone call. Not at his grandmother's or his sister's, they'd be sure to overhear. Not at Ellen's, for she must not know of his activity until it was successfully concluded. He'd have to find a public phone booth, and one where there was no chance of his being observed by either family or friends or police or the unknown man. It eliminated the neighborhoods he knew, and in others he might be intrusive.

He decided to cruise until he spotted a likely booth. He found what he needed at one of the new shopping centers northeast of town. The development was large enough to give him anonymity, but not so large that the phone booth might be in constant demand. Actually there was little reason why the women, darting from one air-conditioned store to another, would need the telephone. They were within a few blocks of their neighborhood homes.

He left the car sandwiched between other cars near the variety store, and went in it, buying a pack of gum to add to the small change in his pocket. Under the arcade he sauntered on to the drugstore, buying a roll of mints, to add more change. Keeping under the arcade, he window-shopped his way to where it ended, and then, as if it were something that had only then entered his head, he walked out into the sun, crossing the sandy expanse to the booth.

There was no one near it. The few cars parked at this end of the area must belong to employers or employees who left the more convenient places for the customers. He closed himself in the booth. It was stifling. He palmed the paper from his pocket, put in his coin, and dialed the number. There was no delay in reaching it.

A metallic recording began without preamble, "If you will leave your telephone number, Mr. Ess will call you. This is a recording. If you will leave your telephone number, Mr. Ess will—"

He hung up. The recording didn't specify how soon the return call might be expected. Minutes? Hours? The sun pouring on the metal roof, the narrow confine devoid of air, made of the booth a dangerous sweat box. Could he remain there safely to await a return call? Did he dare tie up the booth for that long?

He opened the door and stepped outside. There was another possibility. By night Edward's office would be safe from interruption. And Edward knew what he was about. But it would mean giving the doctor's number to the criminal outfit, involving Edward definitely in the dirty business. He had no doubt at all that Mr. Ess would check on a number before he returned the call.

In his frustration and need, it came to Hugh that there could not be a measurable delay in returning the call. Neither party could risk having a third person answer the phone. The area of the booth continued to be avoided. The lady shoppers knew better than to use it when the temperature neared one hundred. Again Hugh entered the box, this time leaving a small aperture for air. Again he dialed the number and reached the metallic voice, but after the repetition of the statement, the recorder stated, "At the beat of five, recite slowly the number to be called," repeated this instruction. The beats were distinguishable and were followed by silence save for the faint movement of the tape. Hugh covered the mouthpiece with his handkerchief, and after the repetition of the five, read off the number printed on the dial. The silent interval was right for a precise reading. He waited and the record went back to its initial statement, "If you will—"

He hung up. He did not dare step out of the booth, someone just might approach to use it. He did open the door wider, not that the hot heavy air brought any illusion of refreshment but it made it easier to breathe.

And he waited. And waited. The perspiration ran down his cheeks like rain, his shirt was like wet paper against his body. He eyed his watch incessantly, then forced himself not to look at it, trying to measure the passage of time in his mind. When he glanced again, three minutes had evaporated. He sucked a mint and his thirst became acute. Why hadn't he bought a newspaper instead of candy and gum? If he had something to read, the time would pass and the phone would ring. He wiped the sweat from his face with the handkerchief, then hung it again over the mouth-piece. And he waited, stepping into the fastness of the booth whenever an occasional car ran to this end of the lot to make its turn. He was tempted to give up, to believe that the organization would not return a booth call for fear of entrapment. But he waited, just a little longer.

And the phone rang. He caught it on the first jangle, pushing the door shut with his foot. "Hello."

A male voice which might have been speaking through a hospital mask said, "Mr. Ess is returning a call to—" and gave the telephone number.

"Mr. Ess . . ." Hugh began.

"Mr. Ess speaking."

It wasn't hard to make the words come haltingly. As they must be spoken by most of those who were forced to deal with this man. "A friend give me your number," Hugh said.

"Speak up," the man commanded. "I can't hear you."

He might be aware that the caller was protecting his voice from identification. But Hugh did not remove the handkerchief. He said louder, "I am speaking up," and repeated, "A friend give me your number."

There was silence at the other end of the wire.

"A friend give me your number," Hugh said again. "You see, I'm kind of in trouble . . . I need some help . . . I got a hundred dollars . . ."

He was interrupted. "The price is five hundred."

Neither Iris nor any friend of hers would have that amount. Hugh invented quickly. "I got a job. I could pay you a hundred dollars now and—"

Again he was interrupted. Dispassionately. "The price is five hundred. Call again." The connection was broken.

Thoughtfully Hugh replaced the receiver. He grabbed the soaking handkerchief and in relief stepped outside. Iris had not been put into the merciless hands of Mr. Ess. If by any chance her friend could have raised that kind of money, he would never have wasted it on a girl he wanted only to be rid of.

Hugh walked back to his car and drove away. The stirring breeze cooled him. There was left Doc Jopher. He wouldn't go there by daylight, it was too close to Scottsdale. He might not be watched as closely as he feared, but he wouldn't mock fate by taking his car to the house of a twice-convicted abortionist until he had cover of darkness.

6

ELLEN WAS PERFUMED, silken, and inaccessible. For once he was on time, exactly six-thirty as he knocked on her door. Venner's visit and the ordeal of the telephone booth had been washed away from him by leisurely dressing for the evening.

"I thought we'd eat at the airport restaurant," he told her. "The food's good, the air conditioning is good, and no one will hurry us." It was also the first fine restaurant in Phoenix to ignore segregation.

She asked, "Would you like to mix a drink while I gather up my things?"

"Not tonight. This is my party. We'll have our cocktails with dinner."

Her purse and gloves, a furred sweater were at hand. She checked her key, cut the air conditioning, and they moved to the door. He had it opened when the phone rang. Neither of them moved. It rang again, long, demanding.

Ellen put her hand on his arm. "Don't answer it."

He hesitated while the after-tone of the bell reverberated in his ears. It began again. He said, "I must." She let out a forlorn sigh as she followed him into the room.

He had a prickle of excitement as he lifted the handset. This could be what he needed. It was still daylight, easy to spot the man if he were using the phone in any of the neighboring places. Hugh gave a tentative "Hello."

"Dr. Densmore?" It wasn't the voice he awaited.

"Yes?"

"Marshal Hackaberry would like you to come out to his office."

This time Hugh did venture a protest. "I was just going to dinner. Would it be possible to come later?"

The officer said, "You'd better come now. He's waiting."

Hugh choked, "All right. I'll come." He hung up. Disappointment was lead in his mouth. "The marshal wants me."

She said, "Don't be worried."

"I'm not worried," he lied. "I'm hungry." He spilled out futile anger. "Why does he always have to call me at dinnertime?"

"Possibly because he can't reach you earlier. At any rate, he's still asking you to come in, not sending someone to bring you in."

Be grateful for small favors. He said, "You'd better not wait to eat dinner. If I can't get back to take you to Skye's—"

She broke in. "For heaven's sake, Hugh, by now you should know that I won't be left behind."

"No," he began, but she walked past him, out the door, and into the car. He was in time to close the car door after her. He said, "I don't want them to see you. I don't want them to know about you."

She waited until he was at the wheel before she answered him. "It's no good. They know about me. This is the second time they've found you at my apartment. I'm not afraid of anything they could say to me. I'm Ellen Hamilton and they can't change that."

She didn't know Venner, she could never have been exposed to a Venner. When they approached the Scottsdale station, he asked, "Won't you drop me and get something to eat at Victor's? To tide you over?"

"No," she replied, as if her answer had been waiting for this question since they left the motel. "You and I have a dinner date. We dressed for it, we're ready to go on with it as soon as the marshal finishes his business with you. I'm going in with you simply to remind him tacitly of these items. Maybe next time he'll be more considerate."

She didn't intend to change her mind, therefore he didn't argue with her. Instead he helped her from the car and down the steps into the station. The two deputies in the anteroom did not conceal their wonder over Ellen's entrance. Hugh stopped before the nearest man and said, "Marshal Hackaberry called," as if he had never before entered the place.

"He's waiting for you." The man was eying Ellen, but not offensively, rather with a cool curiosity. "You can wait here, miss."

"Thank you very much," she said. She walked with Hugh only as far as a corner chair. "I hope it won't take long." She smiled, as if they both knew the call was trivial. The play-acting carried him to the marshal's door without tremor.

Hackaberry wasn't alone. Ringle's chair was pulled close to the desk and he was prodding with a heavy forefinger the contents of a report. Venner wasn't present; it was too much to be hoped that this respite would continue.

When Hugh entered, the two men were immediately silent. They glanced down the room at him, not speaking; Ringle with a ponderous satisfaction, Hackaberry rather as if he'd never seen Hugh before. Hugh waited just inside the door, unsure, unable to understand the changed attitude of the marshal. They could not have found anything damaging in the medical kit or on his car tools. There was nothing to find.

The marshal pushed back his chair. "Did you drive out here this evening?"

"Why, yes." He didn't comprehend.

"Will you show us where you left your car?" The marshal strode down to Hugh, nodded at him to follow. Ringle ambled in the rear.

Hugh said, bewildered, "It's outside, right in front of the Town Hall." He didn't glance toward Ellen as he accompanied the men through the outer office, out the door and up the steps to where the car was parked. One of the deputies, the one who had been in charge of Mr. Crumb, joined Ringle as he passed. For one awful moment Hugh wondered if something had happened to Iris' father, if somehow his car could be involved. But this was impossible. The car had not been left by the motel long enough last night or today to be borrowed and returned. It could not have happened at his grandparents' home; if the killer knew that Hugh had moved there, the harassment would also have moved.

He asked, "Do you want the keys?"

He was ignored. Ringle was half stooping, examining the fenders. Marshal Hackaberry was close by his side. The deputy was there to guard Hugh. Not overtly; he stood apart, but when Hugh moved, he too moved. And his thumb absently rubbed over the leather gun case at his hip.

Ringle was surprisingly agile as he suddenly squatted beside the left front fender. His hand disappeared under it and he looked up at the marshal. "Something's there."

Hugh swept forward, his shadow with him. "That's crazy," he said. "There couldn't be."

The marshal had bent down and pushed his own hand under the curve. He stood up again. He said to Ringle, "Let's see it." Then he looked at Hugh and he sighed. He said nothing, turning his back to watch Ringle. The heavy man was on his knees, his hands working to free something affixed beneath the fender.

Hugh watched, hypnotized, unable to believe. When had this frame been stealthily fitted to him? Last night at Ellen's? The night before? Or as early as Sunday night; while he slept, did the murderer prearrange proof of guilt, to be divulged at the right moment?

Ringle puffed to his feet. What he held was wrapped in a grease-stained piece of flannel, one that might have been discarded at any garage. It was wound with copper wire and heavy black masking tape. The ends dangled unevenly. Ringle loosed the wire and unwound the tape without destroying the pattern made by the cloth. He shook out the contents on his open palm. It was a small, common wrench, indistinguishable from any other of its size and years of use.

Hugh became aware that all three men were studying his face. He said, and he knew he sounded hysterical, "It isn't mine. Someone's trying to frame me. I never saw it before. You know it isn't mine. You took my tools to the lab."

Hackaberry broke through. "We'll go back inside."

Ellen would know from his face as they passed. She would get to Skye in time, before he could be formally arrested, printed, locked up with no hope of proving the truth. He didn't dare look at her lest he start babbling again.

The marshal marched over to his desk. "Sit down," he ordered. They sat as they had on other occasions, Ringle to one side of the desk, Hugh opposite the marshal. The difference was the deputy guarding the door. Ellen wouldn't know, she couldn't hear through that closed door.

Hackaberry bumped down into his chair and picked up his pipe. Ringle carefully deposited the weapon on top of the marshal's papers, as if it were another paperweight. The silence was unendurable, but Hugh kept it during the interminable time it took the marshal to pack his pipe and set it to smoldering. He then said to Hugh, "You're entitled to call your lawyer." There was no more hope, he was to be charged with the murder. "I'll get him if you like."

There was no trickery to the offer, the phone was at the marshal's hand. "Thank you. I would like him here." At least the hysteria was out of his throat, he could speak as factually as the others.

Hackaberry spoke into the mouthpiece. "Get Skye Houston for me."

Would Skye be at home yet? Or was he at the airport meeting Meg? Or with some other clients at dinner? He must be found in time to prevent this arrest.

Hackaberry said, "You deny knowledge of this?"

"You know it isn't mine." Hugh tried to make the words reasonable. "You went all over my car the other night."

"Not under it," Ringle stated.

Hugh continued, separating his thoughts with care, "If it had been mine, if I had used it to murder, you can't believe I'd have kept it in such a precarious hiding place. I'd have had plenty of time and opportunity to get rid of it."

"I don't know about that." Ringle's absent smile held all the knowledge and vagaries of uncounted criminals met in years of service. "Might have been you'd be afraid somebody'd see you throwing it away. Might have worried you that somebody would stumble across it, somebody always does, and it would be traced back to you. Might be you'd figure it was safer to hide it until we let you go home, where you'd know how to get rid of it so it would never turn up."

Hugh said, "You can't trace it to me because it isn't mine."

"We won't find your fingerprints on it." Ringle poked at it with a pencil. "You can tell it's had a good run. But may be we'll find out where it was bought and who bought it."

"I hope so," Hugh declared.

"May be we won't. May be it was bought a long while ago at the five-and-ten or some big hardware store where they won't remember. Could be it was sold in L.A."

It would confirm his guilt to them. It was too much to believe that the murderer had once gone to Los Angeles and bought a simple tool.

The telephone jangled and the marshal grabbed it. "Yeah," he said. "We've got your boy here. The probable murder weapon was hidden under his car." He scowled at the crackling of the earpiece. "That's your opinion. Do you want to get over here before I charge him?" Briefly he listened, then said, "I'll wait just that long." He broke the connection with an angry hand. He said to Hugh, "The lab will find out if this is the weapon. You know that. We'll wait for your lawyer to get here before we continue."

Ringle took out a cigar and lit it. It was a good cigar. He spoke almost affably. "Why don't you make it easy on yourself and tell us what happened?"

Hugh repeated hopelessly, "I've told you and told you. I never saw Iris alive again after I sent her away Friday night. I had nothing to do with the operation or with her death." His words fell into a vacuum of unbelief. And there came to him what should have come before, if he hadn't been disturbed beyond reasonable thought. "Who told you to look under the fender of my car? Did you have another anonymous tip?"

The marshal had the decency to look abashed, but Ringle said, "I don't mind where a tip comes from. As long as it proves out."

Hugh cried to the marshal, "And you don't believe I'm being framed?"

The marshal studied his face, then his eyes went beyond to the door. Skye Houston was entering. He greeted Hugh with a quiet "Hello there" in passing. He stood before Hackaberry, tall, arrogantly disgusted. "Just what is this all about?"

Hackaberry said, "A call came in late this afternoon from a man who identified himself as staying at The Palms. Two nights ago he saw a man—the description fitted Densmore—hiding something under the fender of a white Cadillac with California license plates. This is what we found there." He indicated the wrench.

"Did your informant have a name?"

Hackaberry flushed angrily. "He'd been reading about the murder and worrying about what he'd seen and decided to call us before he left town. No, we didn't get his name. He wouldn't give it. He's a businessman and doesn't want the publicity of being involved in a murder case."

Ringle said without interest, "Venner's looking into it but he won't find out anything. They come and go at the motels. This guy was checking out right then."

Houston was icy. "On this you intend to arrest my client?"

The marshal snapped, "On this and other evidence, I intend to hold him on suspicion of abortion and murder." The scorn on Houston's face made him break out in an appeal to the lawyer, "For God's sake, Skye. With all I have, how long do you expect me to sit on my hands?"

"Until you have one shred of proof."

"Proof? How much proof do I need? He brought the girl here, he admits she came to him to ask—"

Houston interrupted, "You might like to learn the name of the man the girl was involved with."

Ringle's sleepy face quivered to alertness. Hackaberry stared up at the lawyer. He asked finally, "What kind of a gag is this?"

"It's no gag. I can't give you his full name yet but I do have a description and dates of some of his visits to Indio."

"Sit down," Hackaberry ordered.

Skye pulled up a chair, on the far side of the desk.

"Where did you get this dope? How good is it?"

Skye waited, as if considering whether or not he would answer. Eventually he said, "You know I don't have to tell you my source. You could have had these facts before I did if you'd half believed my client's story." With a touch of acid he added, "My information isn't anonymous, it's good. I have a witness."

"Damn you, Skye," Hackaberry began.

"Do you want what I have or don't you?"

Ringle's smoldering anger became a roar. There would no longer be hope of any favor from him, if ever there had been.

The scowling marshal drew paper under his pen. "Shoot."

"His first name is Fred. His surname begins with an O. He lives in Phoenix."

"How many Fred O.'s are there in Phoenix?" the marshal disparaged.

"I haven't checked them out yet. But not too many, I daresay. Not that will fit the other facts. He is young, probably in his twenties. Medium tall."

The description was too vague. The marshal continued making notes but Ringle made no pretense of his loss of interest.

"He wears his hair long, it's bleached blond. When my witness saw him, he was wearing a dark leather jacket and dark trousers."

"And where did this witness see him?"

Skye said with pleasure, "With Bonnie Lee Crumb. When he brought her home after a date."

Ringle was awake again. The marshal put down his pen. "You going to put a name on your witness?"

"Are you going to hold my client on this piece of junk?" Skye's forefinger jeered.

Hugh waited in the awful silence. He could be held; there was more than sufficient circumstantial evidence to hold him on suspicion, the marshal was right when he'd said that. That Houston by legal process might have his client released by morning was of little value. Once Hugh was arrested, once his name became public property, his family was shamed, his medical future without hope.

"You going to give me a name?"

In the silence, Ringle grunted, "Who needs it?" but the two men facing each other didn't hear him. The two were friends. But at this moment there was nothing between them but the contest of their wills shaped by their legal knowledge.

Skye barked a laugh. "All right, I'll give you a name." Hugh felt suddenly weak. It was that close, his being under arrest. Otherwise Skye would never have capitulated. "Lora Mattinor."

"Where does she live?" Ringle was stubbing the name in his book.

"You want me to do all your leg work?" Skye stood up. "Indio, of course. I don't know the address. My client is free to leave, Marshal?"

Hackaberry gave a grudging inclination of his head. "You'll be responsible for his appearance when I want him again?"

As if the suggestion of Hugh's running out was too absurd for comment, Houston gave a short "Yes." He gestured to Hugh. "Let's go, Doctor."

Without a backward glance, Hugh walked out with him. Ellen rose from the chair in the office outside, her eyes deep with anxiety. Hugh had forgotten she was there waiting. Skye put a strong hand under her arm. "It's all right," he assured her. He moved her to the door and up the steps, Hugh behind them.

Night had come down; there was a cold freshness to the white of the stars. Hugh breathed deeply of it.

Skye suggested, "You follow to my house."

Without seeming to move, Ellen was at Hugh's side. "Yes, we'll follow."

Skye waited until they were in Hugh's car, then roared away. His rear lights were pinpoints far up Scottsdale Road when the stop lights held the white car.

Ellen spoke for the first time. "They didn't arrest you." She lit a cigarette and passed it to Hugh.

"It was close. Until Skye came in like the Marines." Why couldn't his appreciation for the rescue be unalloyed? Because Skye had touched Ellen and Ellen had accepted it as if accustomed? Because he wasn't used to dependency on a white man, on a lord of the manor? The light changed, and as he drove on he briefed Ellen factually on what had happened. In silent apology, making Skye the strong man, the hero.

Ellen was excited. "So Meg did find someone who'd talk."

"Evidently. And got the information to Skye in time. Two Marines."

The pinpoints were ahead, cutting a left turn at the sound of Hugh's approach.

Ellen was confident. "They'll have this Fred O. by tomorrow." Her intonation was that it was all over, just this small detail to be attended.

They'd find the man. This he did not doubt. But it was then that Hugh's acute danger would commence. The steps Fred O. had taken might be crude but they had already proved effective in smearing Hugh with guilt. The man had had plenty of time to concoct the story he'd tell; its culmination would be that Hugh was the abortionist and the murderer. He wouldn't have to prove it, only to accuse and let circumstantial evidence convict.

The foolish days when Hugh had thought the finding of Iris' friend would exonerate him seemed as distant as another life. The car was approaching Skye's place, Skye's car had already turned through the gate.

Hugh tried to speak with enthusiasm. "I'm sure they will." Perhaps Ellen accepted it as such. Perhaps not. She wasn't easy to deceive.

✻

Skye waited at the door for them. "Meg's here." That would be the third car parked by the house. "A good thing she had sense enough to phone me when she landed. Without her information I don't know how I could have talked Hack out of it tonight. What about that wrench under the fender?"

"It was put there. Plenty of chances."

They had entered the living room as they spoke. Meg uncurled from a large chair. "I thought you'd never get here," but her voice fell away as their faces revealed they hadn't been idling. Hesitantly she asked, "Is everything all right?"

"Temporarily," Skye said and stopped. By then they all had seen the little girl on the couch.

Meg said, "This is Lora."

The girl bobbed her head. She was looking from Skye to Ellen and Hugh, then toward Meg for direction.

Meg said, "Lora, this is Mr. Skye Houston, the lawyer. Miss Hamilton and Dr. Densmore."

Again the head nodded but didn't understand. She hadn't expected Negroes. She'd doubtless never before been in a living room with them. She was a homely little thing. She didn't look more than ten, but she must be in her early teens, to be a confidante of Iris—Bonnie Lee. Her hair was in a long unfashionable braid down her back; she had a gopher mouth and eyes set too close together.

Houston said, "You didn't tell me you brought her with you!"

Meg said, "It was a surprise. I thought you'd prefer to hear her story first-hand. It's quite interesting."

"Wait till Hack finds out about this!" But some communication passed from Meg to him and he turned to the bewildered child with his most charming smile. "I'm delighted you could come, Lora. What do you say we have something to eat and then you can tell us all about it." He swerved to Ellen and Hugh. "You haven't had dinner!"

"It isn't important," Hugh said.

"Nonsense. Of course it's important. You can't think when your energy's depleted. As a doctor you should be telling me. Go along. We've got a lot of thinking to do tonight." He herded them toward the kitchen. "See what's in the icebox, Ellen. I'll take the orders here."

Ellen opened the icebox as if she were at home. "What kind of sandwich would you like? There's everything."

Hugh said, "I'd like to take you to dinner—" breaking off as Skye joined them.

"Ice cream and chocolate sauce for the girl and a Coke. God. They've had dinner. Meg just wants coffee." Skye wasn't helpless in the kitchen, like some men; like Hugh's own father, for one. He turned the coffee making over to Hugh and set himself to helping Ellen with the sandwiches.

The intuitive knowledge of each other which had been evident in the first meeting of Ellen and Skye seemed heightened as they worked together. It didn't come from the words they spoke, the meaningless light phrases, it simply was there. It set Hugh silent, apart. If they noticed they would believe it was the weight of tonight's near thing. Not the jealousy which he grudgingly admitted. Not the self-pity he was fighting with every atom of his pride. These two could be gay as tropical fish; they weren't truly in this. Whatever happened wouldn't happen to the personal them. And why shouldn't Skye be conscious of Ellen's charm? He wouldn't be a man if he didn't respond. Being married didn't make him a eunuch.

There was no touch of impropriety in his attention. He could admire without touching. He knew Ellen wasn't a slave wench; she was Judge Hamilton's daughter, of impeccable background. There was no sanity in Hugh's jealousy. Ellen wasn't his. He too dared not touch.

He carried the coffee tray to the living room. Lora imperceptibly shrank back into the cushions as he placed it on the coffee table before the couch. He knew he hadn't been explained to her; she was puzzled, unsure of his presence. She could accept him servicing the tray, but not sinking into the cushioned chair after Meg said, "I'll do that," and took the cord to plug in the urn. The little girl was more disoriented when Ellen and Skye returned, when they all ate together.

Meg eased into the story they waited for. "I didn't have any luck today until I met Lora." The girl preened and smoothed the garnet and pink flowers of her skirt. "I'd talked to all the high school crowd at the malt shop but none of them knew anything about Bonnie Lee having a secret boy friend."

"She only told me," Lora boasted.

"I was about to give up—most of the crowd had gone home —when Lora came up and whispered to me that she could tell me about Fred."

"I didn't want them to know about it," Lora explained as she must have over and again to Meg. "I promised Bonnie Lee I'd never tell. And I wouldn't have only—"

"Only she wants to help us catch the man who killed her friend," Meg said for her.

Lora nodded vigorously. "I certainly do. It's simply awful what happened to her. You don't know who'll be next." It might have been her mother speaking. "It might be me!"

"That's why Lora was willing to fly to Phoenix with me. To tell you the story in person, Mr. Houston."

"I'm grateful, Lora." Houston lived up to Meg's shaping of the scene.

"At first my mother wasn't going to let me come," Lora prattled. "She was afraid it might be a ruse to get me killed too. But after Meg called the Judge—"

Meg's eyebrows were expressive. "I remembered Judge Long was from Indio. Fortunately he was at home and we drove down there, Lora and her mother and I. And fortunately he remembered me from when he was working on that extradition case with you, Skye."

"I just had to come," Lora sighed. "I'd never ridden in a plane before."

Hugh remembered from service days, how many of the boys had never been in a plane before the call-up. In the winged century, if they traveled it was as far as their cars would take them, no more. Most had never been on a railroad train. It was as true for the city dwellers as for the country cousins. He understood Skye's amazement, he'd felt the same reaction.

Houston was growing impatient but he covered it with the practiced smile at Lora. "Bonnie Lee actually told you about this man, this Fred?"

"Oh yes. She told me about all her boy friends. She was terribly popular. Probably she was the most popular girl at school."

Bonnie Lee had to have someone she could talk to; girls were like that in their teens. Hugh's sisters were always rhapsodizing to friends over the phone. Lora was the safe confidante because obviously she wasn't one of the popular crowd. And just as obviously she'd never betray the secrets entrusted to her. Bonnie Lee was her ideal; it was in her voice and shining face as she remembered the girl.

"But Fred wasn't in your school?"

"Oh no. He was older." To Lora twenty years would be old. "He was from Phoenix. But he used to come to Indio two or three times a week."

"On business?"

"I don't know." Young people never thought of such matters. To Lora, Fred came to Indio to see Bonnie Lee.

"Where did she first meet him?" Hugh asked.

By now she'd accepted Hugh as part of the room and she answered with recollected excitement. "It was terribly romantic. It was during the Christmas holidays when she was working at the ten-cent store, you know, to make extra money, and this gorgeous blond guy came in to buy some candy and she waited on him. It happened just like that! They took one look at each other and fell madly in love." For the moment she'd forgotten the murder. "He was waiting for her when she finished work." She came back to them. "That's how it started."

A married man, picking up an easy girl. To pass the time. Not thinking then of murder.

"Did she know he was married?"

"Of course not!" Lora was indignant. "She wouldn't go with a married man."

Houston said, "You saw him."

"Yes, I did."

"With Bonnie Lee?"

"Of course."

"Did you meet him?"

"How could I? I'm not allowed to go out on dates. My family's so old-fashioned," she interjected. "Besides, they never went where anyone might see them."

To his motel room? The back of a car?

"It was a secret romance," Lora dreamed.

"Why?" Ellen asked. "Did she tell you why?"

"She didn't want her father to find out she was running around with an older man. Besides, he had been cracking down on her going out school nights and Fred only came over during the week. So she had to tell Mr. Crumb she was baby-sitting, and if she and Fred had been seen around town, her father might have found out she wasn't."

It might have been part of it, Bonnie Lee herself might have believed that the secrecy was her idea. But it wasn't hard to believe that it had been initiated by Fred.

"She lied to her father," Houston stated.

"Yes, but she had to or she couldn't ever have seen Fred."

"How did you get to see him?"

Lora smiled. "I knew she had a date with him that night. It was last February, the night before Washington's Birthday, just before he stopped coming to Indio. There wasn't any school next day so I stayed up reading in my room until I heard them come home. They were laughing it up, not loud enough to wake anybody who wasn't awake, but I heard them. And I looked out my window, I live just across the street, and there he was." She sighed. "Just like she'd described him. Tall, pretty tall, and blond hair with a ducktail, and the leather jacket—"

"You'd recognize him if you saw him again?" Houston put in abruptly.

Lora's mouth drooped. "Well, I didn't see his face, only his back. On the porch." It wasn't good enough. She knew she'd disappointed them. Hopefully she offered, "I'd know him from the back. There's a street lamp at the corner. I had a real good look at him."

Houston helped her regain status. She might be all they'd have to link the unknown man to Bonnie Lee. "You're sure his name is Fred?"

"Oh yes. Bonnie Lee wrote his initials all over her schoolbooks. F.O. Sometimes O.F. Of, you know, in case anyone got nosey."

"But she never mentioned his last name?"

"No, never. But it starts with an O for sure. She was always swooning Fred O, Fred, O Fred, O Fred! She never said the last name though."

And was this too something the man had thought up?

Lora was wound up now, pouring it out, not knowing how much of Bonnie Lee she gave away. A wild girl, the envy of the other girls at high school, the wisecracks of the dirty boys. A girl of whom Lora's parents disapproved yet pitied, remembering a half-neglected child keeping her father's house when she wasn't more than eight years, when the mother left them. A girl who got away with murder—wrong word—when her father was downtown working the night shift at the railroad. A girl who could lie her way out of anything.

"She must have been caught out sometimes," Houston said.

"She was. She was always in trouble at home and at school. But she didn't care as long as it worked out first the way she wanted it."

Lora was right on that. Bonnie Lee, who called herself Iris romantically, wasn't a psychopathic liar; she lied for convenience. After she'd attained what she wanted, she didn't care that the lies were discovered. It wasn't her fault she was what she was; she'd never had a chance to grow up straight. Maybe she would have been a wild kid, anyway. But maybe she wouldn't have been if a mother had been there to help her through adolescence. Men didn't have the gift of mothering. Her father must have tried but he wouldn't know how, and there'd be the job to hold, and all the problems of the household that ordinarily could be shared with a wife. If there'd been someone at home to give the child love and guidance and security. As Hugh's mother gave his sisters. If there'd been someone to talk to other than this unformed worshipping neighborhood child, someone to tell Bonnie Lee that there was a right and a wrong. Someone to say, "Wait" and "Be careful" and "Darling, don't go away yet. Be a little girl just a while longer." Someone to care what happened to her.

Hugh broke through his thoughts. "Did Fred bring her home in a car?"

Lora stopped talking and thought about it. "I don't think so. I didn't see any car. Of course they might have parked it down at the corner but I didn't hear any car. The first thing I heard was them laughing." She explained, "They didn't have to have a car. We don't live far from town. Indio isn't big like Phoenix."

Fred O. didn't have a car; he went over there with someone else, someone else who'd know about his trips.

Now Houston was asking, "Did Bonnie Lee tell you she was planning a trip to Phoenix?"

Lora confessed reluctantly, "No. But we hadn't had a chance to talk lately. She'd been running around with Inky Miller and that crowd." Her nose expressed her distaste. "Inky says she wanted him to drive her to Phoenix to visit her aunt."

The boy with the jalopy. And the aunt wasn't a lie of the moment, she'd been planned.

Lora recalled with pride, "She wouldn't have told me that. I knew she didn't know anyone in Phoenix. Except Fred." Her voice became small, childlike. "Do you think it was Fred murdered her?" She didn't want it to be true. She didn't want her first touch with real romance to be spoiled.

"We think so," Houston said gravely. "We don't know, but we think so."

Her eyes darted to Hugh. Houston caught the implication. He asked, "Have you ever seen Dr. Densmore before tonight?"

"Oh no!" She was outraged at the question. "I never have."

Houston nodded acceptance, then smiled. "I don't think we should keep Lora up any longer, Meg. She's staying at your house?"

Meg nodded.

"I'm sure it's been a long day for her. You'll bring her by the office tomorrow?"

He'd get a signed statement before he turned her loose.

"I'd planned it," Meg said.

He turned the big smile again on Lora. "Maybe we could have lunch together?"

"I don't have to go back to school tomorrow?"

"I don't think we could get you there in time."

The little girl grinned. "That's too bad, isn't it?"

Meg spoke good nights, Lora nodded. Skye went out with them to their car.

Ellen said, "If only she'd met him just once. Face to face."

"If only she knew his full name," Hugh echoed Houston's remark. "But there can't be many Fred O.'s who went to Indio two or three times a week, spent the night, and returned to Phoenix next day." And he thought aloud, "He might not be in the Phoenix directory. Most truckers don't live in the city. If he's a trucker."

"A bus driver," Ellen offered.

"Or a railroad man." Iris would have enjoyed that, the joke on her father. It had to be someone who didn't have a car in Indio. Or whose car or small truck would give away his identity.

Houston returned. "We'll start eliminating the Fred O.'s in the morning. The police may be doing it tonight. But we might get there first. We know more. Someone who had an Indio run at Christmas but no longer has it. She wouldn't have had to come to Phoenix if he was still available in Indio."

Hugh said, "It might be he just stopped seeing her."

"Not in Indio. Too small a town. She'd have found him there if he was still around."

"He could have told her to meet him in Phoenix."

"Not a chance. He wouldn't have had her come here to learn he was married. Too chancey. He wouldn't have wanted her on his hands here." He figured it as he spoke. "She knew where to find him. Not his home, he'd never let her know that."

Ellen said, "The bus station." She repeated it. "A bus driver. She asked to be let off at the bus station."

For a moment there was silence as they looked at each other, hoping. "It could be," Houston said slowly. "It seems too easy but it would fit with his Indio schedule." He took a deep breath. "Sometimes things do fall in line after you get a break."

"Lora is a break?" Hugh asked. She seemed a tenuous one.

"She certainly is. After I get her signed statement in the morning, I don't care how much the police question her." He was thinking of the trial, of his witness, the brilliant defense, the victory of good over evil. He wasn't afraid of the outcome. There might be minor setbacks but the triumph was already in his hand. Academically he might be aware that this triumph would be dust and ashes to Hugh. But he wasn't able to understand that public proclamation of Hugh's innocence would not be able to take away the stain of guilt. "You'll have a drink before you go?" He didn't wait for the answer but began pouring. After handing out the glasses, he sat down beside Ellen. "It's shaping nicely. I didn't expect things to move so fast. Once Fred O. is brought in—"

Hugh could no longer remain silent. "That's when it begins. When Fred O. talks."

Ellen denied him fiercely. "No, Hugh. The marshal won't believe his lies."

"Why not? It's all so logical. He brings her to my doorstep. I say I turned her away and never saw her again. He'll say he left her there and never saw her again. Who is speaking the truth?"

Houston frowned. "There'll be evidence—"

"The evidence is against me. A witness? Not to murder."

"There'll be evidence in his car, or the car he drove that night."

There was a possibility that the scientists by some infinitesimal grain of matter could prove Fred guilty of murder. "But not of abortion," Hugh said. "He will accuse me of the abortion. That will be his revenge because we led the police to him." He said distinctly, "That's all the police are waiting for. Someone to confirm their suspicion."

Skye attempted to speak with the assurance he had earlier but it was a failure. "Let's not borrow trouble. By the time Fred O. gets through lying to the police about everything else, they're not going to be so ready to accept his lies about you as you seem to think. If you didn't abort that girl—"

And still it was the if, even now Skye could have that doubt.

"—no one's going to prove you did."

But who was going to prove he didn't? From a cell he couldn't prove it.

"There's one thing you should know." Houston no longer attempted to hide his troubled frown. "That kid said it at the door. Around school they're saying that Bonnie Lee went to Phoenix with a Negro."

Behind a set face, Hugh's reaction was held.

"She asked me if you were the one."

His voice sounded strange. "What did you answer?"

"The truth. What else could I?" Houston tossed down the rest of his drink. "If only you could remember the license number of that jalopy. I could get those little bastards to tell the truth about your meeting with Bonnie Lee."

"What good would it do?" Hugh asked wearily. "It wouldn't prove I'm not the abortionist."

Not Inky or Guppy or Lora or the ones she spent the night with in Blythe could prove that.

Hugh and Ellen drove away in silence, over the winding deserted roads that led to town. The moon was high and white; each fence post, each clump of cactus was as distinctly outlined as by the sun. The mountains were moon-gray against the deep night sky. A dog barked from a distant house, the only reminder that they were not on another planet.

Hugh said, "Tomorrow I will be arrested."

"This is morbid," she began conversationally, but he cut her off.

"As soon as they talk to Fred O. Skye expects it. He knows he can't prevent it any longer. He's planning my defense."

"He has to plan. What's a lawyer for if he doesn't? Isn't the best offense a strong defense?"

"He'll prove me innocent. When Skye gets through with Fred O., no jury will believe a word he says. But before that the headlines will scream: Dr. Densmore Accused of Abortion. That's what will be remembered, not that I was proved innocent. That's what will stick, my name and that vicious word." He tried to keep the bile from his tongue. "It's all over once I'm arrested. No one wants a doctor with a dubious reputation."

"Why don't you really wallow, Hugh?" she asked quietly. "Make that headline: Negro Doctor Accused." There was anger in her now. "Skye is just as aware as you are of what an accusation can do to your professional life. That's why he's using his prestige, even going outside channels into his personal relationship with the marshal and the police chief and the press to keep you from being officially charged—"

"The press?"

"You don't believe they haven't been around because they don't know about you," she scorned. "They agreed to keep your name out of it because of the circumstances. But they don't like it. If both the marshal and Skye weren't exerting pressure—"

"I'm sorry. I didn't know." And Hugh wondered how often Ellen and Skye had been together, at lunch, cocktails, a swim, for her to know so much more than he did of what was going on. It was none of his business what she did with her spare time. He mocked himself, "No one ever tells me anything."

"You're in good hands, Hugh," she said firmly. "Skye can't make miracles but he can conjure wonders."

They had reached the motel but neither made a move to get out of the car.

She continued, gently now, "If it should happen, don't worry about your family. They'll hear the whole story from me before they can get a garbled account."

"From you and from Edward."

"Dr. Edward knows?"

He had spoken without thinking. "Yes. I've talked to him. I had to."

She didn't seem to wonder why. She only murmured, "Good," as if it were a relief to her that someone in the family shared the knowledge of events. In the interval of silence, each with his own thoughts, the insistence of sound was audible. She said, "I believe that's my phone."

He too had recognized the faint bell. "Answer it!" He was out of the car as he spoke and running lightly from the drive onto the sidewalk and toward Van Buren. When he reached the corner he could see without pausing that in the dispensary across the street there was no one but the clerk, seated behind the counter, a magazine in hand. He chose to turn right toward the service station with the convenient telephone kiosk. But he was halted as a car turned into the main driveway leading to the motel office. For that moment his view ahead was blocked. When the car had passed, he remained rooted where he was. The police prowl car had materialized in that interval. It was stopped near a car at the station curb, a dark unrecognizable sedan. One of the officers was bending to the driver's window, another stood on the corner, not far from the phone booth, talking to two youths. Hugh was too far from the corner to distinguish faces or the make of the car.

He turned and retreated into the motel drive, taking the nearest crosswalk through the green to Ellen's room.

She responded to his knock. "There was no one on the line."

"No." He couldn't contain his disappointment. "The prowl car was there first."

"You think it was Fred O.?"

"Who else?"

"You don't need to go looking for him any longer," she said. "You don't have to take that chance. The police will have him by tomorrow."

She was right. But he had an uncontrollable urge to confront the man in the act of telephoning. With all his theorizing about non-violence, what he wanted was to smash Fred O.'s dirty words down his dirty throat. He said wryly, "The Lord helps those who help themselves."

She countered, "They also serve who only stand and wait." She stepped back from the doorway. "Come in for a cigarette. Until you cool off."

"Not tonight." He made the refusal less blunt. "I'll be underfoot as usual tomorrow. Until our friends arrive—"

What had been banter, by some transubstantiation suddenly was not. If either had spoken in that moment, if either had moved so much as a finger . . . He remembered her laughter, counterpart to Skye Houston's. He kept his hands rigid against his thighs. He managed to make the good-bye casual. "I'll see you in the morning," and she echoed, "Good night."

The palms of his hands were wet. When he was in the car, he rubbed them dry on his coat sleeves, and he was all right again. It was too late to try to find Jopher's home tonight. Particularly with the prowl car active.

✳

He couldn't sleep in the morning. By seven he was dressed, by seven-thirty he heard his grandmother rackety in the kitchen below. He went downstairs. His grandfather was bringing in the newspaper from the front porch.

"You're up bright and early." He smiled. "Would you like to see the paper?"

Hugh's fingers itched but he said, "Thanks, I'll read it later." He might betray his uncommon interest. "Any particular news?" he asked as the old man unfolded it.

His grandfather sat down in the easy chair and looked over the headlines. "Nothing startling. They haven't found that girl's killer yet." No suspicion. Merely the comment of any other man or woman in Phoenix. "Terrible thing that."

"Yes," Hugh agreed. Fred O. hadn't been identified by the prowl officers. You couldn't arrest a man for making a phone call late at night. Hugh went on to the kitchen and visited with his grandmother.

"You going to bring your girl to dinner tonight?" she queried.

"She can't make it tonight." He dared not until he found out what was going to happen to him.

She fussed a bit because she liked to sputter but she didn't insist. It was only out of her hospitality that she was urging the invitation, she was too old to enjoy cooking all day in this heat.

After breakfast it was still too early to go to Ellen's. His mother would be up, she'd be turning to worry if she didn't see more of him. He excused himself. "If Ellen calls, tell her I'm on my way over, will you? I'm going to Stacy's first." That should take care of any calls today.

He found his mother lingering with Stacy and Edward over breakfast. There was no possible way for either the doctor or himself to create a moment alone. Edward left on his calls with the unanswered questions in his eyes.

By ten, Hugh could no longer endure the strain of leisurely conversation and he left for Ellen's. On the way, he decided to stop at the corner station for gas; he was running low. There were two attendants; neither had any special knowledge of him. They were casually efficient.

He went on to the motel, parked outside Ellen's door, but he didn't knock there. Instead he went around to the lanai entrance. If the curtains were opened, he'd know she was up. They were wide, the sliding doors as well. He called from outside the screen, "Anybody home?"

Her voice came from the dressing room. "Come in. It isn't locked."

She reached the living room as he entered. She was buttoning a beach coat over her swim suit. As always she gave him the quick searching glance, to read in his face if things were good or ill. Reassured, she said, "Skye called. He wants you to come down to his office."

"When?"

"As soon as you can. I'm not invited."

"You don't know what he wants?"

"He didn't say." She made it clear. "He deliberately didn't say, so I didn't ask. Come back afterwards?"

"If there is an afterwards."

"Oh, Hugh, don't be silly," she said. Her spirits were high today. Did a morning talk with Houston so elate her? "If this were serious, don't you think he'd have warned me?"

He couldn't deny that. He smiled. "Very well. I'll be back."

The morning's cool was burning away with the mounting sun. The downtown streets were always more intense than where there was grass and sprinkling water. The First Avenue parking lot was full but he eventually found one on First Street. By the time he'd walked from there to the old bank building, his optimism had been depleted by the temperature. He took the narrow stairs slowly; their darkness was relief from the outdoor glare.

Meg was at her desk in the outer office. She said, "It'll be a few minutes. A client just came in."

He should have telephoned before coming. "Where's Lora?" he asked.

"My mother's taken her shopping. I'm meeting them for lunch. Mr. Houston can't make it. Then she'll fly home."

"The police must be wondering where she is."

"They can wait," she said cheerfully, returning to her work.

The morning paper was strewn on the oak bench. Hugh gathered it together. The canal murder was retold to make it seem new. The marshal had given an interview about the search in Indio for clues to the murderer. The autopsy results were repeated in detail. There was no mention of Lora or a man named Fred or of a Negro doctor.

The brown-haired secretary came from the private office with her stenographic notebook. She greeted Hugh, "All clear." Meg spoke through the door to Houston and held it for Hugh to enter.

Skye was involved with papers at his desk. He said, "Find a chair, Hugh. I'll be with you in just a minute," and returned to his work. The owl horn-rims were on his nose; he was as impeccably dressed in a tailored suit as if he practiced in a temperate clime. He looked as if nothing important was on his mind. He completed his notes, clipped them together, and set them in a wire basket. "We've located Fred O.," he stated.

Hugh waited, half in excitement, half in dread.

"The O. is for Othy." He drew a paper in front of him and

read from it. "Age twenty-five. Blond, blue-eyed, five ten, weight 164. Drives a 1950 blue Ford sedan." Skye glanced up. "This is from his employment record at the bus company office. He worked for this company from last September until the first of March. He asked then for another run. When he didn't get it, he quit. The manager was pleased rather than otherwise at the solution. Othy was hired as temporary help originally; older men are preferred by the company." Houston set the paper aside. "He is not married."

Hugh pulled up sharply.

"He lives with his mother. She owns a beauty parlor. Out in the 24th Street district."

"No!"

"Her name isn't Mayble. It's Dorcas. That information is from the City Directory."

"Do the police know?"

"We came up with the information about the same time. In reverse order. I did the bus company first. They did municipal records."

Hugh was only half hearing. He was driving into Phoenix, seeing again the excitement mounting in the little girl as she neared the city, neared her meeting with the man she loved, the man she'd come to marry. He could not bear to remember the next night, her despair. He broke in grimly, "He lied to her. To get out of marrying her."

"Yes," Houston said. "He lied to her. He'll lie to us."

"To us?"

"We're going out to talk to him. He works in a garage not far from his mother's shop."

"You want me to go with you?" Now that the moment of facing the man was at hand, he didn't know if he could.

"Definitely. If anyone can start him talking, you can. Because if you're right in thinking he drove the girl to your motel and waited for her, he can't be absolutely sure that you didn't catch a look at him. You know it was impossible. But if he was in sight of your door, he can't know. At least that's how I see it."

Hugh made himself speak calmly. "Have the police talked to him yet?"

"Venner has."

"Venner." His intonation said it all.

"I made the same comment to Hack. Ringle's on the Indio end today. According to Venner's report, Othy never heard of the girl except in the newspaper."

"But his Indio run—"

"There are dozens of men who make that run," Houston said flatly. "It'll take more than that to make him a murderer." He pushed papers into his briefcase and lifted it. "Shall we go?"

Of course Venner would believe Othy. Houston's car was in a private lot nearby, assigned to the building. Its air-conditioned interior made the trip northward a brief one. But the density of the heat was deeper when they left the car and crossed to the open shed with its corrugated iron roof. A porcine man was pounding on an old car in its shade. There were other old cars, all dark sedans, standing in haphazard pattern on the surrounding sandy yard.

The man lifted his red face as Houston queried, "Fred Othy?"

"Round back." He wasn't curious, but then the police had been here earlier. He didn't seem to see Hugh.

They skirted the shed to the rear. Here were dismantled cars, engines and chassis and fenders like crazy players arranged for some monstrous game. At the far end of the premises, a man was dumping debris into one of the empty oil drums standing there.

Skye called out, "Mr. Othy?"

He pushed in his load of rags and metal before turning. "Yeah?" he took his time sauntering toward them.

When he saw the face, Hugh's pulses quickened. He knew this was the right man. It wasn't a good face, it was bony, the complexion bad, pasty despite Arizona sun. The mouth was mean with small unclean teeth. Othy was blond, as Bonnie Lee had told Lora; his hair was lank and yellow; it looked dyed, whether or not it was. It could be that his mother touched it up to keep it from turning dark. He wore it too long into his neck and below his temples.

He was young but not boyish, he could never have been

boyish. He wore no shirt, only old, grease-covered khakis. His shoulders were round and freckled but his arms bulged with the muscles of heavy work. He came almost to them, then leaned against an old chassis and lit a cigarette. "What can I do for you?" His feet were long and narrow; he was wearing limp maroon socks and broken brown and white latticed summer oxfords.

"You're Fred Othy?" Skye asked.

"I'm Fred Othy." He paid more attention to the cigarette than to Skye. He might have known Skye Houston by sight. Phoenix hadn't yet grown to the size city where a prominent figure would be lost in the populace. But he was neither suspicious nor frightened at Skye's interest. There was an underlying cocksureness in him; he could afford it, he'd passed the police test this morning.

He was conscious of Hugh's presence and he knew who Hugh was. But after one quick flip of his pale blue eyes to Hugh's color, he ignored him, as if Hugh were chauffeur or handyman to the lawyer.

After his affirmation, both he and Skye waited, testing each other. It was Skye who continued the identification. "I'm Skye Houston."

"Yeah?" Othy's eyes flicked Hugh again but Skye made no introduction. He was so sure of himself, he could ask, "What you want to see me about?"

"You don't know?"

"How'm I supposed to know unless you tell me? I'm no mind reader."

Skye spoke as diffidently as he. "I understand you were a friend of Bonnie Lee Crumb."

Othy was unperturbed. "You're wrong."

"You know who Bonnie Lee Crumb was?"

"Sure. I read the papers. She's the girl got drowned in the canal."

"You didn't know her?"

"I never heard of her until she got drowned." He pitched his cigarette stub at Hugh. It didn't connect.

Skye let his eyes rest on the young man's face for the moment, not too long, just enough for Othy to be forced to wonder what would come next. And it came. "You drove a bus between Phoenix and Indio this past year."

He didn't like the reference but it couldn't shake him; he'd been through this before. "So what. It was a living."

"You didn't meet Bonnie Lee Crumb in Indio?"

"I didn't meet no girls there. I drove the bus over, I drove the bus back. I didn't have no time to screw around with girls."

"You didn't lay over there?"

He was ready to deny it but changed his mind. Instead he shrugged it off. "Once or twice maybe." He was as sure of himself as if he were telling the truth. "I don't remember. You'd have to ask the checker."

Skye paused, then asked, "Why did you quit your job with the bus company, Mr. Othy?"

Maybe Venner hadn't bothered with that. Othy snarled, "I got sick of it. I wouldn't of quit if they'd give me a shorter run but they wouldn't. So I quit."

Without change of expression or inflection, Skye continued, "It wasn't because Bonnie Lee had told you she was pregnant?"

Just briefly, the real Fred Othy was visible, vicious in hatred. Then his face closed as if he'd pulled down a curtain. Although he tried to recover his previous assurance, he achieved no more than an imitation. "What's the matter, don't you believe me? I told you I didn't know no Bonnie Lee." He hoisted himself off the chassis. "Look, if this is all you got to say to me, you might as well cut out. You're wasting my time."

"Suppose I were to tell you I have a witness who saw you in Indio with Bonnie Lee?"

"I'd say she was a liar." He shot back the words but he was shaken.

"She?"

"She or he." He beetled, "Look, what business is this of yours, anyhow? What right you got to be asking me these questions?"

Ignoring the question, Skye indicated Hugh's presence. "Mr. Othy, have you ever seen this man before?"

Fred O. looked long at Hugh. Framing his answer. If there was, initially, contempt, it changed to actual hate. His lip curled. "No, I never."

"You're quite sure of that?"

He gave Hugh a quick, contemptuous stare. "I'm sure."

Skye then addressed Hugh. "Is that the voice you heard on the telephone, Dr. Densmore?"

"Yes, it's the same voice." Of this, Hugh was certain.

Othy took a step toward Skye. "What is this? A frame? I never talked to no spook on the phone."

"And you didn't inform the police by telephone that Bonnie Lee Crumb had come to Phoenix in Dr. Densmore's car?"

Othy shouted, "I don't know what you're talking about."

Evenly, Skye stated, "I wonder if the sergeant who took that call will also be able to identify your voice."

Othy's grease-stained fists balled. "I don't like this. I don't like it at all."

"You'll like it less when the police go over your car and find Bonnie Lee's fingerprints in it," Skye said sharply. "You may think you've got rid of them all but you can't, not the latent ones."

The boy's fury was diminished by the beginning of fear.

"It's only a question of time," Skye continued. "The police have the same leads I have and better ways of obtaining information. They'll catch up with you." He shot the final question, "Why did you kill Bonnie Lee?"

Othy yelled back at him, "I don't have to listen to no more of this crap. I didn't know no kid named Bonnie Lee and anybody says I did is a liar." He swerved away, smashing through the rear entrance to the shed.

"Come on," Skye said quietly to Hugh. "We won't get any more from him now."

They moved on toward the street, Skye nodding to the boss as they passed. The pudgy man was hammering like thunder on an angular part of a truck. He would not have heard anything that was said.

As Skye steered the car away from the curb, Hugh slanted a look toward the shed. Within the shadowy interior, the figure of Fred Othy could be discerned. He was watching the car drive away.

Skye drove west to North Central. "They'll get him. But you

might be a bit careful of dark alleys tonight." He turned south for the downtown district.

Hugh wondered, "Why did you warn him about evidence in his car? He'll get rid of it."

"Oh no, he won't." Skye's lips curved. "He can't. The police took his car this morning for a going-over."

Then Othy had already scrubbed up. His fear was that he'd missed something.

"I told him the truth, there'll be some evidence. He'd better start thinking up a new story."

If only he wouldn't change his story too soon. There must be time to tackle Doc Jopher tonight.

As they neared First Street, Skye said suddenly, "Let's check on what they've found." He parked in his lot and led the way across to the courthouse. Reluctantly, Hugh went along. It could be he was risking his last previous hours of freedom. The wrench was also in the hands of police technicians.

Skye had no hesitancy. He strode hard-heeled to the door of the police chief, entered. The secretary, a handsome, black-haired woman, greeted him by name.

"Is he in?"

"Yes. Just a minute, Mr. Houston." She buzzed the office, spoke into the box. "Skye Houston is here." She disconnected the machine. "You can go in." Her glance went beyond him. Curiosity touched her eyes but not because she wasn't aware of who Hugh was. Rather as if she knew this was it.

Again he followed the lawyer. The chief was a distinguished gray-haired man, tall in a dark summer suit. He didn't look like a career cop.

Skye made an offhand introduction, "My client, Dr. Densmore," and said, "I want to know what the lab got out of Othy's car."

The chief delayed response. He photographed Hugh from crown to toe, he probed Houston's features, he rubbed a thoughtful finger on his cheekbone. Hugh changed his first opinion. The chief might be a political appointee but he came from legal background. He had enough years and experience on Houston to force the younger man to attack.

"For God's sake, Bruce," Houston exploded. "I could get the report from Hack without asking."

"Why don't you?"

"Because I don't want to drive all the way to Scottsdale when my office is across the street from yours. You don't think I want to tamper with it, do you?"

"I don't know what you want with it. I don't even know what gives you the idea you can barge in here and demand access to a police report before it's been released to the public. We can't have our reports—"

Skye broke in, "If I cross my heart and hope to die I'll not reveal the contents until they're splashed all over the front of your newspaper—"

The chief answered with asperity, "I'm no longer connected with the paper, which you damn well know. What's more, you know the family's played ball with you keeping this case under cover—"

"All I want," Skye interrupted patiently, "is to preserve the reputation of an innocent client. If the lab report says what we think it will, he can go back to his hospital and forget this nightmare."

The chief looked over at Hugh, then smiled at Skye. He flicked his intercom. "Where are those lab reports?" He disconnected and said, "The car is clean."

"It can't be!" Skye exploded.

"Absolutely, totally clean."

Without speaking, the secretary brought the requested papers to the chief's desk and quit the room. The chief held them out to Houston.

"I don't believe it!" Skye put on his horn-rims before taking the report.

The chief continued amiably, "There isn't one smidgeon of evidence that the girl was ever in Othy's car."

Then why had Fred O. been disturbed when Skye spoke of latent fingerprints? There had to be proof in the car. And it came to Hugh. Othy hadn't used his car, for some reason or other. He'd borrowed—from his mother! Of course, from his mother. He wouldn't have been so upset if it had been the car of a friend, a car which couldn't be traced right back to him. Hugh wanted to blurt out the idea but it was best for him to be silent in this office.

Skye returned the paper. He swung his glasses for emphasis. "This is the boy's car? He didn't make a trade for a new one this week?"

The chief's manicured thumbnail tapped the report. "It's all here. He's had that piece of junk for three years."

It came to Skye then. "He used another car."

"Or he's as clean as his car," the chief said. "And you've got the wrong man. If there is a man."

"My witness—"

"We're looking for your witness. Have you returned her to Indio yet?"

"She's on her way home now," Skye snapped the half-truth. "For the record I didn't know she was in Phoenix when I talked to Hack last night. Yes, I know she came over in my plane with my secretary, but I didn't know it then. Also for the record, we've got the right man. I know when I'm being lied to and Othy just lied in his teeth to me." His voice was flint. "What we haven't got is the right car." He turned on his heel with a short "Thanks," and nodded Hugh toward the door.

The chief's calm voice followed them. "Wouldn't you like the report on your client's fender wrench?"

Hugh froze. Skye half turned. "Yes, I would."

"It was clean too. Or at least, it was rubbed down so thoroughly that not a print can be lifted." He smiled professionally, "Nice seeing you, Houston."

"The same."

Hugh waited until they were outside the building before saying, "It was his mother's car."

"How do you know?" Houston's temper was short.

"I don't know. But if his is ruled out, he must have borrowed a car. There's no other safe way he could take her to an abortionist."

"Why the hell would he borrow a car when he has one?"

"Maybe he was out of gas." Hugh's own temper was raveling. "Maybe he didn't want to waste his gas driving her around town. All I say is that it's logical he'd borrow from his mother. Kids do. Everybody does. Whose car do you think I'm driving here?"

"All right, all right." Houston ended the discussion at the corner. "I'll see if the police are on that angle." His eyes were as distant as if he'd lost the case. And then he saw Hugh and frowned. "Keep yourself scarce today. If there's more news, I'll call you."

Hugh said mechanically, "At Ellen's." He could call in to Ellen. He wouldn't go there; he wouldn't go home. But where to spend the rest of the day? Not driving the white car; it would be a lodestone for the police. He left the lawyer and moved in the direction of the shopping streets of the town. He sauntered with the pavement crowds, feigning interest in display windows. It didn't seem that he had been followed from the chief's office, but because he had no experience in such things, he couldn't be sure. He'd just have to hope he was right. He couldn't spend the entire afternoon walking the hot streets. He crossed and headed in the opposite direction to the nearest motion picture theatre. He was alone, as visible as a rocket, as he approached the cashier's window and bought a ticket.

He didn't know what the current rules were for seating but, remembering childhood, he took a seat in the balcony. There were only three other customers up there, refugees from the truant officer. He hadn't noticed what the picture was before entering; it turned out not too bad the first time around. And the air was cool. The second time was a screaming bore and his summer jacket too light for the continued chill. But he remained in his seat into the third showing, until it would be dark outside.

Emerging at seven-thirty, the warmth of the day past was pleasant on his face. He was inordinately hungry. He'd had no lunch and had been afraid to leave his safety of the balcony for the lighted refreshment counter. If he weren't too late, Ellen might meet him somewhere private for dinner. He passed a news vendor, swung back to buy the evening paper. There was no scare headline, no news of an arrest in the canal murder. They were still seeking clues in Indio.

He began walking toward the parking lot where he'd left his

car but he didn't go all the way. Before he returned, before he quit the comparative safety of being just another man on a city street, he had better find out if there were new developments. There were phone booths in the big garish drugstore he'd passed. He returned to it and drank a milk shake while waiting for an empty booth.

In due time, the young girl with dirty blond hair arranged in a grotesque haystack left the booth. She and her duplicate girl friend continued to block the entrance with a detailed retake of her call. He waited in outward patience until they flopped away. He rang the motel and Ellen answered at the first ring from the switchboard.

"Where have you been?" she protested.

"Round and about. Any calls for me?"

His unworried response allayed her anxiety. "Yes, Skye called hours ago, before dinner. He wanted you to get in touch as soon as possible."

"Have you had dinner?"

"I'm just finishing it."

"I'll be out as soon as I get a bite. If I may."

"Don't stop to eat. You can order something here."

He agreed. "I'll be there as soon as I can."

She asked in alarm, "You're not at the police station?"

"No." He could laugh. "I'm downtown. I'll be there soon." He rang off and called Skye's home. There was no answer. Although certain it was futile, he tried the office. No response. He vacated the booth, meeting the glare of the frizz-headed fat woman waiting.

He wove through the crowded store without hindrance and again started to the parking lot. Once out of the main district, the streets were empty and poorly lit. He walked rapidly, close to the buildings. All, with the exception of a small café, were closed. The courthouse loomed across the street, a darkened mass decorated with a few golden globules of light. No longer were old men seated on the benches under the shady trees. After passing the building he cut over to the parking lot. It too was closed and dark, his car was one of few remaining. But it was a park-and-lock, the keys were in his pocket. No one deterred him from driving away. He went out Jefferson, passing the family home, its lighted windows gentle in the night. He'd call the family from Ellen's, let them know he was all right. His absence since early morning might worry them.

At 24th, he went across to Van Buren and drove on to the hotel. But he passed Ellen's unit; he wouldn't leave the car there tonight as identification of his presence. He followed the outside drive and pulled into the circular parking area which serviced the cocktail lounge and restaurant. It was always crowded, his car would be just another one here.

He walked through the grounds to Ellen's. The draperies were luminous across the picture window. A knock at the lanai might alarm her. He went on to the rear door and rapped.

It was opened only a few inches. Then seeing him, Ellen pulled the door wide, locked it after he entered. She looked at him and said, "You're all right."

"I told you I was."

The television set was on in the living room; she turned down the volume, saying, "I couldn't help being worried. Not hearing all day. And Skye sounded disturbed—he wouldn't tell me anything."

"I tried to reach him."

"He's gone out to dinner. He'll call back." She was still examining his face, as if he wore a mask to deceive her.

He said, "I've been to the movies."

"You've what?"

"It was the safest place I could think of. The cliché." He sat on the arm of the chair. "Skye told me I should be scarce today. After we saw Othy this morning."

Her alarm heightened but she controlled it. "You haven't eaten all day?" Her dinner dishes were on the table. She unearthed the menu card from beneath the coffee pot. "Order something now, you can tell me about it while we're waiting for service."

"Skye didn't tell you about that?"

"No," she said. "Nothing."

He called in a steak order. He had just returned to the chair when the phone rang. "Skye." He started up but she was on her feet.

"Wait!"

From her face, he knew. "He's been calling."

"I don't know. I answer but no one speaks."

He was at the phone before she finished, shouting, "Hello."

But it was Skye. He said, "You were right, it was the mother's car."

He couldn't help the lift of excitement.

"It was in the shop. For new seat covers. A present from her son."

"Oh no."

"A good try but not good enough. They found pieces of the old covers. Bloodstains."

"Has he been arrested?" It could be he wouldn't involve Hugh. It could be he'd be too frightened to tell anything but the truth.

"He's skipped."

Hugh couldn't believe the words.

"They let him get away." Skye was angry. "He could be in Mexico by now."

"He isn't," Hugh told him. "He's been calling the motel." He was thankful he'd had sense enough to keep the car away from Ellen's door. He could reconstruct what was going on, alternate telephone calls and driving by the unit, waiting for Hugh to appear.

"You will be careful."

"I will. But I don't think there's anything to worry about. The marshal put a prowl car in the neighborhood."

"If he's picked up, I'll ring you again. Don't stay out late. I'll feel safer when you're home in bed."

If Skye knew his plans, he would worry. Actually Hugh didn't expect trouble from Fred O. tonight. If the boy were running from the police, he wouldn't want to chance falling into their hands by tackling Hugh. He'd carry on with the harassment, the dirty words, but nothing that he couldn't accomplish from under cover. For the first time since Saturday night, Hugh felt free to come and go without danger. The police wouldn't be looking for him, Othy had practically declared his guilt by skipping. This was the night to visit Doc Jopher.

Yet Hugh rang off quickly as a knock sounded at the outer door. He moved in front of Ellen. "I'll get it." It would be his dinner but he wouldn't let her take any chances. Despite his reasoning, Fred O. could be lurking.

It was the dinner, the same boy who'd served them before. He took away Ellen's dishes. Hugh said to her, "I must call home before I start eating." Fortunately it was his grandfather who answered. He could be brief and unconcerned with Gramps.

While he ate, he related the day's developments. "Why don't you let me take you to Stacy and Edward's for the night?"

"And tell them there's a killer after you?"

There couldn't be a good-enough excuse, she was right. The same was true for taking her to the grandparents'.

She said, "I'll take the same precautions as before."

"But you opened the door tonight."

"I knew you were on your way."

"It didn't have to be me."

"I won't open it again. And I'll tell the desk not to put through any more calls after you leave."

He had to be satisfied with it that way. He finished his dinner. The late movie had come on TV. It was vintage cops and robbers; the girls wore knife-blade marcels and the men lip rouge. He was too restless to watch it.

Ellen said, "Why don't you go home?"

"I'll go after he phones."

"He may not again."

If the prowl car had spotted him, he wouldn't. There was no actual reason why Hugh shouldn't start on his private mission. But he waited. At the next commercial, he got to his feet. "I think I'll go over to the dispensary and get a bottle. We could have a drink."

"There's plenty on the shelf."

He paced, stopped by her chair. "Would you trust me out of your sight long enough for me to go to the office for the L.A. papers?"

Her eyes probed. "Just there?"

"My word I won't leave the motel grounds."

She was reluctant but she said, "Very well." She opened the lanai door. "Go this way. It's safer from outsiders. I'll latch the screen after you."

Outside he took a deep breath of the cooling air. He couldn't have endured the confinement much longer. He had to have a look around. If Fred O. was in the vicinity of the motel, he had to know it. Before he set out for Doc Jopher's. If Fred should sense that Hugh was heading for Jopher's, he'd stop it, whatever he had to do. He couldn't allow Hugh to talk to Jopher. Because it had to be Jopher, there was no one else.

He followed the white walk bisecting the green lawn. At regular intervals there were low-standing amber lamps, like jungle flowers growing along the path. They gave little-enough light, yet if Fred were nearabout, he could recognize Hugh. A middle-aged couple was ahead of him; they turned off at a cross angle. Two high-flying Texas types came out of the cocktail lounge with two nasal, talkative middle-young women. Hugh let them get a good start toward their quarters before he continued on his way. He didn't want to run into minor trouble.

The lobby was enclosed by glass and chrome on three sides. Within it, he would be spotlighted. He entered. Two elderly men were on a couch, boring each other with reminiscences. They gave the inevitable flicker at Hugh and put their heads closer together. One clerk, a woman, was at the desk. The newsstand counters were covered for the night but the dailies were stacked outside, by the magazine and pocketbook racks. He hadn't seen an L.A. paper for some days, he took one of each lying there, the *Times* and the *Herald.* He paid at the desk and went out again.

He walked along the boundary fronting on Van Buren. He didn't step off the grounds. He didn't have to for a look into the dispensary. The lonely clerk was as usual alone and there were no cars parked at the curb. From here he could see only a part of the service station lot. It was peaceful.

When he started back to Ellen's rooms, no other guests were in sight. It would have been a good time for Othy to face him. But there was no incident. Hugh tapped on the frame of the screen and immediately Ellen pulled aside the draperies. She must have been standing there. She said, "You were gone so long."

"I walked a bit. Fresh air. But not off the premises." He asked, "Any calls?"

"No calls. There aren't going to be, Hugh. If there were, it would have been before now. There were three in the hour before you came."

He agreed but not aloud. He'd wait until midnight. In Los Angeles, the case of the girl in the canal had been relegated to unimportant inner pages of the papers. There were fresher murders to report. At midnight the picture ended and he turned off the set. Neither of them had watched much of it. Ellen read a book—it was *Sartoris*—while he dallied with the papers.

She raised her eyes. "Do you give up?"

"I'm afraid I'll have to. Although I don't like to leave you alone." He'd said it so often.

"I don't like to have you go out there."

"I always check a bit before I head for Jefferson." He outlined his circuitous movements of the preceding nights. He walked to the front doors. "I'll go this way. I didn't park outside tonight."

For a moment they stood there looking at each other, then as if she sensed he held private plans, she lifted herself taller and touched his cheek with her lips. "Don't be brave," she said. "You're in enough trouble."

She waited in the lighted doorway until he lifted his hand and moved away. He heard the door close but the light still swathed his path and he knew she was watching. He didn't look back.

7

THE AREA where he'd parked wasn't crowded now, only the cars of late celebrators remained. A young couple backed their convertible out as he approached. The man wasn't Othy.

Hugh got in his car, waited until they'd gone before turning on the engine. Instead of circling out onto Van Buren, he took a side exit. For safety he would have a better look around the neighborhood before traveling to Scottsdale. The prowl car could only be on one street at a time.

The cross street he had inadvertently chosen wasn't a good one. It was too dark, too narrow, too lonely. A small frame house stood on the northwest corner. It was either vacant or everyone in it was long asleep. On the west, for the length of the block, there were only vacant lots. On the northeast corner was a machine shop of some sort, long since shuttered for the night, its back lot littered with rusty shadows. The only indication of life was at the far end of the block where there was a night club of sorts with a painted sign on its roof, lettered black on red: THE CAN-CAN. The building was an ugly frame shack of a depressing dark red color. The windows were painted black. Here and again on them were vivid scratches, as if the inmates had, in a sudden attack of claustrophobia, clawed a glimpse of a cleaner world outside. In driving to and from The Palms, Hugh had noticed the shack, with an idle wonder at the kind of need for companionship, or hope for pleasure, which would lure a person to it. The dim light over the door, the reflector for the roof sign were the only illumination on this entire block. The street lights from Van Buren on the north and Washington on the south did not carry to the long stretch of the midblock.

He did not know where the car came from. At one moment, he was solitary, driving toward Washington; within a breath, a car without lights darted like a snake into his rear-view mirror. In another breath, he was forced to swerve to a sudden stop, half on the dirt sidewalk; there was no curb. It had happened so rapidly, Hugh was yet without comprehension of its meaning when he pushed open his door and started to get out, demanding, "What the—"

Not until that instant did he understand. Fred O. was getting out of the other car. An ugly smirk was on his face, his muscles and fists were tensing. At the wheel of the marauder car was some friend, hidden by the night, no more than a silhouette with a high-pitched jeering laugh.

In the split second of comprehension, Hugh had the choice of getting back into his car or of continuing his outward movement. He couldn't drive away; he was penned. He got out. It wouldn't be a fair fight but he too was ready. He had inches on Fred, that alone could help him. He did not have the experience or the cruelty. Nor did he have reserves in his car.

Fred waited for him to push shut the door of the Cadillac. The youth's eyes in the night light were hot with satisfaction. Hugh backed away a few steps, hoping to reach open space before he was attacked. If he was maneuvered into the narrow end of the funnel created by the cars, he would be at Fred's mercy. It could be a common strategy of young hoodlum gangs.

He spoke as he inched backwards. "What's the idea? You might have wrecked both cars."

In response, Fred spit directly at the Cadillac. From within the other car, the titter sounded again.

Hugh continued his cautious backing but he didn't make it to clearance. Fred moved up with cold menace. Hugh would not turn and run; he wouldn't have that humiliation forced on him by this scum.

As of yet, Hugh had not openly given recognition. He did now, as a delaying tactic. He said, "You'd better get going. The cops are looking for you."

The smirk twisted to hate. Fred's voice was a monotone.

"You goddamn dirty nigger, you won't tell the cops no more about me when I get through with you. You won't tell nobody nothing. Never."

"Aren't you in enough trouble?" Hugh was taut, controlled, waiting for the initial lunge.

"Not the trouble you're going to be in, nigger."

The weight of Fred's whole body followed his fist, a low blow that knocked Hugh against the rear fender of his car. By making a fast half-turn, he had avoided taking it in the groin. But it put him off balance. He struck back and heard his fist land somewhere on Fred's face, but it was no deterrent. Fred moved in, chopping at Hugh, spinning him, and backing him into the narrows. Irrelevantly, the thought kept jangling through Hugh's mind: he's neglected to turn off the car lights; would they run down the battery?

He was being beaten cruelly. But he kept fighting back. Only his height, offering some protection to his eyes and point of chin, and his reach, which kept forcing Fred to protect his own features, kept Hugh on his feet. He knew he was losing ground, he hadn't the training. And it was possible a rib had been cracked in that first powerful blow.

From the car, the laughter screamed, close to hysteria now. "Give it to him, Fred! Give it to him good!" It was a girl's voice, breathy, shrill. It had never occurred to Hugh that Fred's companion might be a girl. It could have been his reaction of disgust which for that fleet moment took him off guard. A shoulder blow staggered him and, before he could recover footing, Fred's knee thudded into his groin. Hugh doubled over, crumpled to his knees, and automatically covered his face and head with his arms.

"Now you got him!" the girl whimpered ecstatically.

A boot crunched into his side but he held his position, crouching in sheer agony, trying to recover breath. Trying, before he was beaten unconscious, to get to his feet and kill Fred.

"Go on, give it to him," the girl was squealing, and then she broke into a sudden scream. "Jesus, Fred. The cops!"

The boot caught Hugh again but not full strength. There wasn't time for completion. He heard the swoop of Fred getting into the car, the metallic slamming of the door. The girl must have had the motor running but he didn't hear the wheels churn the gravel, the pipes roar. He passed out.

He must have returned to consciousness shortly after. At least no one had delivered any first aid, he was where he had fallen. In the muscle relaxation of unconsciousness, he must have rolled over on his back, but his arms were still rigid, covering his face.

He heard voices, male and female, as from an echo chamber. "He's coming to . . . he moved . . . he isn't dead . . ." And he heard a disgruntled girl who might have been sister to the girl who drove Fred's car. The words were distinct. "It's only a nigger."

He managed to slit his eyes and he saw the boots. Without volition, his knees jerked up to his chest for a shield. He remembered at once what he must do, get to his feet and kill. And then he realized that these weren't cycle boots, they belonged to a police uniform.

In the background the staccato of a police radio was audible. With effort, he forced his eyes open and glimmered up at the circle of faces illuminated in the spotlight of the police cruiser. He distinguished first the young and anxious uniformed officer, behind him a blur of curious bystander faces, western-looking men, farm-looking women. One of the women had her hair up in leather curlers.

And then he saw Venner. Venner with sly amusement on his lips. Venner who must have identified him before now from the white Cadillac with the California license plate. Someone had turned off the lights of the car.

He kept trying to push up to his feet. The young officer came to his assistance. "Take it easy now," he said. "We've radioed for the ambulance."

Hugh shook his head and blackness spun about him. Someone's strong arm kept him from falling. He slurred, "I don't need an ambulance. I'm all right."

"Now you just take it easy," the policeman repeated. "We'll see."

He heard Venner on the periphery telling the onlookers, "It's all right, folks. Go on home. Go on now."

And he heard a woman twanging, "Well, if they want a witness, I'll testify. It's dreadful." It wasn't the voice which had dismissed Hugh on seeing the color of his face.

The policeman opened the rear door of the Cadillac. "You'd better sit down." He directed Hugh, helped him to sink down to the floor of the car. Hugh's head was thudding, there was blood in his mouth. But he remained almost upright, his feet pressed to the dust of the road, his shoulders held by the door hinges. He managed to say, "Thanks." With his elbows on his knees, his head propped in his hands, he could possibly keep from passing out again.

When the mist cleared, he saw that Venner was standing in front of him. There was a satisfied stench about him. "If you were looking for trouble, you found it."

Hugh managed to extract his handkerchief from his pocket. He dabbed at his mouth. The teeth seemed intact, the blood was coming from a cut or tear of his lip. He couldn't talk too well but he said, "It was Fred Othy."

"That figures." Venner didn't seem too interested.

The officer came into the shadows. "Do you feel up to talking? Do you want to tell me what happened?" His pencil and notebook were visible.

"They ambushed me." Hugh might as well tell it now, he wouldn't be feeling any better later.

"They?" The officer was one of the new type, educated, courteous.

"Fred Othy and the girl. She was driving the car."

Venner snickered, "She must have been a wildcat."

"She didn't get out of the car." To the other man, Hugh said, "I didn't get to see her."

"How'd you know she was a girl if you didn't see her?" Venner jeered.

"I heard her voice. A girl's voice. She was laughing. She kept laughing."

The officer was writing it down in his little book.

Venner said, "You sure do have trouble with Othy and his girls."

Out of sick anger, Hugh asked, "Why aren't you chasing

Othy instead of standing here cracking lousy jokes?" He was past caring about Venner's reaction.

There was reaction, immediately. Venner made an abortive forward movement but the officer was there, Hugh's protection. At the same time a siren screamed around the Van Buren corner.

Venner snarled, "Mind your tongue, nigger. I could give you some real trouble."

The police ambulance came to a short stop. The attendants were out of the cab advancing to Hugh. He would not, must not, go with them.

Venner turned his ill-temper in their direction. "It took you bums long enough to get here."

As they converged on Hugh, one said, "We had a three-car crack-up on the Mesa highway."

He was afraid to come to his feet, he might spin out again. He managed to lift a painful grin. "I may not look it but I'm okay."

"That's what they all say," the stocky one said. "Let's ride in to the hospital and find out."

"I've heard all the excuses, I've ridden the wagon myself." With difficulty, Hugh fumbled his wallet from his hip pocket. "I'm a doctor." He passed over his credentials. "If I find I need help, I'll call Dr. Willis. He's my brother-in-law."

Dubiously, the attendant returned the wallet. "You're sure we can't do anything for you?"

"Not a thing. Thanks just the same."

His companion said to the policeman, "You'll put it in your report? Refused medical assistance."

"It'll be there."

Hugh expected possible trouble from Venner but the detective merely bared his teeth. It might be a laugh. Hugh was beginning to breathe more normally. He'd be able to drive home, it wasn't far.

The ambulance wheeled away. The policeman said, "Now if I can finish the report—"

The ambulance diversion had given time for Hugh's head to stop spinning. He gave his name, the reason he had been out at this hour—returning home from a visit to a friend, even the fear of trouble which had caused him to take a circuitous route.

"You mean you're still getting phone calls?" Venner smirked.

"Yes," Hugh said, still not caring. "My lawyer telephoned me that the police couldn't find Fred Othy. He was afraid Othy might be hunting for me."

Venner said to the officer, "How do you like that Skye Houston, running us down after all the errands we do for him?" He jerked his head toward Hugh. "His lawyer." As the officer continued to look puzzled, Venner snorted, "Don't you know who this guy is? He's the nigger brought the canal kid to Phoenix."

Somehow the officer hadn't connected it. He was surprised, then thoughtful. Hugh tasted fear. Possibly the police could take him in on some charge. Disturbing the peace? Or for his own protection? Any excuse would suit Venner. A second beating couldn't be distinguished from the first. Particularly after Hugh refused attention from the ambulance crew; there'd be no report on his injuries.

Hugh appealed, "I've given Marshal Hackaberry all the information I have. It's my lawyer who located Fred Othy."

The officer wrote something, then directed, "Go on with tonight."

Hugh continued his recital, omitting the racial slurs only. Before Venner, he would not speak them. He concluded with a ghost of a smile, "It's a good thing you came when you did. I would have killed Othy."

Venner snorted but the young officer understood. And he asked again, "You didn't get a look at the girl?"

"No. I didn't know it was a girl in the car until I heard her voice. Then it was too late."

"Could you describe the car?"

Hugh shook his head and hammers thudded. "A dark sedan. That's all I know."

"That's the best we could do. He wasn't using lights." The officer put the notebook away. "We were cruising the neighborhood looking for Othy when we spotted the fight. As soon as we turned into the block, this dark sedan took off. It was souped up."

He said, "I put it on the radio at once but I couldn't go after the car. I didn't know but what you were dying—or dead."

Hugh was grateful for the kindness but he wished they'd taken after Othy and let him wait.

"He won't get away, don't worry about that." The officer straightened his cap. "Do you want to come down and file a charge against him?" He knew that Hugh wouldn't but he had to ask.

"No," Hugh told him. "He's wanted for something more serious than assault and battery."

Venner shrugged. "Maybe he is. Maybe he ain't."

Hugh said flatly, "He is." He hoped to hell he'd be around when Venner ate dead crow. Slowly he started to push himself to his feet. He wavered and caught onto the door frame.

The young officer was quickly at his side. "Don't you think you'd better let me get you to a hospital?" he appealed.

"It won't be necessary." His entire body agonized with the pain; he didn't know if he could make it but he must. To remain under police jurisdiction meant under Venner. "My head's clear. It's just that I took a thumping." He pushed shut the rear door of the car. The slam of it was like a nail sledged into his brain. But he kept smiling. "If there's any damage I can't repair myself, I won't hesitate to call a doctor."

Every step was agony as he shuffled to the front of the car. He hoped it wasn't showing too much. They stood watching him, the officer anxious, Venner with malicious satisfaction. Hugh managed to open the front door and to slide under the wheel.

He remembered to turn his head to the window to say, "Thanks for turning out my car lights." He didn't know if the officer was responsible but there was no one else to thank.

The motor caught. The wheels came out of the soft dust onto the road. He hoped the police car wasn't going to follow him. He had realized by now that he couldn't go home, not near two in the morning in this condition. There was only one place he could go, back to Ellen. She might be frightened at his appearance but she wouldn't panic, she would cope.

The policeman and Venner had returned to the cruiser. Their

engine sounded, their headlights went on, their blinker off. Hugh held his car, lighting a cigarette as excuse for the delay. It looked as if they were waiting for him to make the first move, but something must have come on their radio, for they made a sudden U turn and sped to McDowell. Hugh drove on slowly, cautiously, to Washington, at the next corner taking the cross street to The Palms. From one inch to the next he didn't know if he would be able to make it.

He had to make it. If he fainted at the wheel, he would be picked up by the next cruiser. He would be at Venner's mercy. And Ringle's. He took particular care in making the turn into the motel grounds. He knew the twisting pain it would bring. There was a black Jaguar in front of Ellen's unit, he had to park four spaces away. He inched his car into the curbing, cut the engine and the lights.

He couldn't move, but he must before the blackness closed in again. A few more moments and he could rest. He slid out of the car, cautiously closed the door. He mustn't disturb the guests, if one should see him they would call the police in panic. Not until he reached Ellen's door did he realize that through sleep she would never hear his knock on it. Not unless he hammered loud enough to wake others.

Painfully, pushing one foot in front of the other, he felt his way through the arch and around to the front of the apartments. One more slow step, one more, just one more and he was there. To his relief, the drawn draperies were yet alight. She must still be reading. With one hand pressed against the door screen to keep himself from falling, he tapped with the other.

Almost at once the curtain was pulled aside to reveal her startled face. He swayed away from the screen while she unlatched it and held it open for him. He tried to say something but words wouldn't come. He shook his head and that was wrong. His eyes were swollen almost shut but he saw ahead of him a chair. Blindly, he stumbled toward it. Just before he fainted, he thought with incredible surprise that he saw Skye Houston's outraged face bending over him.

✳

When he half opened his eyes, he was in a strange bed in a strange room. It wasn't a hospital room, you couldn't fool him on a hospital room. He went under again at once but not completely. Far, far away he could distinguish voices. He couldn't hear what they were saying.

He was drugged. At least he was conscious enough to recognize that. He fought against drifting away, fought to force his eyes to reopen. He couldn't see faces, only shapes, but the voices were coming through. In particular Skye's voice, cold, decisive. "You can't question an unconscious man."

"How long's he going to stay unconscious?" That was Ringle.

"Do you think he's feigning?" The anger was more intense. "You've had your own doctor check Dr. Willis' hospital report. What do you want, a miracle?"

"Take it easy." That was Hackaberry. "We know he's in bad shape. Othy lost his temper and—"

"Lost his temper!" Skye exploded viciously. "He tried to kill Densmore."

"All right. So he defended himself brutally when Densmore ran him into the curb—"

Hugh struggled to speak and felt a quick hand on his pulse. He opened his eyes full wide upon Edward's grave face. Edward gave the slightest shake of his head.

Ringle shouted, "He's coming out of it." He must have been at the foot of the bed.

Before his words were completed, Hugh's eyes were reclosed and he had already started to drift into oblivion.

Distantly he heard the marshal's quick "Is he conscious?" and the beginning of Edward's explanation.

As easily as he'd faded out, he returned to the room. Edward's thumb and fingers were still holding his wrist.

The marshal was still declaiming, "—he turned himself in as soon as he found out we were looking for him. Does that sound like he's lying?"

Only moments had passed.

Skye said, "He knew he'd been spotted when he tried to kill Hugh."

"That's just it, he hadn't been. No one but Hugh had seen him. Othy didn't have to tell us about it."

This time Hugh didn't open his eyes; Ringle might and probably was still hawk-watching the bed, waiting for the least quiver of lids. But he did rub his thumb against the doctor's wrist, in order that Edward might know he was listening. Edward's fingers tightened in understanding.

"We'll prove he's lying," Skye orated. "About everything."

How? Hugh wondered bleakly. So far, without Othy's lies, they hadn't been able to prove Hugh's innocence. He wondered more bleakly what Othy had said, whether he'd accused Hugh of both the murder and the abortion. The police wanted to believe Fred O., he was one of their own, not a dark alien stranger.

All at once Hugh was again ebbing and flowing. He mustn't go now, it was important he hear this. Frantically, he tried to remain on shore, but helplessly, he was wafted away.

When he woke there were no voices. He was in the same bed in the same room. He saw his hands on the whiteness of the sheet. They were clean hands. Swollen, stained with methiolate, bandaged across the right knuckles, but unbloody, ungrimed, clean. He noticed the sleeves above his hands. Someone had undressed him, washed him, put him into white pajamas. Not his own pajamas, his were blue.

He didn't know if his voice would carry. His mouth hurt. "What time is it?" It was twilight.

"He's coming out of it."

He smelled Ellen's perfume. He managed to lift his eyelids. Just to see her face. She was a blur bending over him. He croaked, trying to grin, "Hello. I must look awful."

"You do." She turned away. He couldn't lift his hand to deter her.

But his eyes were focusing and he saw at the foot of the bed Skye Houston and Dr. Edward. He said, "Hello," to them too.

Their faces suddenly seemed to fill out. Edward came around to the side of the bed and took the pulse again. "He'll come out of it in a few minutes." The police must be gone.

"I am out of it." They didn't seem to hear him. If he could

turn his head, he could find Ellen. He tried to say her name but it wouldn't come forth. He tried whispering, "What time is it?" He said aloud, "What time is it?" He didn't know why he kept asking.

Skye looked at his wrist. "Almost six o'clock."

"I thought it might be tomorrow," he whispered. It didn't hurt as much to whisper.

All he wanted now was to sleep, but Edward kept saying, "Come on, Hugh. Open your eyes. Come on, you can open your eyes." The new medical theory, only enough drug to accomplish what must be done for patients, then bring them out of it as quickly as possible.

"I'm not asleep," Hugh said, and, "Ellen?"

"Yes, darling."

He didn't know if that was what she said but she was beside him, holding his hand.

He closed his eyes. "You know I didn't do what he said."

"I know."

"It was he who ran me off the road."

"We know," Skye said. "You've told us often enough."

He couldn't remember. He tried to joke. "I've been talking in my sleep?"

"Constantly."

"Othy hit me. And she kept laughing, laughing . . ." He opened his eyes and peered for Edward. The doctor was on the other side of the bed. "Hysteric, you know." Politely, he redirected his attention to Skye. Skye was his lawyer, the one who was going to get him out of this trouble. "The police officer has the report. And Venner. White-trash Venner."

"I've seen it," Skye stated.

Then they must have known Othy attacked him. Unless Damnvenner altered the report. He'd been asleep all day, he shouldn't be so tired. But of course, it was the medication, to kill pain, maybe an extra dose to keep him quiet when the marshal came. He had to know why the marshal came. His voice sounded slow, too faint, and he shook his head in annoyance. That was a mistake. A million pains jumped within his skull. But they woke him up. He saw the patio beyond French doors. He was at Skye's.

"Why was the marshal here? And Ringle?"

"You were conscious?" It was Ellen who asked.

"Briefly." He didn't look at her but his fingers tightened on hers. "Why?" he asked.

Houston's expression was troubled.

"I have to know," Hugh said. "I'm strong enough."

Without embellishment, Skye recited, "Othy turned himself in early this morning. Admitted he'd lied before, out of fear. Admitted Bonnie Lee came to him in her trouble. He still denies he fathered the baby, insists it was one of her Indio friends."

That much could be true. She would have fastened onto the one who could do the most for her. Unlike the high school boys, Fred O. had a job, lived in a big city.

"She had fifty dollars."

"No! She had seventeen cents and the little I gave her."

"Fifty dollars hidden under the lining of her handbag." She'd kept it clutched to her. "Some of it she earned; some she took from her father's wallet. Othy drove her to your motel. When she came out, it was done. The police lab has moved into that unit; Ellen is staying here."

"They won't find anything."

Skye said, "Let them probe. It will give us more time. I've spent the day asking questions of anyone and everyone who admits knowing Fred O."

Hugh demanded, "He says I killed her?"

"He's read the autopsy report too; he knows how badly she was cut up. He says he didn't know where to take her, what to do with her. She couldn't travel back home in that shape. Neither of them had motel money. He'd parked the car while he tried to figure out what to do, it just happened to be on Indian School Road. Suddenly she started gasping, and keeled over, dead."

If true, it made the abortionist and the murderer one man.

"He admits he panicked. He put her in the canal. He says the head blow was caused by some debris in the canal. He brought in a jacket and travel bag he says were hers."

"The police believe his story?"

"They don't reject it."

Because part of it was true. Because he had driven her from

the abortionist's, had stopped on the Indian School Road. But she wouldn't have died of the operation, not that soon. Not unless her heart gave out.

"They came here to arrest me."

"To take you in for questioning," Skye amended.

"Has Othy been arrested?"

"He's out on bail. His part was minor; he could get merely a suspended sentence."

"He killed her!" Hugh cried hoarsely. "Don't you see, that's why he's made this confession. He's running scared."

Skye said, "Don't despair. The police are checking and double-checking and looking for witnesses—"

"When are they coming back for me?"

"Not until the doctor lets you out of bed. I hope that won't be for several days. I need the time."

It was essential he talk to Edward alone. He closed his eyes. "I'm awfully tired." The reaction was what he wanted.

Ellen released his hand. "We'd better go, let him rest." She was, of course, speaking to Skye.

"Yes, it's almost dinnertime anyway. Would you join us, Dr. Willis?"

Hugh narrowed his eyes. Edward was moving to the doorway where the others were standing. "I wish I could but I haven't seen my family since yesterday. They're sort of expecting me at home."

Hugh waited, timing it for Skye and Ellen to step out of the room, the doctor on the threshold. It hurt to raise his voice, "Edward, before you go . . ."

But it worked. Edward excused himself and returned. The others went on down the corridor.

Hugh whispered, "Close the door." Edward gave him a dubious glance. "Close it. As if you're going to do another examination or are getting me the bedpan."

Silently Edward walked back, closed the door. He returned to the bedside.

"How bad is the damage?"

"Not bad."

"Level with me. I'm in the business myself."

"I'm leveling, Hugh. You have a couple of cracked ribs. I've bound them. You're badly bruised but no bones broken."

"Kidney damage?"

"Nothing that shows up. I took a couple of stitches in your lower lip."

Hugh scowled. "He kicked me. Bastard." No wonder he couldn't talk right. He was afraid to ask the main question but he did, watching Edward with care. "What about skull damage?"

"None." Edward sighed soft relief. "None at all."

Was he leveling? Hugh pressed it. "My eyes. They blur."

Edward grinned. "With the dope I've pumped into you, it's a wonder you can see your hand in front of your face."

Hugh lifted his swollen hand. He could see it plain. "Steady too."

Edward said, "Fortunately, when you keeled over on them, they didn't try first aid. They got you to me at the hospital without delay."

"Skye was there."

"That was a bit of luck. Ellen couldn't have managed alone."

And why was Skye there at that hour? He didn't ask Edward. "Does the family know?"

"You're bunking with an old friend for a day or so. Reunion celebration."

"They believe it?"

"Why not? I'm quite good at dissembling." Edward touched his shoulder. "Don't worry about that part of it. I'll cover. You're in good shape considering everything, Hugh. Another day in bed—"

Hugh interrupted bluntly. "I need some medicine."

The suggestion confused Edward.

"I want you to shoot me full of B-12. And I want some biphetamine. Strong."

Edward wasn't slow to understand. "You can't—"

"I have to. I haven't seen Doc Jopher yet."

"Someone else can go."

He remembered not to shake his head but he made it emphatic. "I have to do it myself."

"Tomorrow."

"Tomorrow may be too late."

Edward knew this was true, but refusal was on his face. "I can't let you do this—"

Hugh interrupted factually. "I'm going to do it. With or without help."

Edward capitulated. "When do you want these things?"

"As soon as you can make it back here."

On reluctant feet, Edward started to the door. "I can probably get the supplies in Scottsdale."

"I'm trusting you to say nothing."

"You can trust me." Edward closed the door after him.

The medication was wearing off and his strength was returning. He ached in every bone and muscle but he was no longer in danger of fading out. He had a terrific thirst. He managed slowly to turn himself and raise onto his left elbow. It was a bit more difficult to reach across with his right hand and lift the water glass on the bed table, but he did it. He drank a little water, slowly. When he'd finished and put down the glass, he didn't sink back onto the pillow as he wanted to do. Modern medicine taught you to try your strength, to get on your feet as soon as possible; to get on them even when you couldn't believe it was possible. There was no head injury. Medically, it wouldn't hurt him to try to get up.

He waited until he had become accustomed to the half-reclining position and then, using the palms of his swollen hands for leverage, he pushed up until his shoulders rested against the headboard. The effort set his head to spinning like a phonograph record.

When he had rested a little, he would try to swing his legs out of the bed. If he could stand upright, he could stagger into the adjoining bathroom. There was a soft rap on the door. It had been too much to hope that he would be left alone.

It was Ellen who looked in. When she saw his position she rushed across the room. "You shouldn't be sitting up."

"I was just changing position." He tried to smile. "To see if I could."

"Why didn't you ring?" She indicated the small china bell on the bed table.

"I didn't need help," he assured her.

She was settling him with her lovely, strong hands. Scolding as his mother would have. He let her arrange the pillows, tuck him in. "I just came to see if you needed anything. Are you hungry?"

"I couldn't eat. And I don't need a thing." He thanked her.

"If you want anything, please ring," she urged. "You know I'm staying here tonight." There were circles under her eyes. She probably hadn't slept at all.

"Edward's coming back to give me another shot. After that I'll get settled for the night," he told her. She started back across the room. "If you sit up waiting for that bell to ring, you'll be the one in the hospital. Promise me you'll go to bed soon."

"I'll sleep if you will," she smiled.

"Skye too."

"He has to go back to town. He's interviewing more of the bus drivers."

Hugh asked point-blank, "Have either of you slept today?"

She said, "I rested a bit when the police were here." Her hand turned the doorknob. "If you want anything—"

"Good night," he said firmly.

Once they got to bed, they wouldn't wake easily. They'd be too worn out to be checking on him all evening. After her footsteps could no longer be heard in the corridor, Hugh managed to push out of bed and get to his feet. Once the dizziness had cleared, he was able to make it to the bathroom. He hurt all over, he was weak; however, it wasn't too much of an ordeal. He didn't stay up long. He was only too glad to return to the bed. But next time it would be easier.

He was too impatient to rest for long. Edward wouldn't let him down, not Edward, but he should have returned by now. Again Hugh forced himself up and out of the bed. By slow stages he walked the length of the room, to the door. He rested briefly against it before starting his tedious return. Halfway, he stopped before the mirror and forced himself to look into it. The gargoyle who gazed back at him was uglier than he had imagined. Well, Ellen had Skye for company.

He heard the doorknob turn, and moved too quickly. The

room tilted, the Navajo rug at his feet quivered like sand. Quickly he clutched the bureau, held tight. It was Edward who opened the door.

Hugh groaned. "I was afraid Ellen had caught me out **again**." He let go too soon and swayed like a metronome.

"Here, let me help you."

"No." Hugh grimaced. "I've got to learn." Slowly but with increasing confidence, he covered the space to the bed, sank down on it.

Edward prepared the shot. "Double dose?"

"Yes, please." The needle connected. It hurt.

"It won't help too much tonight. But you'll be in better shape tomorrow."

"It'll help some. The bennies?"

The doctor handed him a glassine container of capsules. "Go easy on them."

"I only want one. To keep me on my feet."

Edward put away his materials. "I can't dissuade you?"

Hugh sat up again. "I don't want to do this. I have to." He touched Edward's arm. "One more favor. Give orders outside that I'm not to be disturbed for several hours. I need that much time."

"I'll tell Ellen. Skye has gone out."

"Thanks for everything. And say a prayer this is it."

"I've been on my knees all week," Edward said.

When Edward was gone, Hugh got up again and walked to the closet. They had taken his clothes away. For the ragbag, or perhaps Skye kept them as evidence.

He couldn't go to Jopher's in pajamas. He'd have to borrow from Skye. If Ellen should catch him at this, it would be necessary to tell her of his plan. He didn't want to add that trouble, but if it happened, he could handle it. The capsule had already begun to work; he felt capable of handling any problem.

Soundlessly he opened the door to the corridor. The light had been left on. From the living room he could hear music; Ellen was there. Using the wall for support he padded in the opposite direction, until halfway along he found what must be Skye's room.

He entered, put on a light, and closed the door behind him. In the dressing room, there was a king-size walk-in closet. He leafed through the clothes with growing concern at their immaculate tailored condition. But he found what he wanted on a hook, a pair of worn Levis, bleached to a mottled blue. With them over his arm he stepped over to the shoe cabinet and easily found a pair of old tennis shoes, stained beyond repair, fraying at the seams. Skye was human, he didn't discard his old shoes. Against all his upbringing, Hugh forced himself to open drawers. He collected a faded-blue sports shirt, its freshness would be gone by the time he struggled into it, a pair of shorts, and a pair of heavy white tennis socks. The latter would take up some of the extra space in the tennis shoes. Skye was bigger than he. He remembered a belt as he started away. He didn't select the oldest one of well-rubbed leather, it could be a cherished relic. There was a fairly old black one which could be replaced. He'd have to punch some extra holes in it.

He was weaker now, not alone from the exertion but from the tension of haste, the fear of discovery. He retraced his faltering way to his own room, closed the door and locked it. He didn't stop to rest but crossed to the patio doors, drawing the curtains across them, after they too were locked. Dressing wasn't easy. Each move awakened a fresh vise of pain. That Skye was several inches taller didn't matter with Levis, he could roll the legs above his ankles. The belt took care of the waistline inches. That the shoes were oversize helped give him the appearance he needed, that of a poor lout wearing hand-me-downs.

It was essential that he find the keys to the Cadillac. He would have to drive it, notorious as it was; he couldn't borrow. His personal belongings should be here in the bedroom. At the hospital the nurses always stashed them in the top bureau drawer, the natural place. He found them there, the wallet, the keys, as well as all the peddler's pack from his pockets, loose silver, the half roll of mints and the open pack of gum, his cigarettes and lighter. He transferred them to his pockets. He could go.

Quietly he unlocked the corridor door. On his way back across the room, he noted the glassine bottle and put that into his pocket. He left by way of the patio. The car was parked where he expected, in the rear, shielded by the whitewashed walls from the road.

Hugh edged himself under the wheel, careful not to wrench his battered bones. He drove without lights out of the grounds. The gate was ajar; he left it open after he'd nosed through. He put on the lights as he started over the meandering lane back to Tatum, and found the jog which would carry him to Camelback Road. He slowed here to a standstill. There were no other cars to harry him. From his wallet he took the precious scrap of paper and in the dash lights read again the directions to Doc Jopher's house.

*

Camelback was long and dark and sparsely traveled at this hour. Hugh held a steady pace, not too fast, not too slow, to Scottsdale Road. At the intersection of lights, he turned north. Within moments, he had left all town traffic behind. One pickup truck rattled past him, otherwise he saw no cars as he proceeded.

He continued on, as slowly now as he felt he might without attracting stray attention, until the speedometer showed he had covered the designated miles. With the moon low on the horizon, it was difficult to recognize the turn-off lanes until you were upon them. Not that there were many. He turned on mileage alone, and wasn't sure he had the right lane until he reached the venerable cottonwood growing undisturbed in the middle of it.

As all travelers must over this road, he circled the tree and crept on along the bumpy, narrowing way. Over a rise, down a decline, on into rural darkness until he saw far ahead a prick of light. It could have been a distant firefly. But as he came closer, it became a miniature green-glow square of a shaded window. Soon the house took shape, a kindergarten scrawl against the night sky. It was away from the road, on a rise, across a neglected field.

Before he reached its gate his wheels clattered across the warped boards of a bridge spanning a dry stream. Within that house, the sound would give warning of an approaching car. A few yards and he had reached the gate, never mended, the paint peeling from the white palings.

There was no need to dismount to open the gate. It swung loosely, nudged by how many cars over the years? Hugh's headlights picked out no driveway, only the choice of crisscrossing tire tracks on the stubble. Hugh made his own as had those who had come before him, in slow approach over the beaten field toward the knoll. His pulses were beating too fast, not in fear but in desperate hope.

Close up the house was frame, once white, built country style, a box with a pointed roof set atop it. The small porch and the front door faced to the west, overlooking the lane he had traveled after leaving the highway. Someone could have watched his lights from the time he first turned into it. Yet the place was so motionless, it was impossible to believe that there was anyone within.

He drove past the porch and parked at the far side, where his car would not be seen. As he silenced the motor, the drone of crickets seemed to increase sharply. Hugh climbed the three sagging steps to the porch. The moment he set foot there, the barking of a dog sounded in fury from inside the house.

Hugh did not stop moving. He crossed to the screen door. It sagged on its hinges and in several places the screen had broken from the frame. But when he took hold of it, it was hooked fast. He felt around for a doorbell and found where it had been. The push button had been wrenched out of its socket.

He gave a tentative knock on the frame of the screen, rattling the entire door. The sound of barking increased and Hugh pushed the door tight with the flat of his hand while he waited. From the appearance of the screen, the dog might be in the habit of charging at strangers.

He waited. He was considering another knock when a dim porch light came on over his head. It startled him and he stumbled back, releasing his hold on the screen door. Someone was fumbling with a bolt. In another moment, the front door was opened to give a partial view of a big man standing inside. There was no sign of the dog. When the door opened, it had ceased barking.

Hugh put a touch of the South in his voice. "Are you Doc Jopher?"

The man peered out. "Yes, I'm the doctor." He pushed into the aperture and peered more intently. "What you want with me? Speak up, boy, what you want?" The sour smell of old wine came from his breath, fouling the clean night air.

"I got a little trouble," Hugh began softly.

"What kind of trouble? Speak up."

"Well, it's like this—" He tried to say what the doctor might expect of a boy in his position. "I'm in trouble. My girl friend— you see, she—"

"You get your own kind of doctor," the old man returned almost angrily. "I don't do no work for the colored."

He started to push the door shut and Hugh spoke up fast. "I got money." There was little evidence of a decent living in this broken-down house and the broken-down segment of man visible in the doorway. It didn't appear that Doc Jopher was in the business. If so, he drank up his fees. "I got plenty of money," Hugh emphasized. At least he was holding Jopher's interest, the door remained ajar. "I can get hold of most a hundred dollars." If he had operated on Bonnie Lee for fifty, the double amount should be tempting.

He had awakened cupidity. Even in the poor light, he could see the flicker of it over the shadowed face. Doc Jopher wet his lips and asked suspiciously, "How'd you know to come here?"

"I heard some fellows talking where I work."

"They didn't tell you I do colored folks. They didn't say that."

"I guess they didn't say." Hugh drooped his head. "I didn't think about that. I got most a hundred dollars to spend—" He couldn't believe that Jopher would care about the color of skin if the money was there.

"It ain't that I'm bigoted," Doc Jopher said as if arguing with himself. "It's just they ought to go to their own doctors." He peered, but not at Hugh now, over his head. He might have spotted the pinpoint lights of a car. If so, the motor was not yet audible. His eyes moved back to Hugh's face and unwillingly he opened the door wider. "Well, come in," he said crossly. "I can't talk business with you out there on the porch." He unhooked the decrepit screen and pushed it open with his other hand.

Hugh caught the screen and followed the old man across the threshold. He forgot about the dog until he heard the throaty growl. Across the room he discovered it, an old molting collie, shapeless in a shapeless soft chair.

"Come in," the doctor repeated. "He won't bite you."

Hugh closed the front door. "I'm not afraid. I got a dog of my own."

"Get out of that chair, Duke." Doc Jopher waggled his puffy hand in the direction of the dog. "Let the company sit down." The animal didn't move.

"This is all right," Hugh said, taking quick hold of a straight chair, unpadded, once part of a dining-room set. He didn't sit down, for Jopher was still standing, but he would quickly if the man insisted on ousting the animal. The sagging cretonne on Duke's chair was gray with old dirt.

"I can't teach him, seems like. Minute I turn my back, he's up there like he owned it." Obviously Duke did. "Sit down, boy," he told Hugh. He himself went to the table in the center of the room under a green-shaded hanging lamp. He took up a wine bottle and poured sparingly into the sticky tumbler beside it.

He was a shapeless mass of man, shapeless as the dog and the chair, yet he had retained height. He was almost as tall as Hugh. His head was large, his jowls sagged, his large nose was pocked as a drunkard's. His rheumy blue eyes peered from overhanging eyebrows. He needed glasses, possibly he wore them for work. His hair was white and thick and the only clean-looking thing about him. His baggy gray trousers were stained with wine, his western shirt with sweat.

Although the back windows were open, the heat of the day was motionless, unbearable, under the low ceiling of the small square room. The room wasn't dirty, it just wasn't clean. There was a threadbare old carpet on the floor, several chairs like the one Hugh had taken, the center table, an old sideboard at the rear, and against the wall by a closed door an old-fashioned sofa with a raised headrest. Its black leather covering was cracked into brown lines like a crazy map. Was this the operating table?

It wasn't the heat and the smell which sickened Hugh's stomach. A half-opened door at the rear, just beyond the dog's chair, gave a glimpse of a kitchen sink and drainboard. There were no dirty dishes visible, no clutter at all. Under the sink was the dog's plate, a small scatter of food remaining on it; beside it a bowl of water set on a newspaper. The closed door near the couch undoubtedly led to bedroom and bath.

There was a picture in a gold frame hung on the mottled gray of the wallpaper. It was of a country cottage, smothered with roses, banked in green, shaded by leafy trees with a brook at their feet. In spite of what this man was, in spite of what he had done, the pathos of that picture smote Hugh. That it was there, a home, an old home far from this desert wasteland. That this misshapen old relic was once a country child, was once a boy with dreams, once a student with aspirations, once a Doctor of Medicine. The poignant cry rose silently in him: What can happen to a man? Why?

As if in answer to the unspoken question, the old man sampled the wine, licked his lips, and took another small suck at the glass. He then sat down in an old-fashioned rocker, pushed aside the evening paper, pushed aside a small wooden-cased radio, so that there was no obstruction between his eyes and Hugh across the room. He said, "I wasn't expecting company."

He never stopped drinking while Hugh was there, although he never replenished the glass with more than an inch of the yellowish wine. And he never did more than sip of it. He wasn't drunk, perhaps it was too early for that. But he was probably never sober.

He asked again, squinting in the direction of Hugh, "Who was it you said sent you here?"

"I didn't say no one sent me," Hugh replied. "I heard the fellows talking. One of them said you took care of his girl."

"And he said I did it for a hundred dollars?"

"He said he didn't have no more'n a hundred dollars and you took care of her." He wouldn't name a name. The doctor listened to the radio and read the papers. The police had cleared him, but if he had done the operation, he must know that eventually the truth would out. Fred O.'s name might not yet have been made public, and it was doubtful if Jopher would know him by his right name, yet Hugh wouldn't chance naming him. Not yet.

"Where'd you get that much money?" The dim eyes could see Hugh's battered appearance and they were suspicious.

"I worked for it. And some I borrowed from a loan company."

The answer must have been satisfactory. The doctor rocked in his chair. "Why don't you marry your girl?"

"I can't." Hugh wasn't expecting this kind of questioning, he hadn't prepared for it. He made it up as he went along. "She's already married. She's got her a husband in the army. Over in Europe. He's been gone most a year."

The sudden cackle was startling. "You're in a pretty bad spot, aren't you, boy?"

"Yessir, I am. I sure am, Boss." He mustn't pile it on too thick. Wino though the doctor was, he had the remnant of a shrewd brain.

The doctor measured out another drink. There wasn't much left in the bottle. "Well, I just might take care of you." He sipped and rocked. "If you got the money on hand, cash on the barrel. That's the only way I do business, cash on the barrel."

"I got it," Hugh affirmed.

"All right." The eyes sharpened. "You bring her out here tonight."

"Bring her tonight?" Hugh couldn't control his shock at the words. He hadn't planned on producing the imaginary girl, only the money for the trap. "You mean tonight?"

"That's what I said. Tonight. If you want me to do it." A slack smile came to the big mouth. "I'm thinking of taking a little trip down to Nogales tomorrow."

Did he need the hundred dollars to skip town while the heat was on? Possibly the police hadn't canceled out the possibility of Jopher's guilt; it could be Ringle was still nosing around. Innocent or guilty, Doc Jopher, unless his need was great, surely wouldn't be doing business until this canal case had been resolved. But the need could be for drink alone; it could be to replenish his wine cupboard that the doctor was going to Nogales. A hundred dollars would buy more spirits across the border than here. And the doc doubtless had half a dozen secret ways to carry it back over into Arizona. Exchange of favors.

Hugh was reluctant. "What time would you want me to come back?"

"Soon's you can make it. I'm not going nowhere tonight."

"I'll have to go tell her," Hugh said. He didn't know what he was going to do. But the boy he was acting would have been no less uncertain about it. It was difficult to get up from the chair; movement activated his pain.

"Don't forget to bring the money. It won't do you no good coming back here unless you can put cash on the barrel." The voice was good-natured.

"I'll bring it." Hugh started to the door, clumsy-footed, but the doctor wouldn't figure it was from pain. He'd expect "boy" to walk that way. The dog raised a lazy head and growled.

Doc Jopher's voice chuckled. "Where'd you get that fat lip, boy?"

Hugh half turned. There was no evil knowledge on the sodden face. Simply amusement.

Hugh touched his hand to his swollen mouth. "I got in a little trouble," he mumbled.

He went on out, closing the door on the doctor's wheezing laughter.

✳

Hugh returned to the house by way of the kitchen door. He hadn't the strength to walk further. He went through to the living room. Ellen was alone in front of the fire, a book in her hands but she wasn't reading. There was coffee on the table. When she saw him, it was as if she were seeing a specter. The book dropped; she was on her feet. "What are you doing here? Where did you get those clothes?"

He just made it to the couch. "I borrowed them from Skye. I didn't have time to ask his permission." He tried to light a cigarette; his hand fumbled.

She held her lighter. She asked, "Where have you been?"

The smoke made his head whir, but he needed it. "I've been to see Doc Jopher."

She disbelieved, and then she accepted the truth. "He is the one?"

"I don't know yet. I'm to return. With my girl. And a hundred dollars."

"He accepted you?" She indicated his appearance.

"To him I'm a poor colored boy who's got a girl in trouble. He doesn't do colored, but for a hundred dollars he'll forget his principles." He said hopelessly, "Where can I get a hundred dollars at this time of night?" He'd expected Skye to be home; Skye could arrange it.

"I cashed a check yesterday. I could almost make it."

"I have about twenty." He hoped again.

"Won't he be suspicious of your producing that much to-night?"

"I've explained that. Work and a loan company." He put out his hand. "Will you—"

"You can't go now." She was appalled. "Not until you've rested."

"I must get back. Before he's too drunk to answer questions."

Her hand on his arm restrained him. "Wait until Skye returns. He can go with you to help."

Hugh's mouth flicked a smile. "There are plenty of white Negroes but I'm afraid Doc Jopher doesn't know it."

"Skye is as dark as I am," she returned. "Sun glasses would take care of his eyes—if Doc Jopher doesn't know about blue-eyed Negroes. And he could darken his hair."

"Skye is too well known. I can't take any chances now of Jopher getting suspicious." He rejected the idea entirely. "I must do this myself, Ellen." He tried to make her see it. "All I need is his admission that Iris was there, and the police can take over. They'll find the evidence. Not only of her presence but with luck of Fred O.'s as well." If nowhere else, on the old screen door.

"Then why can't they do it without you?"

"Because they don't believe he's guilty."

"But you think they'll believe you if you say he is?" There was a touch of scorn.

He didn't think they would, with no witnesses, only his word. But they wouldn't dare not check it out. He said, "It's the only hope left."

Without further word, she left the room. He poured himself a cup of coffee and with it swallowed another capsule. He needed as much artificial energy as he could tolerate for this night's work.

He was drinking a second cup of coffee when she returned. Her handbag was held close to her; she didn't open it. She asked, "What about your girl?"

He had this planned. "I won't have to produce the girl. I'll tell him she's out in the car. I'm sure he'll answer questions when he sees the money. He needs that money."

She said decisively, "I'm your girl."

"No!" The tortured word sprang from him. To think of her in that foul room was inconceivable. "I don't want you there."

"You need me," she said.

"I don't. I won't take you there. You don't know—"

"I'm not milk and sugar," she said. "I'm not afraid. I can play a part as well as you."

He looked long at her and made the final decision. "No."

"Then you aren't going, Hugh." Her hands tightened on the closed purse. "Because I won't let you go alone. Not in your condition."

He could wait for Houston. Wait for how long? For Doc Jopher to open another bottle of wine, to be too fuddled to speak? Ellen would not change her decision. He knew her strength too well to hope for that. He was defeated.

She saw it without his admission. "It won't take me five minutes to get ready." She handed the purse to him. "You'll wait for me?"

He took it. "I'll wait." It was his word.

He put the money together, crumpling the bills, some into one pocket, some into another. He kept out three twenties for her to carry. He might need to play for time.

She returned in little more than the five minutes. She hadn't disguised herself; she wore the same dress but had changed her pumps for beach sandals. With her lipstick rubbed away and her hair pulled back from her face into a rubber band, she didn't look the same girl. "I'm ready," she said. She put on a dark plaid coat. It was too big for her. "I found it in the hall closet."

He gave her the twenties and explained why. She divided them, two in the pocket of the coat, another in her handbag.

"The car is out back," he said. It took a little time to get to his feet but he was all right, no feeling of blackout, only the constant aching pains.

Half across the room she said, "Let me make sure I have the house key. Skye lent me one." She opened the purse, resting it on the back of the couch.

"The kitchen door was unlocked." He was impatient to get on with it.

"Marcia must have forgotten it when she left. We mustn't leave the house open."

While she searched, the portable bar caught his attention and with it a half-formed idea. He went to it and found among the bottles one of bourbon, half filled. Winos drank wine because wine was cheap. The promise of a real drink might make Jopher more talkative than the money.

"I found it," Ellen said.

Hugh shoved the bottle into his jacket pocket. It was very visible.

When they reached the car, she asked, "Shall I drive?"

"I can manage it." Physically it would have helped but he didn't want the effort of giving directions. He knew the way.

As they covered the now seemingly brief miles, neither of them tried to make conversation. The roads were lonely, only occasionally did the lights of a car flash in the rear-view mirror and disappear. He wished Ellen a million and one miles away, yet he knew his chances of success were better with her along. After they had turned into the country lane, he asked, "Can you talk southern?"

She shrugged. "I've been told not too well, northern comes through. If I have to speak I'll stay with 'Yes, suh' and 'No, suh'—" She saw the lonely house ahead. "That's it?"

"Yes. Don't be afraid, he won't touch you." But he was the one who was afraid.

As before, he put the car where it would be partially hidden at the far side of the house. He didn't dare add a drink to his medication but he opened the bottle and rinsed his mouth with the bourbon. Then he spilled a little on his hand and rubbed it on his shirt. He wanted Jopher to thirst. When he and Ellen approached the house, the dog set up his noisy barking. Under his breath, Hugh said, "He barks but he doesn't leave his easy chair."

They climbed the broken steps to the porch. Again Hugh rattled the screen. This time the porch light did not go on. The door opened its cautious slit, revealing the blurred eyes and big nose.

"So you're back," Doc Jopher said. He unhooked the screen. "Come in, come in, don't stand there."

Hugh pushed Ellen ahead, keeping himself between her and the doctor. While Jopher locked the door, Hugh pointed her toward the side windows where she could breathe a little fresh air. The dog muttered sleepily from his easy chair.

"You got the money?" Jopher demanded.

"Sure, I got it," Hugh answered, somewhat truculantly.

The doctor poked his eyes at Ellen. "You sit down and keep quiet, girl." His voice was thick. "We'll take care of you after we get our business out of the way."

He saw Hugh's bottle as he passed. "You been celebrating, boy?" he asked slyly. "I might join you for a little drink when I'm through working." He shambled to the table and drained the last traces of wine from his glass. For some reason the dog lifted his head and growled. "You be quiet, Duke." The doctor nodded at Ellen. "He won't hurt you. He's a good old dog. I don't know what I'd do without old Duke." As if the sip had revived him, he turned to Hugh with sharp eyes. "Now, boy, you give me that hundred dollars and we'll get this over with."

Hugh didn't move. He let his voice be laden with doubt. "You're sure you'll do a good job on my girl? I wouldn't want nothing to happen to her."

Doc Jopher didn't take offense. "I'll do a good job." He held out his shaking hand for the money.

"I wouldn't want nothing to happen to her," Hugh repeated

with hesitation. "Like what happened to that little white girl who got drowned in the canal."

"It wasn't my fault what happened to that girl," Doc Jopher said amiably. "She was all right when she left here."

Hugh began shaking as if with a chill. Fearful that the import of what he'd said would trickle through the doctor's sodden brain. And then he realized the doctor didn't care; this poor colored couple couldn't give him away without involving themselves. That business was over and done, and he couldn't wait too long between drinks.

"If you want me to take care of your girl, you just put up your money." The doc was losing patience. "Stop worrying about what don't concern you."

Hugh reached into his pocket. He began bringing out the crumpled bills, one at a time. "Fred O. says it's your fault," he whined. "He says you killed Bonnie Lee."

Ellen gave a little moan in the background. He didn't know if it was she or the assumed character giving way.

"Then he's lying to you, boy. He knows that girl walked out of here on her own two feet." Doc Jopher's palsied hand stretched out greedily.

Hugh fed it with a few bills. "That's what you say." He made his distrust evident by withdrawing, holding fast to the money in his fist. "But I don't see no operating table here. How you going to operate on somebody without no place to do it?"

The doctor's arm swept toward the battered couch. "Right there's where I'm going to do it. Like I always do. If it's a hospital you want, what'd you come here for?"

He mustn't let the doctor reject him, not this near to success. Hugh was quickly obsequious, the way he should be. "Oh, nossuh, nossuh." He made the accent strong. "I don't want no hospital, nossuh!"

"Then let's get this over with." The outstretched hand quivered across the table.

Hugh began to smooth a bill, and again he hesitated. "Don't you have no"—not instruments —"no tools?"

Doc Jopher's face twisted into a mammoth scowl. "Of course

I got instruments," he thundered. "I'm a doctor, not a damn hat-pin quack!" He lifted his glass to drink but it was empty. He slammed it on the table; it didn't break. The money was there in plain view, the money he evidently needed so desperately. For he made the great effort, erasing the wrath, putting on the kindly-old-man demeanor he wore for all the world to see. "Come here, you."

Unsure, Hugh followed him across to the couch.

"Stoop down, boy, you're younger'n I am. Stoop down and hand me that bag you find underneath there."

Hugh went to one knee. From the lint and dust he brought out the doctor's bag. Like his own but so old, so very old.

"Hand it here," Jopher said.

Hugh passed it up. He started to rise but the doctor halted him.

"Reach under again. There's a washbasin there. Feel it? Bring it out. That's right."

Hugh stood up, holding the chipped basin. Folded into it was a rubber sheet.

The doctor's forefinger indicated it. "Shake it out, spread it over the couch." There were old stains on the fabric but it wasn't dirty. It had been scrubbed. "That's right. Set that washbasin down, at the foot. There. Now, come over here."

Doc Jopher returned to the table, plumped his instrument bag in the center, under the pool of light. Hugh edged himself to a place across from him.

"Now, you look here." Jopher opened the bag. It wasn't locked. "You see this 'tool'?" He mocked the word. He was humoring a dumb, ignorant colored boy. Because he must have that money. Now. Tonight. Not when another case turned up. "And this?" He laid the clean, worn instruments in a row on the wine-mucked table. His hands were tender, fondling them. "Doctor's tools," he said, but this was to himself. "The finest you can buy." He straightened up tall; his watery eyes prodded Hugh. "You satisfied, boy?" He took silence for assent. "Then pay up and we'll get this job done. You can stay right here and watch I don't make no mistakes."

Hugh had more than he needed to go to the police. He passed across the rest of the money.

Doc Jopher counted in a monotone. The dog growled. "Keep quiet, Duke." He finished counting, not quite believing his tally. "There ain't but forty dollars here."

"She's got the rest of it," Hugh said quickly. He went over to where Ellen was. She looked up at him for direction. He gave an imperceptible nod and she got up from the chair. On some excuse, they must get out of here now. Unexpectedly, the dog's growl menaced.

The doctor said sharply, "Do you have that money or don't you?"

Ellen opened her purse and found the one twenty. The others she took from the coat pocket. As he took them, Hugh muttered, "Get ready to run if I can't. Send police . . ."

Holding the bills, he started back to the table. And saw the kitchen door opening. In the opening Ringle towered, a monstrous shadow. He moved without sound into the room. Behind him crept the cat smile of Venner.

Ringle spoke. "I'll take that money, Doc."

Slowly Doc Jopher turned and saw them. For a moment he stood there, peering through his bleared eyes, not understanding. Then as Ringle advanced into the pool of lamplight, all hope sagged out of his old body, leaving it an empty sack. He fumbled for the wine bottle; its emptiness was the final betrayal. Still holding the bottle, he sank into the rocking chair. After a moment he put it to his mouth. His tongue licked the stain from the rim.

Ringle took a ponderous step toward Hugh. With satisfaction he recited, "I'm arresting you and Doc Jopher on conspiracy to commit an illegal operation. And for contributing to the death of a minor."

Hugh cried out, "Don't you understand?" but he saw that it was useless. He shouted, "Run, Ellen," as he himself advanced toward the two detectives. The club of Ringle's hand knocked him to the floor. She didn't make it. Venner, triumph staining his eyes, caught her at the door.

Hugh didn't lose consciousness. He knew every anguished

moment of being hauled up and away, half flung into the back of the police car with Ellen and the old doctor. He knew the writhing pain of every yard of the drive back to Scottsdale. Ellen held him against her shoulder. His mouth was bleeding again.

Half along the way he became aware of Jopher's whisper. "The bottle. You didn't break the bottle when you fell?" He hadn't. The two detectives in the front seat weren't paying any heed. Venner was riding the wheel, Ringle growling into the radio. Hugh worried the bourbon from his pocket and thrust it into the avid hands. The doctor opened it, wiped the rim with his open palm and took a long, shuddering swallow. He recapped and fumbled it back toward Hugh.

"Keep it," Hugh slurred. "You need it."

Doc Jopher sighed. "You're a gentleman." He tipped it again briefly before putting it into his own pocket.

The expression on the faces of the deputies on duty at the Scottsdale station was to be expected, an almost weary and matter-of-fact acceptance that two shabby young Negroes were guilty until proven innocent. There was confirmation, seeing Ringle and Venner in charge. When they recognized Jopher, their mouths took on cynical knowledge.

"Sit down over there." Ringle pointed to the straight chairs against the wall. "We're waiting till the marshal gets here."

Hugh came out of despair. Marshal Hackaberry had been summoned, either by Ringle or as a result of Ringle's radio communication. Ellen helped him to a chair, eased him into it. She sat beside him. The shine of anger never left her eyes. Hugh spoke under his breath. "When the marshal comes, he'll let us telephone Skye," and he said, "Take that crazy rubber band off your hair."

She said, "Skye isn't home." She let her hair fall about her face. Without apology she told him, "I left a note where we'd be. On the couch when I was opening my purse."

At the time he might have been annoyed. Now he was grateful.

She said, "I'll try, but if he was home, he'd have traced us by now."

And if he didn't get here in time, Hugh wouldn't be believed. He'd be formally charged. But Skye should have returned by this hour—and then he saw by the wall clock that it wasn't yet midnight. It had seemed near to dawn.

Doc Jopher was incongruously at ease in this room with its too-bright lighting. He knew all the officers by name. And it would seem they had a special niche for him, as for one of the pet regulars, no matter the crime. He didn't move toward the chairs but away from them.

Ringle ordered again, "You too, Doc. Over there."

"I just want a cup of water." He drew his mouth into a pout. "Can't I have a cup of water?"

"Get your water and sit down." Ringle went to the desk just outside the marshal's door. He had a report to write.

Doc Jopher walked to the water fountain and filled a cup.

The deputy at communications said, "Sorry we got no ice, Doc."

"How do you like that?" Venner had spied the bottle. "Now Scottsdale's furnishing setups." He brayed laughter. "How do you like that?" He went over to make sure Ringle had caught the joke.

Jopher drank the water with dignity and filled the cup again. He ambled over to the chair next to Hugh and sat down, not spilling a drop. He proceeded to mix bourbon in the cup. If he was drunk, he was brilliantly so. The laughter at his antics was his applause. No one made a move to take his bottle.

He tasted and smacked his lips. But mixing a highball at the police station wasn't just a stunt to amuse an audience. Hugh recognized again the shrewd brain, the doctor who knew his tolerance to alcohol and who measured his dosage. There had been no room in the cup for more than a flavoring. In spite of the drinks on the way, the drive in must have brought to him a measure of sobriety. Which he had no intent of destroying. He knew the ropes. He knew the buffoon got a better deal from the cops than a straight man would.

He sipped and smacked until the laughter died. Then he began to talk. "Look, Mr. Ringle, you know I wasn't going to do nothing to this girl. I was just leading the niggers on to see how far they'd go." His appeal was jovial. "Then I was going to kick them out, you bet I was, right on their butts. First thing in the morning I was going to get me to a telephone and tell you all about it."

Ringle didn't look up. "Save it for the judge, Doc."

"You got no right to arrest me," Jopher complained. "You're a Phoenix cop. I live in the county."

This time Ringle looked at him. "Come off it, Doc. If you want to get technical, Marshal Hackaberry's got the right. He's county and city both."

"Well, I don't call that fair," Jopher said.

"You'll have to take that up with Hackaberry."

Jopher sulked audibly while he emptied his cup. "Is there any rule about getting a drink of water?" he began.

But the sound of boots on the outside stairs hushed him. He pushed the paper cup quickly under the chair.

The marshal came in. A swift glance covered the room and filed essential information. His boots were noisy as he stalked across to Ringle at the desk.

Ringle was standing. "We caught them both red-handed," he said with satisfaction. "Densmore was setting up another girl with the doc."

The marshal's side glance at the three was brief.

"You have your report?"

"I'm working on it."

"We'll go inside," Hackaberry announced.

He waited for Ringle and Venner to precede him. One of the deputies came over to the three. He gestured with his thumb.

"Me too?" Jopher asked in disdain.

"You too."

With Ellen's assistance, Hugh fumbled to his feet. The deputy asked, "Need any help?"

"I can make it."

The marshal was waiting. He didn't say anything about Hugh's condition, he merely observed it. When they came abreast, Hugh asked him, "May I call my lawyer?"

"He's not home. Go on, call him. I did, but he's not home."

Ellen went to the booth. The marshal motioned Hugh into the office. The deputy went with him. There were chairs for everyone tonight. This wasn't the informal gathering. The deputy helped Hugh to sit down. He didn't know how long he could last. His pain was frantic, but he mustn't black out until he could defend himself.

Ellen joined him, shaking her head. A deputy stood guard at the door. Ringle ignored everyone, pushing his pencil stub across the paper. Venner scuffed about the small room, whistling tunelessly between his teeth, too excited for silence. And Doc Jopher protested his innocence in a dozen maudlin ways. Still the marshal didn't join them. Not even when Skye came rushing in.

He scraped a chair over to where Hugh and Ellen were. "My God, what have you got yourself into?" he asked under his breath, and of Ellen, "Why did you let him go out?"

"I couldn't stop him." With fury, she said, "Ringle knocked him down."

"He just pushed too hard." Hugh smiled wryly and felt the encrusted blood flow again. He covered it with his stained handkerchief.

"When I read Ellen's note I checked here before tearing out to Doc's. I was afraid your idea might backfire."

"I've got Jopher," Hugh mumbled. "He admitted Bonnie Lee was there."

"Can you make it stand up?"

"The police can. We tried to call you."

"I've spent the evening at the bus depot," Skye said. "I found some men who can quote Fred Othy on Bonnie Lee. Before he got cautious." Before she was with child. "Just what happened at Doc's?"

It was too hard to talk; Hugh let Ellen whisper it. She hadn't finished before Fred O. was brought in by an officer. And the marshal followed.

When Othy saw Hugh and the doctor, he began a shrill protest. "Whose idea is it dragging me down here in the middle of the night? I've told you what happened."

The officer said, "Sit down and shut up." There was a small scuffle before the officer put him into a chair.

"I'm not going to be framed," Othy yelled. "I want a lawyer."

"Look, you're not arrested," the officer said. "What you want with a lawyer, when you're not even arrested?" Temporarily, Fred O. subsided.

Skye intercepted Hackaberry. What they said was private. When Skye took a place by Hugh's side, he didn't speak. The marshal went to his desk. "Okay, Ringle."

Ringle's report made it clear that he and Venner hadn't just happened to turn up at Jopher's. A Scottsdale cruiser had spotted Hugh's car heading north. The deputies didn't have to move in; they knew the road. Knew that particular lane, where Hugh turned off, led only to Doc Jopher's and tilled fields beyond. The information was relayed to the Phoenix detectives.

Ringle abandoned the report for discourse. It was easier for him. "We didn't drive up to the house. That dog of Doc's would raise the dead the way he barks when he hears anybody coming. But his ears aren't as good as they once were if you come quiet. I noticed that the last time we were out at Doc's. I had on my crepe soles and he never heard me till I was on the porch. So tonight when we got the call, I changed to them."

Venner said, "I had a pair of sneakers," but he didn't try to take the stage from Ringle.

The big detective continued placidly, "We knew we'd have to catch Densmore red-handed or not get nowhere. We left the car down the lane and the dog never heard us approach. We saw the whole thing through the window." His chuckle was only in the shape of his lips. "With that old dog snoring in his chair right on the other side." The moment of fun was so brief it might have been imagined. "Densmore passed some money to the doc, then the two of them went over to the couch and Densmore took out the doc's bag from underneath and handed it to him."

Oh, God, they hadn't been able to hear, only to see what went on!

"Next thing Densmore took a basin and a rubber sheet from under the couch. He spread the sheet on top and put the basin on it. They came back to the table then and the doc took some instruments out of his bag. After he and Densmore looked them over, Densmore gave the doc the rest of the money he was holding. Then Densmore went over to get the girl, and that's when we moved. We weren't going to let them go through with it."

"You don't understand!" Hugh repeated his cry.

"Keep quiet," the marshal barked. "You'll get your chance to talk."

Ringle went on smoothly, "We entered by the kitchen door." He didn't mention how they had made entry through Jopher's locked doors. "Took them red-handed. I had it figured by then why we couldn't get nothing on Densmore. He didn't use the motel room or his own stuff. He was working in partners with Doc."

Venner said, "Yeah." With satisfaction.

"That's it?" the marshal asked Ringle.

"That's about it." He put his big hands on his knees. "The details will be in the report."

The silence seemed long before the marshal addressed Hugh. "What have you to say?"

Hugh didn't try to rise. It was difficult enough just to speak. He said, "I never saw Doc Jopher until tonight. I was never in that house until tonight. Doc Jopher was the one who aborted Bonnie Lee."

"He's lying," Othy snorted. "It was him."

"You keep quiet," the marshal ordered. "Wait your turn." He gestured Hugh, "Go on. So why did you go to Doc's tonight?"

Hugh told him. Forcing down the pain which enveloped him; forbidding it to take over until he was done. He told how he knew what he must do, and what he did; from the hapless search for Mahm Gitty to the conclusion at Jopher's.

The marshal must know it was the truth. It was the truth. Yet he said noncommittally, "That's your story." One story against another story and another story.

Hugh insisted, "Send your lab men out there. They'll find her fingerprints. Othy's too. Doc Jopher admitted he did it." He had a witness. He indicated Ellen. "Before both of us."

Othy hooted. "You going to listen to two niggers and a drunk old hoss doctor?" But fear was on him.

It could have been the professional insult. It could have been the bottle Hugh had given him. It could have been Doc Jopher knew when to sing. "Othy brought the girl to me. He waited while I took care of her."

Othy was on his feet. "Shut your mouth, you fat slob!"

Doc Jopher's eyes became venomous stones. "She walked out of there with him. She was just as live as him or me when she walked out with him."

Marshal Hackaberry said dispassionately to Othy, "The lab's found some dog hairs in your mother's car. You folks don't have a dog. Doc does. Might be they'll match up."

Othy shouted, "I didn't kill her. It was the doc!" The officer restrained him.

The marshal raised a decisive voice. "She was killed by a blow on the head. It was inflicted while she was alive. There was no debris in the canal. The Zanjaros checked after the locks were closed for the night. The locks were still closed when the girl's body was found. Nothing could have gone through them."

Doc Jopher's words quavered. "You know I didn't kill that poor little girl, Marshal. I wouldn't do a thing like that. Maybe I tried to help her in a way I oughtn't. Like I've tried to help other poor little girls that come crying to me. It's not my fault I got a soft heart. I can't stand to hear them crying when I'm a doctor and know I can help them. But I wouldn't kill anybody."

It could have been a performance, the tragedian now. But at least a part of it was real. And it was real later when the deputy started to take him away.

"If you lock me up, who's going to take care of poor old Duke?" He began to cry. Real tears.

The marshal said brusquely, "Don't worry about that, Doc. We'll see to Duke until you get back."

For he would come back. Even if it came to complicity in murder, he wouldn't serve too long. He knew the ropes, the ingratiating deeds, the good behavior, the sentiment he could engender. He'd come back to carry on with his butcher's business.

Before that, a cursing Fred Othy had been led out. Last of all, Ringle and Venner went away. Ringle, stolidly; so he'd made one miscalculation, but on the whole he wasn't dissatisfied. He'd helped run Othy and Jopher to ground, not by risk and chance but by unspectacular routine. Venner departed with the hate still ugly in his eyes, with more hate for an innocent Hugh than for a guilty. The Venners would not be changed in their generation.

Hugh witnessed it all. And the aftermath hubbub of Ellen and Skye and the marshal filling in details. He didn't want to spoil their celebration but he knew he couldn't hold on much longer. If he could get outside to the car, he could lie down and wait.

He heard the marshal's slow western twang. It wasn't triumphant. "With any luck, we'll send Doc Jopher up for a longer spell than usual. But there'll be another Jopher. And another telephone number. And another old woman. Another and another and another. There'll always be abortionists just as there'll always be prostitutes and pimps and pushers. When man wants an evil, he'll always find someone evil to supply him."

Carefully, Hugh lifted himself from the chair. He took one step, and the floor rose up and crashed into his face.

8

SUCH A SHORT TIME AGO, he had traveled this road from Westwood to Phoenix. Now, such a long time later, he was traveling it from Phoenix back to Westwood. He had been light-hearted then; he wondered if he would ever again know that same careless happiness. He wondered if he would ever be cleansed of his innocent guilt.

By mid-afternoon he would be in Blythe; before sundown, in Indio. He would not stop in either place. After being treated as an invalid for almost a week, he was in pretty good shape. Even if his face did still bear considerable resemblance to that of a broken-down prizefighter's. By evening he would be making the rounds at Med Center. Just as if nothing had happened. Just as if he'd never been away.

His name had been in the papers. Not in the headlines, not as a suspected criminal, not as a Negro. Embedded in the story of the arrest of Fred Othy and Dr. Oren Jopher was a paragraph:

"Marshal H. C. Hackaberry stated that the discovery of Dr. Jopher's part in the case was made through the co-operation of Dr. Hugh Densmore of Los Angeles, a visitor in Phoenix. Dr. Densmore first became suspicious of Dr. Jopher's activities after learning from a friend, Skye Houston, attorney, of the conflicting stories given the police by the suspect, Fred Othy."

No more than that. It all might have to come out at the trial. He would return as a witness. Along with little Lora and bewildered Mr. Crumb and a handful of bus drivers and Doc Jopher turning state's witness. But he wouldn't be afraid to speak up then. He was no longer the expendable one.

Fred O. continued to deny killing Bonnie Lee. And why had he? She must have threatened to expose him, as they sat there in the car on Indian School Road after it was over. She hadn't come to Phoenix for this ugly thing; she had come with her secret hoard to buy a beautiful wedding dress, to begin a grand new life. Had she demanded that he free himself and marry her? Or did she make what would be the first of interminable demands for money? Whatever it was, he had panicked and killed her.

There was so much to remember. Not just the sad and the bitter moments, but the good ones as well. You'd think he was a bloody hero the way the family carried on. And Skye. And a friendly marshal. Everyone but Ellen. She didn't care to talk about it.

The road was winding through Wickenberg. Hugh spoke to her. "Hungry?"

Her smile was wide. "After your grandmother's breakfast?"

He wondered if she had been remembering too. The big farewell dinner his grandmother served last night. With Skye the honor guest. And Skye and Ellen silhouetted in the doorway as they said good-bye to each other.

Hugh had walked away, leaving them together. That was

when Edward, just emerging from the dining room, put an envelope in his hand. "Houston asked me to give you this." The bill. Hugh didn't open it until he was alone. Not that he was afraid to see it. Whatever the amount, he could pay. He had a future ahead. When he did look at it, he couldn't believe. Carefully itemized, the total read: $10,000. Across it was stamped: *Paid in Full.* And scrawled, by Skye's own hand, was the notation. "I told you I was expensive. I didn't tell you my war chest was already full. I don't need your money. I'll take it out in trade when I get my ulcer."

Remembering so many things he would never forget. They were in open country again. Sand and horizon and the far-off hills. Hugh said, it had to be said, "If things had been different, it might have been you and Skye, mightn't it?"

She didn't hesitate. "They would have had to be very different."

"If he hadn't been married—"

Her words were simple. "If he hadn't been white."

Somehow it surprised him. "That would matter to you?"

"Yes," she said. "It's too soon. I'm not that strong."

"You have more strength than any woman I know."

"Not enough for that."

She was silent for a little while. Then she said, "I love Skye. I'll always love him. There are different ways of loving. Even if he weren't white, even if he weren't married, I wouldn't marry him unless I couldn't have the man I want."

Hugh couldn't look at her. There was a truck ahead, he had to keep his eyes on the road. He waited until the truck driver gave him the signal to come around, and until he had negotiated the passing. Then he spoke, quite casually, he hoped.

"How long will you be in Los Angeles?"

"It depends upon how interesting I find your campus."

"I won't have much time," he despaired. "I've two weeks' vacation to make up."

"I'm in no hurry," she said.

For an instant, he took his eyes off the road. She was smiling. Not at him, but at the certainty of the coming-true of the plans they both were making.

AUTHOR'S NOTE

Place names in this book are factual, but locations such as
Three Oaks and Dr. Jopher's country acreage are invented, and
to the best of knowledge, there is no motor hotel in Phoenix named
"The Palms" and no café in Scottsdale called "Victor's."

All characters are entirely fictional; any fancied resemblance
to any persons, living or dead, can only be the product of imagination. Marshal Buster Shaver and the deputy marshals, who so
generously furnished information on law enforcement in the
Phoenix-Scottsdale area, can vouch for the fact that no law officer
in this book bears even an imaginary resemblance to the actual
officers of the area.

In the comparatively brief time it takes to produce a book,
a number of landmarks in the Scottsdale area have given way to
progress, including the police headquarters as described herein.
A handsome new police station now stands next door to the
Town Hall.

1963

AFTERWORD

A WHITE CADILLAC is on the road from Los Angeles to Phoenix, driven by a young man on his way to a family wedding. The young man is single, on the rise in his medical career, a good son and brother. His car, borrowed from his mother, is one my father would have admired: a solid and luxurious example of American engineering.

Behind him is Los Angeles, a modern city of new beginnings and glossy stars; a desert city that pipes in enough water to transform itself into a false paradise. The world this car moves through, once it leaves Los Angeles behind, is a different kind of desert, the American West that still remembers old myths about tough men finding justice in their own way. It's a hard-edged landscape that looks abandoned, primeval. It's a dangerous place for this particular young man at this particular moment in our history, something he knows instinctively—and yet he ignores this instinct.

Trouble begins when he notices the girl, a young woman, at the edge of the road and stops to give her a ride.

With its spare language and depictions of men and women and their outsized desires, *The Expendable Man* is the epitome of American noir —but there's something more beneath the surface. Dorothy B. Hughes, a white woman working as a book reviewer in Los Angeles and New Mexico, captures an unease under the skin of everyday life in a way that is all her own. Her understated description of the young driver's rising nervousness as he moves through this world has us wondering: Why is he questioning himself, what is he afraid of? She calibrates the tension carefully: What could be more innocent or decent than this young doctor helping out a young woman in a dusty town?

By the time he has reached his family we know all too well what could and will go wrong. Race has come into the equation and will distort everything in much the same way that the desert light and its heat does the perception of anyone caught outside their air-conditioned offices and homes. Hughes captures in her seemingly straightforward mystery a signal truth of mid-twentieth-century American life: under the façade of equality the uglier divisions of racism have their own story to tell about who will pay for the death of a runaway white teen.

Not unlike the characters Hughes portrays in *The Expendable Man*, my father came to Los Angeles to create a new Jim Crow–free life after World War II. He understood though that every rung he climbed up that American ladder into a world of owning real estate and having middle-class aspirations was going to be negotiated by race. Los Angeles might on its surface seem like the promised land, but at its back door was that other America, that place that still wanted the old narrative to hold true where black men and women had no right to that dream of true freedom. My father understood: born in Louisiana, grown to adulthood in Houston, he would have been on guard driving that car to Phoenix.

The poison this too-little heralded writer uncovers is as lethal as arsenic. Hughes's hero wants to believe in the country Los Angeles represents to him. He wants to believe that his education and his family's hard-won social position will protect him. He talks about his family's connections; he worries about social status and the circles his family's success has yet to propel him into—is he good enough for the beautiful woman from Washington, DC, he's just met and has begun to fall in love with? But that distance—between his hopes and what he encounters—is much greater than he imagined.

He doesn't want to be beholden to a powerful white lawyer to save him from injustice and so he tries to unravel the strands of the story of the girl's death himself. He takes us to the secret places where illegal transactions are only periodically checked. We feel the sun on our skin, disorienting and dispiriting, as he walks the long blocks trying to work out how he can protect his family from the shame this bogus crime will entrap him in. We are with him and become him as he regards the world he thought he knew come undone.

A white woman writing of a young black man's problems with the law was certainly a kind of gamble—but Hughes often chose to write from perspectives far from her own. She studied to be a journalist, actually plied that trade in Missouri, New Mexico, and New York. Though married to a man with long roots in New Mexico, she moved to Los Angeles, was one of the founding members of the Screen Writers Guild. More than a decade before she wrote *The Expendable Man*, she wrote *In a Lonely Place*, a book adapted for film and made famous by Humphrey Bogart's performance. The story is told both in the third and first person, a complex dance of characters whose failures have left them all marked in some way—the reader isn't sure until the end who is murdering the young women in postwar LA. Hughes wrote about men and women of means—a fashion designer, a doctor—and she also wrote about poor white girls, ex-GIs, jazz musicians, and a war profiteer. What she brought to them all was a poet's eye for detail and feel for language. Her first book had in fact been a collection of poetry, published in the prestigious Yale Series of Younger Poets.

Hughes only published that one book of poetry and then turned away to invest herself in the mystery genre, ultimately writing fourteen novels and a scattering of short stories. Then just as her novels began to move from the standard motifs of noir and started taking on the politics of the cold war and race, she quit. The reason she gave was that she needed to tend an ailing mother and grandchildren. She never stopped writing about that literature—she was a book critic for almost forty years. She wrote an acclaimed biography of Erle Stanley Gardner, the writer known for his Perry Mason series, in 1978. And that same year, more than a decade after she stopped writing novels, she was anointed Grand Master by the Mystery Writers of America.

So why has she not been more celebrated? Why hasn't her work been anthologized like that of so many of her peers? Her novels are carefully crafted pieces, ahead of their time in their use of psychological suspense and their piercing observations about class and race. She was among the best and her work belongs in our canon of classic American stories. Bringing her back is no act of nostalgia; it is a gateway through which we might access her particular view of that road between our glittering versions of American life and the darker reality that waits at the end of the ride.

—WALTER MOSLEY

OTHER NEW YORK REVIEW CLASSICS

For a complete list of titles, visit www.nyrb.com or write to:
Catalog Requests, NYRB, 435 Hudson Street, New York, NY 10014

* *Also available as an electronic book.*